MAGGIE CHRISTENSEN

A Family for Christmas in Pelican Crossing

Dedication

To Jim, my soulmate of over forty years

Also by Maggie Christensen

Oregon Coast Series
The Sand Dollar
The Dreamcatcher
Madeline House

Sunshine Coast books
A Brahminy Sunrise
Champagne for Breakfast

Sydney Collection
Band of Gold
Broken Threads
Isobel's Promise
A Model Wife

Scottish Collection
The Good Sister
Isobel's Promise
A Single Woman

Granite Springs
The Life She Deserves
The Life She Chooses
The Life She Wants
The Life She Finds
The Life She Imagines
A Granite Springs Christmas
The Life She Creates
The Life She Regrets
The Life She Dreams

A Mother's Story

Bellbird Bay
Summer in Bellbird Bay
Coming Home to Bellbird Bay
Starting Over in Bellbird Bay
Christmas in Bellbird Bay
Finding Refuge in Bellbird Bay
Escape to Bellbird Bay
Second Chances in Bellbird Bay
Celebrations in Bellbird Bay
Happy Ever After in Bellbird Bay

Pelican Crossing
The Restaurant in Pelican Crossing
Secrets in Pelican Crossing
A New Dawn in Pelican Crossing
A Christmas Surprise in Pelican Crossing
Safe Harbour in Pelican Crossing
Waves of Change in Pelican Crossing

One

It would soon be Christmas, Lou Chalmers thought, another Christmas she'd spend alone. It wasn't Halloween yet, and Christmas items were beginning to appear in the shops. It seemed to happen earlier each year.

Over the years she'd become adept at pretending it wasn't a problem, that she enjoyed the break from her shop, enjoyed spending the holiday alone in her cottage with only her ginger cat, Tilly, for company and the pile of books she hadn't had time to read all year. In a few months' time she'd be sixty-five. Where had the years gone?

Lou's heart filled with pride as she gazed around *Books and Coffee*, the combined bookshop and café she'd established over twenty years ago when she was in her forties and had been fortunate enough to attract a couple of young guys, Ron and Denny to run the café section. Their coffee and Ron's cakes were legendary in Pelican Crossing, and the bookshop proved an attraction to locals and tourists alike.

Other women she knew had families, a husband, children. Some were even in a second relationship while she… Lou brushed away a tear. There was no sense in getting upset over what couldn't be changed, but sometimes she wished her life could be different.

If only… But there was no sense in lamenting the past either, even if over the years the sharp pain of betrayal had faded to a dull ache of regret.

Lou had been twenty-one and in love, when Darren told her he was in love with her younger sister. Fleur was nineteen and had always coveted what Lou had, Darren was only the last in a long line of boyfriends she'd managed to steal from her older sister. It was the one that hurt most, the fact that the man she'd hoped to marry had been taken in by the younger girl's sweet smile and flirtatious ways.

It had been a relief when Fleur and Darren left Pelican Crossing, when Lou didn't have to see her sister every day, see the couple together, but now so many years had passed, Lou felt differently. Fleur was the only family she had left.

In the first few months after her departure, Fleur had written to Lou, letters which Lou had returned unopened. She'd had no wish to read about her sister's happiness, achieved at the expense of her own ruined future. She'd concentrated instead on her own life, on her work as a librarian, which Fleur had mocked as being boring, saving madly to achieve her dream of owning her own bookshop.

Books and Coffee was her dream come true, the result of years of hard work and planning. But in the process, she had lost touch with her sister.

As the years passed and Lou's anger dulled, she often thought about Fleur, wondered how she was, if she and Darren were happy together, if they'd stayed in Sydney, if they'd had children. But the letters had stopped, and Fleur had even ceased communicating with their parents. Lou had tried to find her when first their mother, then father had died, but her searches proved fruitless. It was as if her sister – and her husband – had vanished off the face of the earth.

It had all happened so long ago, but despite forgiving her sister, Lou had never fallen in love again, preferring to concentrate on her home and her work, both of which were within her control.

Lou gave herself a shake and pulled herself together as the shop door opened and a group of women walked in. From the way they were dressed, she knew they were tourists, one of her most lucrative sources of income. Pasting a smile on her face she said, 'Good morning, ladies. Welcome to *Books and Coffee*. How can I help you?'

By the time they had chatted about Pelican Crossing and the weather, and the women had chosen their books, half an hour had passed, and Lou was in a better frame of mind. This was why she had established her business, to share her love of books with others – and her love of coffee, she thought, as the group headed into the café.

After the women left, there was a flurry of customers which slowed down towards lunchtime, then the usual trickle of elderly souls who Lou suspected came here to escape from the heat and catch up with friends. It was seeing them discussing books that had sparked an idea in Lou's mind, and tonight at eight o'clock there would be the first meeting of the *Book Café*.

She knew there were already several book clubs in Pelican Crossing, but this would be different from those groups whose members all read the same book each month then met to discuss it, often over a glass of wine. She had friends who belonged to them. At the *Book Café*, each person would bring along a book which they had enjoyed and wanted to share and recommend to the others. It might even lead to further sales, but that wasn't the purpose of the group. Lou saw it as an extension of what she had already established and was delighted Ron and Denny were on board, offering to provide coffee and some of their popular sweet treats.

Lou hoped it would be a success. She might live alone with her cat and have lost touch with her only sister, but here in Pelican Crossing, she was providing a service to the community in which she'd grown up. She was, she hoped, making a difference in people's lives.

*

At five minutes to eight, Lou was attempting to calm the butterflies in her stomach. Everything was ready, the circle of chairs in the section of the bookshop reserved for special events, the table containing plates of Ron's signature salted caramel brownies and tiny muffins. The room was redolent with the aroma of coffee. *What if no one came?*

Then, at two minutes to eight, just as she was beginning to give up hope and admit to Ron and Denny that this had been a mistake, a few people began to trickle in. By ten minutes past eight, all the chairs were filled, and Denny had brought in extras from the café.

'Welcome, everyone, to the first meeting of the *Book Café*. If tonight is a success, I hope this will become a regular event. As I indicated in the flier, it's an opportunity to share a book you've enjoyed, and which others might enjoy too. I expect a variety of genres will be shared and not every one of them will appeal to everyone here. But that's what it's all about, being exposed to something which you might never have chosen for yourself, perhaps even being taken out of your comfort zone.'

She looked around to see smiles and nods and a few uneasy expressions. Most of the group were familiar to her but there were a few strangers.

Lou gave what she hoped was an encouraging smile. 'Since this is our first meeting, I'll start.' She held up her well-worn copy of *A City of Friends* by Joanna Trollope. 'This is a favourite book of mine by one of my favourite authors which I've recently re-read. I have all of her books on my bookshelf at home and I'm afraid this one has seen better days.' She indicated the creases on the cover and there were a few laughs. 'Books have always been my friends, what I turned to when life was difficult…' There were a few nods. 'I see some of you understand. It's why I built my life around books, first as a librarian, then by realising my dream of opening this shop.' Lou paused. She hadn't intended to reveal so much about herself, but she could see everyone listening avidly. 'Now,' she smiled again, 'to the book. The reason this one has meant so much to me is not only the way it is written, the beautiful way the author has with words, but because of the…' As she continued, Lou could see a few people leaning forward eagerly while others looked bored. She quickly finished up. 'As I said at the beginning, not every book will appeal to everyone here. Why doesn't someone who reads a different type of book go next? But before they do, are there any comments or questions about this one?'

A few people spoke up, one who had never heard of the author and a couple who, like Lou, loved her books. Then one of the male members of the group held up a copy of an Ian Rankin book and talked about his love of the Inspector Rebus series, which led to a discussion of different crime authors. The evening was off to a good start, and Lou was able to relax as the discussion took off.

The rest of the hour passed quickly, and there were a few disappointed groans when Lou drew the evening to a close and reminded them of the date of the next meeting in four weeks' time.

'I hope to see many of you again,' she said, 'but no worries if this isn't for you. You might like to start your own book club and if so, I'd be happy to help in any way I can.'

As Ron and Denny moved around to collect used cups and mugs, most of the group left, with a few staying behind to thank Lou and either say they'd be back or that they'd drop into the bookshop during opening hours. One asked if they'd be able to purchase any of the books which had been discussed, and Lou promised to check her stock. The comment which almost moved her to tears was from the elderly woman who thanked her, saying that it had been so good to get out of the house and meet other likeminded people. It hadn't occurred to Lou that her *Book Café* would provide an antidote to someone's loneliness.

Lou had a smile on her face when she arrived home to be greeted by Tilly who wound herself around her ankles mewling piteously, annoyed at having been left alone. It was good to be home in the small cottage that had once been a fisherman's shack, now renovated and unrecognisable from the original. Lou picked up the cat and gave her a cuddle. Life was good. It would be perfect if only she could find Fleur, but as her old grandmother used to say, if wishes were horses, beggars would ride. Reminding herself to be grateful for what she had, she headed for bed as Tilly wriggled out of her arms.

Two

Blair Stevens gazed at the piles of boxes which filled his hallway and wondered for the hundredth time if he was making a dreadful mistake. It had seemed so simple when his daughter first floated the idea of him moving to Pelican Crossing, but now the time was drawing closer, he was beginning to regret agreeing so readily.

But it was too late to change his mind now. The house was sold, the sandstone cottage on the bank of the Derwent River which he and Prue had purchased when he was a newly appointed lecturer at the University of Tasmania. It was where Katrina and Chelsea had been born and held so many memories. Blair shook away the tears which threatened to leak from his eyes. It was only a house, after all.

In Pelican Crossing, there would be Katrina along with Harper and Noah, his two grandchildren, who he'd be able to spend more time with. And he'd be closer to Chelsea too. Brisbane was a lot closer to Pelican Crossing than it was to Hobart.

It had been a wrench to leave the university, to retire from the work he loved, say goodbye to beloved colleagues and students. But he hadn't wanted to become one of those sad old emeritus professors who hung on with no other life. He had a family he loved and who loved him, and he and Prue had always planned to move closer to the girls when he retired. It was just hard to make the move by himself.

Blair knew if Prue was still alive, it would be different. She would be urging him on, talking about how wonderful it would be to live on the mainland, to be able to see Katrina and the grandchildren whenever they wanted, instead of rushed holidays in Queensland when he could be prised away from the university, or their equally hurried trips back to Tasmania. She'd be reminding him of the novel he'd always been too busy to write, of how the ongoing maintenance of their old home would soon be too much for them, and how the villa Katrina had picked out in an over-fifties community would suit them much better.

But that was the problem. There was no them. There was only him, and without the daily routine of the university, he'd miss Prue even more. He didn't know how he'd fill his days.

He stifled a sigh and turned away from the boxes, willing them to disappear. The removalist was due in the morning, and he'd promised to meet a group of old friends for dinner. The formal farewell at the university had been held a week ago, despite Blair saying he didn't want a fuss. But after being there for over forty years, it was too much to hope he'd be able to slip away quietly, so he suffered the large farewell party with as much grace as he could muster, embarrassed by the effusive compliments and glad when it was over and he could return home.

*

It was a strange sort of evening. The others – two couples and two singles one widowed like Blair, one recently divorced – had been friends and neighbours for years, ever since their children were little. They had gone through the various stages of infancy, childhood illnesses, adolescence and the trauma of the teenage years together, but Blair's daughters were the only two to move away. The others had children and grandchildren they saw regularly, so they understood why he'd decided on the move, even though they'd miss him and their regular get-togethers. He'd miss them too.

Was he too old to make new friends, Blair wondered as he looked around the familiar faces, each one recalling a treasured memory from the past. The new owners of his house were a young couple. They wouldn't fit in with this group, all of whom were, like Blair, in their sixties and either retired or heading that way.

The conversation flowed, helped along by quantities of wine as they remembered days gone by and discussed future plans. One of the couples had recently purchased a campervan and planned to become grey nomads, the other had booked a series of cruises. The two singles were still working but talked longingly of the overseas trips they'd take when the time was right. It all made Blair wonder yet again if he had fallen in with Katrina's plans too readily without stopping to think about what he wanted to do with the rest of his life.

Blair was a homebody. Unlike his friends, he had no desire to travel around or beyond Australia, and the thought of spending weeks on a cruise ship left him cold. He'd done his travelling when he was younger, backpacking around Europe in his gap year and visiting the national parks in the US with Prue when they travelled there to attend conferences in his early years at the university. Now he was content to stay put. Moving to Pelican Crossing would be a big enough adjustment for him.

'So, you're off tomorrow?' Alec said. In addition to being his closest neighbour, Alec also taught at the university and was yet to retire. 'Hobart's loss is Pelican Crossing's gain. We'll miss you.'

'I'll miss you too.' Since Prue's death three years earlier, Blair and Alec had fallen into the habit of spending more time together. He was widowed too and understood the gap it left when the woman you'd spent most of your life with was no longer there.

'But you'll have your daughter and grandkids. That's a bonus.'

'Mmm.' It was the prospect of spending more time with them that Blair was looking forward to, what would make it all worthwhile. Harper was ten now and growing up fast. She reminded him of Prue with her bright eyes and dark curls. She'd been her grandmother's little shadow every time they were together, helping her bake and following her around the house, while Noah, at seven, barely remembered his grandmother. Blair had vowed to help him remember, telling him about her and showing him photographs.

Katrina led a busy life, and he suspected it might fall to him to collect the children from school when she was working. From what she had told him, the massage business which she'd set up in the *Pelican Crossing Wellness Centre* was going from strength to strength, and he was aware his son-in-law led a busy life too, as a reporter with the local paper.

Blair was still thinking about Katrina and Brett when he arrived home, so wasn't surprised when his phone rang almost as soon as he walked in – Prue had always told him he had an advanced psychic sense.

'Hi, Kat, I was just thinking about you,' he said.

'All set for tomorrow, Dad?'

'As much as I can be. The house is packed up, the removalist arrives at seven, and I fly to Brisbane late afternoon. As I told you, I'm spending a few days there with Chels to catch up and give all my stuff time to make its way up to Pelican Crossing. I'll see you on the weekend.'

'Good.' She sounded relieved. *Had she thought he'd change his mind at the last moment?* 'Harper and Noah are so looking forward to seeing you.' She paused. 'I spoke to the realtor, and he said I can collect the keys to your villa. I thought I might take a peek, see if anything needs doing before you move in.' She paused again, as if wondering if she'd overstepped the mark.

It occurred to Blair how like her mother she was. If Prue had been alive, the pair of them would have already arranged to have the villa cleaned, painted and he didn't know what else. But Prue wasn't here, and it was his new home, where he'd live out the rest of his days. He didn't know why the thought made him feel depressed. Several of his former colleagues had moved into similar accommodation when they retired and waxed lyrical about the low maintenance, the company and the number of activities on offer ranging from something called pickle ball to bridge, Zumba and ballroom dancing, none of which held any appeal for him.

'Dad?'

'Yes, sorry. Miles away. Take a peek. Good idea.'

Three

It was Saturday morning, and after last night's first meeting of the *Book Café*, Lou knew it would be a busy day in the bookshop. Not only had some of last night's group promised to pop in, but weekends were always her busiest times, and now the weather was becoming warmer, Pelican Crossing was a favourite weekend getaway for people from the city and interstate. It wouldn't be long before the summer holidays were upon them with all the extra holidaymakers too.

'How was last night?' Lou's assistant, Zoe, asked when she arrived to see Lou scanning the computer. 'Can I help?'

'No,' Lou said, distracted. She'd been checking her list of stock for last night's titles to save herself the trouble of searching the shelves. 'Sorry, Zoe. It was good, went really well. We had a full house and after a slow start when I probably talked for longer than I should, it really took off. Many promised to come back next month, and we should be seeing a few of them come in this morning. I was just checking if we have the books we discussed.'

'Wow! Another of your good ideas. You're still happy about Halloween?'

'Of course.' The idea to have a special Halloween display had been one of Zoe's brainwaves. The younger woman was a fan of fantasy novels, especially those involving witches and magic. She had suggested that they not only arrange a display of the books for the week ending in Halloween which fell on the Friday, but that they turn the children's section of the bookshop into an eerie cave complete with fake cobwebs and spooky masks. She'd managed to arrange with the local primary school for classes to visit on rotation for readings from relevant books and persuaded the teachers to encourage the children to dress up in appropriate costumes.

'Good, it should be fun. Then we need to think about Christmas. It's just around the corner.'

'Not you too,' Lou sighed. 'When I walked into the supermarket last week, I was confronted with a display of mince pies and Christmas crackers.'

Zoe laughed. 'It's big business. You do intend to have our usual tree and decorations, don't you?'

'Of course,' Lou said again, 'but let's wait till closer to the time. I hate this habit of racing through the year from one celebration to another. Let's get Halloween over and our breath back from that before we start thinking about Christmas. At least we're not in America and we don't have Thanksgiving to worry about. No!' she said, seeing a gleam in Zoe's eyes. 'Don't you dare!'

Zoe only laughed, and any further conversation was prevented by the arrival of their first customers of the day.

It wasn't that Lou didn't like Christmas. She did. She loved the lead up to the big day, the excitement on children's faces when they walked into *Books and Coffee* to see the large tree she always placed just inside the door and all the other decorations, the sound of Christmas carols echoing around the shop and the café. It was her busiest time of the year, and she wouldn't trade it for anything. Over the years, she'd managed to persuade her friends that she relished the opportunity to spend Christmas Day alone, to have a respite from her busy life, to spoil herself. But she couldn't fool herself.

Christmas Day for Lou was a day of memories, memories of a time when she was part of a happy family, the house buzzing with people, filled with the aroma of food cooking and the sounds of happy laughter. It was a day when she gave thought to her sister, wondered where she was, if she was happy and if she ever thought about Lou.

Lou dismissed her musings on the past to concentrate on the present. She was right. Many of those who'd attended the *Book Café* did drop in, and she was pleased when they purchased copies of books which other group members had recommended. It might be a good idea to make books available for sale after the meeting, though it would mean a later night for her. It was something to consider. The next meeting was a month away. But it proved that her idea for a *Book Café* had more than one benefit.

By lunchtime, she was more than ready for a break, relieved when the stream of customers slowed down sufficiently for first Zoe, then Georgia, her weekend assistant who was in Year Twelve at the local high school, to grab a quick bite.

'Your turn,' Zoe said when she returned. 'We can manage for a bit.'

'If you're sure.' Lou glanced around the shop to where several customers were browsing the shelves and Georgia was serving a woman with two young children.

The shop door opened, and Lou smiled at the sight of her friend, Rachel, accompanied by a small girl. 'Verity is eager to buy the next Amelia Bedelia book in the series she's collecting,' Rachel said, 'and we hoped you might be able to make time to join us for lunch.'

'Good timing. I was about to take a break. Why don't you find your book, Verity, then we can all have lunch?'

As the little girl rushed off to the children's section, Lou watched Rachel's eyes follow the child with affection. It was almost two years since her friend's son had arrived on her doorstep on Christmas Eve with Verity whose mother had recently died, then had returned to England leaving the little girl behind. It said a lot for Rachel that she hadn't been fazed by what others might have seen as an imposition but had accepted the little girl into her life. Now, although Alexander had returned to Pelican Crossing and was in a relationship with a local woman, Verity still loved to spend time with her grandmother. She loved books and the pair often popped into the bookshop on weekends.

By the time Lou and Rachel made their way into the café, with Verity proudly clutching her new book, the crowd was thinning, and they were able to secure a table without any trouble. It was a relief for Lou to get off her feet. She was finding it more difficult these days, prompting thoughts of retirement, but what would she do without *Books and Coffee* to go to every day, without the friendly faces of her customers, without Ron and Denny's cheerful company?

'You're looking very thoughtful,' Rachel said, when their coffee and paninis had arrived, and Verity was slurping a large smoothie.

'Just wondering how long I can keep going at this pace. Oh, don't mind me,' she said, seeing Rachel's shocked expression. 'I don't mean it. It's just that my feet are killing me and it's been a busy morning. I shouldn't complain,' she added, remembering that Becky, Rachel's older sister and her own best friend from school, had died suffering from Alzheimer's before she reached Lou's age. 'I enjoy it really. It's just that sometimes I realise I'm not getting any younger and I won't be able to do this for ever. I'll have to give it up some day.'

'But not for a while yet, I hope.' Rachel looked concerned. 'You had your first meeting of your *Book Café* last night, didn't you? How did it go?'

Lou immediately cheered up as she described the evening to her friend, finishing with, 'I hadn't realised there were so many lonely people in Pelican Crossing, Rach.'

'You're providing a community service, Lou.' Rachel put her hand on Lou's. 'This town needs you. Don't think of giving up… ever.'

'I won't.' Lou laughed. She knew the day might come when the shop became too much for her, but hopefully not for many years yet.

Verity was lost in her new book, and Lou and Rachel were finishing their coffee when Rachel asked, 'Do you ever hear from Fleur?'

Lou gazed at her in shock. Although Rachel and Fleur had been in the same year at school, they'd never been friends like Lou and Becky had been. This was the first time Rachel had mentioned her to Lou. 'No,' she said, then realising she might have sounded abrupt, added, 'Why do you ask?'

'No reason. It's just we were looking at old school photos the other night, and Luke asked about her. He remembered she was your sister.'

Lou swallowed. She didn't know why she was surprised. It was almost two years ago, about the same time Alexander had appeared with Verity, that Rachel had reconnected with her old flame, Luke Findlay, who'd been in Lou's year at school. They were now living together in her house on the bluff on the outskirts of town with their two dogs.

'I haven't heard from her in years, Rach. I don't even know if she's still alive.'

'Oh!' Rachel said no more, but Lou could tell she was itching for more information. But that was one of Rachel's strengths. Not only was she able to keep a secret, she knew when to keep her mouth shut.

'Sorry, Rach. It's been good to catch up, but I need to get back now.'

'I'm sorry if I held you up.'

'Not at all. It was good to have time to chat.'

'Why don't you come to dinner with Luke and me next Saturday? We're having a few people over for a barbecue. You'll know all of them. It'll be a chance to talk over old times.'

'Thanks, I'd like that.' She hadn't seen as much of Rachel since she and Luke got together, and it would be good to relax in the company of old friends.

Lou put the conversation with Rachel out of her mind for the rest of the working day, as she focussed on her customers. It was only when she was back home enjoying a glass of wine after dinner, Tilly curled up on her lap, that she remembered Rachel's question about Fleur. It had been a long time. They were both getting older. Maybe it was time to try to find her sister again. But where to start?

Four

Blair had spent an enjoyable few days with Chelsea in her cute home in Brisbane's West End. His younger daughter lived in what had originally been a 1920's worker's cottage, before being renovated by a previous owner who was an architect. This was Blair's first visit to her home, and he was impressed at the realisation that her photographic business must be doing well for her to be able to afford it. She'd developed a love of photography in her early teens and after begging for a camera of her own for her fifteenth birthday, hadn't looked back, working part-time for a local photographer and completing her studies at the local TAFE, before heading to the mainland. Now she ran what appeared to be a successful business in Brisbane.

While Blair was there, she'd taken a few days off to spend time with him, visiting galleries, taking a trip on the City Cat and attending a concert at QPAC (Queensland Performing Arts Centre). He loved the river city and promised himself another visit in the not-too-distant future, and Chelsea had promised to visit him and Katrina in Pelican Crossing once he was settled. There was even a moment during his visit when he wondered if he'd made a mistake and would have been better to have bought something in Brisbane where there would be more to do than in Pelican Crossing. But it was too late. He now owned a villa in this over-fifties resort, and Katrina and his grandchildren were looking forward to his arrival.

Soon after arriving in Brisbane, he'd bought a new car, having sold his old Volvo before he left Hobart. The red MG was very different from anything he'd driven before with its bright paintwork and hybrid engine, and it made him feel at least ten years younger. Chelsea's surprised expression when he drove up in it only confirmed his choice. He might be retired but there was still life in the old dog.

Now, as he waved his daughter goodbye to make his way through the Brisbane traffic and onto the Bruce Highway, he was filled with a sense of heady anticipation. He was about to begin a new life.

*

The drive north was uneventful. Blair stopped once for an indifferent coffee served in a cardboard cup and texted Katrina giving her his ETA. She texted back to say they were all excited to see him.

Blair's mood rose even more as he drew nearer to Pelican Crossing. He couldn't wait to inspect the villa and hoped he wouldn't hate it on sight. His worldly goods were due to arrive in two days' time, on Monday, and Katrina had insisted he stay with her and Brett till then.

It was a relief to see the sign to Pelican Crossing, then to finally pull up outside Katrina's home, a neat bungalow in a new development outside of town with tree-lined streets and tidy gardens. It appeared to be inhabited by many young couples like Katrina and Brett and today there were several small children playing in the front gardens and a few older ones speeding along the footpath on scooters. Harper and Noah were standing inside a white fence, clearly looking out for his arrival.

'Grandad's here!' Noah called, haring back inside to reappear with Katrina.

As soon as Blair stepped out of the car he was enveloped in a mass of hugs. Then, with Harper and Noah hanging on to his arms, he followed Katrina inside.

'Welcome!' Brett gave him a hug. 'I bet you're ready for a beer.'

'Brett, let Dad get his breath,' Katrina said. 'Maybe you'd like something to eat, Dad. We've had lunch but I can fix you a sandwich.'

'A beer sounds good,' Blair said. It seemed a long time since his coffee, and he was feeling dry after his long drive. 'And a sandwich would go down a treat, Kat.'

Brett poured him a beer, and the two men went out into the garden, followed by Harper and Noah, while Katrina made a sandwich. 'How was the trip?' Brett asked, while Noah tried to attract his grandfather's attention, and Harper grabbed his free hand.

'Long. It was good to have a few days with Chels in Brisbane.'

'You stayed with Aunt Chelsea?' Harper asked. 'She's so cool.'

Both Blair and Brett laughed.

'Grandad!' Noah tugged on Blair's arm. 'Can you kick a ball with me?'

'Later, son,' Brett said. 'Your grandad has just had a long drive. He needs time to drink his beer and have something to eat.'

'Sorry, Dad,' Katrina said, coming outside and handing him a sandwich. 'They're just so excited to see you. We've been talking about it for weeks.'

Blair smiled. He was pleased to see them too, and to think that he'd be able to see them as often as he liked now, though he expected the novelty of his presence would soon wear thin.

After he'd finished his beer and sandwich, arranged his overnight things in Katrina's spare room and freshened up, he returned to where the family were waiting for him in the kitchen.

'The kids are keen to show you the beach if you have the energy, Dad,' Katrina said,

'Of course.' He may have retired but hoped his daughter didn't intend to treat him like an old man. He was only sixty-seven and didn't feel old. Back home he had still walked every morning and visited the gym at least once a week. He intended to keep up his exercise programme here once he got settled, and now he was living on the coast, it might be good to add swimming to his routine.

As they drove to the beach, Harper pointed out the harbour and the marina which he remembered from his previous visits, while Noah wanted him to look at the pelicans that waddled across the path.

They stopped in a car park close to the main beach which was busy with swimmers, surfers and a group involved in a game of beach volleyball. Blair was glad he'd thought to apply sunscreen and brought a hat. The weather was warmer here than back home, and the sun a lot stronger. He pulled himself up. This was his home now. It was going to take a bit of getting used to.

As they walked along the hard-packed sand at the edge of the sea, the children dashed in and out of the shallow water. With the sand between his toes, the sound of the waves and the calling of the seagulls in his ears, Blair felt his spirits rise. This was a good place to be. Maybe this had been the right decision after all.

It wasn't long before first Noah, then Harper begged for an ice cream, and they all made their way back to Main Street and a gelato shop. 'Thanks,' Blair said as Katrina handed him a mango flavoured ice cream. He couldn't remember when he'd last eaten the frozen treat from a cone. It took him back to when Katrina and Chelsea were small, and he and Prue took them to the beach for holidays.

'What are we going to do now?' Noah wanted to know when he'd demolished his ice cream. Blair had forgotten about the unflagging energy of a seven-year-old. It was mid-afternoon and, after driving all morning, Blair was ready for a rest. But when Katrina said, 'Why don't we take your grandad to see his new home?', Blair perked up. He hadn't wanted to suggest it, but he'd been hoping to see *The Haven* and his villa. So far, he had only seen photos and the floorplan of the place that was to be his new home, and he wasn't completely sure what to expect.

'Yay!' Noah and Harper chorused in unison.

'Okay with you, Dad?' Katrina asked. 'We could wait till tomorrow if you want a rest before dinner. We were planning to go out to the yacht club to celebrate your first night in Pelican Crossing. They do a special early dinner for children and seniors.'

'Fine by me,' Blair said, unsure if he was being categorised along with the children as being eligible for the early dinner. 'I can't wait to see my new home.'

Blair gazed around with interest as they drove through the gates of *The Haven,* and along an avenue bordered by palm trees. They passed a beautiful old sandstone building which he presumed was some sort of restaurant or recreation hall, then a row of tidy villas sitting apart with well-tended gardens.

The villa in front of which they parked was neat and white-painted like the others but with a moss green door and a garden which was in need of care. Blair could picture it filled with colourful plants similar to the one he'd left behind in Hobart, and he itched to begin planting.

He fingered the key in his pocket which Katrina had handed him earlier.

'Why don't you have a look on your own, while we take a walk around,' Katrina suggested, much to Blair's relief. Much as he loved his daughter and grandchildren, he wanted to savour this first glimpse of his new home by himself. Suddenly too overcome to speak, he only nodded, waiting till they'd walked away, the two children chattering like magpies, before fitting the key into the lock and opening the door.

Once inside, Blair moved from one room to the next, visualising how they would look filled with his furniture and belongings, brushing away a tear at the thought that Prue should have been there with him, telling him that the sofa would look best here, his favourite armchair there, and that this would be the best spot for his study and desk.

He blinked to dismiss the image of his late wife who would never see this home, would for ever remain in his beloved Tassie. This was his future, and it would suit him very well.

Five

Lou gazed critically at herself in the bedroom mirror, while Tilly prowled around her ankles mewing piteously as if she knew Lou was going out for the evening. She'd been a chubby child and had slimmed down in her teens and early twenties only to put on weight again when she opened *Books and Coffee* and found Ron's delicious offerings hard to resist. But, she thought, as she smoothed her hands down over her hips and the dress she'd chosen to wear, she didn't look too bad for someone approaching her mid-sixties. Her dark hair, which she always kept short, was only showing a few flecks of grey, and her eyes still had the same sparkle they'd had when Darren… No, she didn't want to think of him, not tonight, not ever again. She leant into the mirror to check her makeup, grimacing at the new wrinkles around her eyes which she could swear had appeared overnight.

She was looking forward to the barbecue at Rachel's, in the house situated on the top of the bluff on the outskirts of town with magnificent views over the ocean and her private beach. It was the one she and her late husband had bought when she was pregnant with her first child and now lived in with her new partner. It was very different from Lou's small cottage.

There were several cars already parked outside Rachel's house when Lou drove up, and as soon as she got out of the car, she could hear the sound of voices and the barking of at least two dogs, not surprising as now Luke's boxer lived there along with Rachel's small West Highland Terrier. She had barely reached the door when the two dogs padded out to greet her, followed by Rachel.

'I thought I heard your car,' Rachel said, giving Lou a hug. 'We're in the garden. Come through.'

Once outside, in Rachel's carefully tended garden, Lou saw a larger group than she'd expected. Besides Rachel's three good friends, Poppy, Liz and Gill, and their partners, there was Rachel's neighbour and local vet, Bob, along with Phil and Troy, neighbours of Lou's who had been at school with her and Luke. Neither had partners, Troy having been widowed and Phil, who now owned the yacht club, divorced. Rachel had been right. Lou did know all of them.

'Welcome.' Luke hugged Lou as did the other women, while both Phil and Troy gave her a peck on the cheek. To Lou's relief, Bob and the other men merely nodded. She didn't know them very well, although Liz's partner, Finn, was editor of the local newspaper, and Joe, Gill's partner, was the local mayor, and he and Gill were now neighbours of Lou's too, having recently purchased the cottage at the end of the row.

At one time, after Darren left, her friend and Rachel's sister, Becky, had tried to set Lou up with Phil or Troy, but Lou knew them both too well to be interested in them romantically, even if she'd been prepared to risk her heart being broken again. They'd remained friends over the years, and now they were neighbours too. It was the way Lou liked it. No emotions. No fuss. No regrets. She was happy Rachel, like her friends, had found love a second time around, but it wasn't for her. She was satisfied with her bookshop, her cottage and her cat.

Once Rachel had poured her a drink, Lou, eschewing stereotypes, didn't join the other women in the kitchen, instead gravitating to the barbecue area where the men had formed a huddle, and the dogs were salivating at the smell of meat cooking.

'Hey, Lou, what's new?' Troy said. 'Not thinking of retiring?'

'Absolutely not! What would I do all day?' The others all laughed. They knew that although Troy maintained he'd handed over the day-to-day running of his landscape business to his son, he still worked there on a daily basis. Of the group, Luke was the only one who could claim to have retired, and *he* helped out at Bob's vet practice on an as-needed basis.

By the time the steaks were cooked, the other women had joined them, and Lou found herself seated between Rachel and Poppy, both of whom wanted to discuss the Halloween event at the bookshop which their granddaughters were to attend. Lou was happy to oblige, and the evening passed pleasantly without any further comments about or thoughts of retirement. This was possibly because both women were still younger and, while Rachel had given up her bed and breakfast business when she and Luke got together, Poppy was still the active owner and manager of *Crossings*, Pelican Crossing's premier restaurant.

It wasn't till Lou was back home and had made her peace with Tilly who was annoyed at having had to spend the evening alone, that Lou had time to reflect on her evening. As she prepared for bed, it occurred to her that out of all the people who'd been at the barbecue, she was the only one without any family, either here in Pelican Crossing or interstate, like Gill's daughter or Luke's son, both of whom lived in Sydney. But she had a sister somewhere. Once again, she felt the urge to find Fleur and to repair the rift that had kept them apart for so long.

Six

It was Monday morning, and Blair couldn't wait to move into his new home. It had been good to spend the weekend with Katrina and her family, but he had found the children's continual presence wearing and would be glad to be on his own again. Since Prue's death, he'd become accustomed to his own company. *Had he become a grumpy old man?* He grinned at the thought and knew Prue would grin too.

He could hear the sound of voices outside the bedroom and knew it was time to get up, shower and dress. This was a working day for Katrina and Brett, and a school day for Harper and Noah. Although his daughter had offered to take the day off to help him get settled, Blair had declined, telling her that her massage clients needed her, when in actual fact, he didn't want her fussing around him while he decided where to put everything in his new home.

'There you are, Dad.' Katrina looked very smart in pale green pants and a matching tunic bearing the logo of the *Pelican Crossing Wellness Centre*. There was no sign of Brett who must have already left for work. 'I need to leave soon to drop the children off at school before I start work. Help yourself to breakfast and lock up when you leave. Are you sure…?'

'I'm sure. I'll be fine. Have a good day.'

'Yes.' But she was distracted, as both Harper and Noah seemed to be having trouble finding everything they needed for school. 'We'll see you for dinner, won't we? Harper! Noah! Give your grandad a hug. It's time to go.'

'Yes, Kat. Don't worry about me. I'll fill you in tonight. Why don't I take you all out to dinner?'

'Not on a school night.'

Duly chastised, Blair hugged Harper and Noah, accepted a peck on the cheek from Katrina, then they were all gone, and the house was suddenly very quiet. Blair gave a sigh of relief, before fixing himself breakfast and taking his coffee and toast out into the backyard where a couple of brightly coloured parakeets were feasting on some bushes. The removalists weren't due to arrive at his villa in *The Haven* for another hour. He had time to relax.

*

This time, when he drove through the entrance to *The Haven*, Blair felt a sense of familiarity. It didn't feel like home, perhaps it never would, but it didn't feel as strange as it had on Saturday, either. He fitted the key into the lock and went in. When he entered the kitchen, he was greeted by bright sunlight coming through the window and the sight of a pair of kookaburras sitting on the back fence. As he watched, they began their loud *koo-koo-koo-koo-koo-kaa-kaa-kaa* as if to welcome him. Blair's face broke into a smile. How Prue would have loved this.

'Hello?' someone called through the front door which he'd left open. It was a woman's voice, not the removalists he was expecting. When he went to the door, the elderly woman standing there was a stranger. She was smiling.

'Hello, you must be my new neighbour,' she said. 'I'm Joan.' She looked at him expectantly.

'Blair.' He held out his hand, which she shook.

'We're a friendly community here. I'm sure you'll enjoy living in *The Haven*. Your furniture…?' She glanced behind him.

At that moment the large removal van drove up, and Blair was saved from replying or engaging in any further conversation. 'Sorry,' he said, gesturing to the van. 'I need to…'

'Of course, but if I can help in any way, you only have to ask.'

'Thanks.' Was this what it was going to be like? Overtures from overly friendly neighbours, from women who, going by this one, were at least ten years older than he was? Blair was glad they'd been interrupted. While it was good of her – Joan – to want to welcome him to the neighbourhood, he wasn't ready to play happy families with strangers.

Blair's furniture was soon unloaded, and he spent most of the rest of the day moving things around till he was satisfied, only stopping briefly to snack on a sandwich he'd brought from Katrina's. She'd insisted he accept a box of food she'd bought for him, saying he wouldn't feel like a trip to the shops on his first day. She was probably right, as it took him longer than he'd expected to get unpacked, and there were still boxes of stuff in the garage.

He'd chosen a bedroom overlooking the backyard as his study and was delighted with the peaceful outlook. The kookaburras had departed to be replaced by a trio of noisy miner birds, and he enjoyed listening to them as he arranged his books on the bookshelf and set up his computer. This would be the perfect spot to write the book he'd been thinking about for years, based on stories his grandmother had told him and which she'd heard from *her* grandmother.

He was sitting there, lost in thought, when his phone rang, and he saw Chelsea's number.

'Dad,' she said when he answered, 'just wanted to check how you were settling in. It was today, wasn't it? Hope Kat isn't trying to organise you too much,' she laughed.

Blair laughed too. It had always been a joke in their family how both Prue and Katrina were the organisers, while Blair and Chelsea seemed to manage to drift through life without any effort. 'No, your sister's at work today, so I managed the move all by myself. I'm currently sitting in my new study, looking out onto the backyard and listening to the birds.'

'Sounds good. So, you think you're going to like it in this over-fifties place?'

'So far, so good.' But Blair couldn't help thinking about the woman who'd appeared at his door and claimed to be his neighbour. But perhaps they weren't all like her. 'I'm having dinner with Kat and family again tonight, then I plan to spend some time getting to know my way around… by myself.'

'Good luck with that,' Chelsea chuckled. 'You know what Kat's like. She'll have you organised within an inch of your life if you're not careful.'

'Don't worry, Chels. I think I can handle your sister. I've had plenty of practice.'

Chelsea chuckled again. 'Well, don't say I didn't warn you. I plan to come up for Christmas, which isn't too far away. Look forward to seeing your new abode. You should be well settled in by then.'

'I hope so. It'll be good to see you again. I'm not likely to make it back to Brisbane before then, but you never know.'

'Well, if Kat gets too much for you, you can always hide out here for a bit.'

Blair chuckled to himself when the call ended. His two daughters were so different from each other, and he loved them both dearly. He was glad Katrina had found Brett and was happy. He only wished Chelsea would find someone special too.

By six o'clock, Blair reckoned he'd done enough. He showered and changed before taking a can of beer out of the fridge, feeling he deserved it after all his effort. Looking around, he was pleased with what he'd achieved. The villa was beginning to look like home.

On the way to his daughter's, Blair stopped off at a bottle shop to buy wine for dinner, adding a couple of packets of the potato chips he knew his grandchildren liked.

He had barely made it out of the car when he was caught up in a whirlwind of arms and legs as Harper and Noah fell on him with hugs. 'Did you move into your new house today?' Harper asked, while Noah, catching sight of what he was carrying asked, 'Are those for us?'

'The chips are for you two, the wine for your mum and dad. Now, how about you let me get inside before I drop something?' But Blair was grinning. This was why he'd made the move, to spend more time with these two scallywags, to watch them grow up and maybe even give them some guidance. He was going to enjoy introducing them to history and literature, just as he had Katrina and Chelsea, and to discovering what they enjoyed doing.

Once inside, he hugged Katrina and handed her the wine – the children had already taken possession of the potato chips with their mother warning them not to eat them all before dinner.

'How was today, Dad? Are you all unpacked? Did you meet any of your neighbours? Did…?'

'Give your dad time to get his breath, Kat,' Brett said. 'Beer, Blair?'

'Thanks, Brett. And today was good, Kat. I'm mostly unpacked, just a few more boxes to go, mainly unimportant stuff that can sit in the garage till I need it. And I did meet one neighbour, an elderly lady called Joan.' He took a welcome sip of the beer Brett handed him.

'Joan?' Katrina's forehead creased, then cleared. I know who she is. Joan Ellis. She's one of my clients, a lovely lady, Liz Phillips' Mum. Liz works in the medical centre and is friends with...'

'Okay, Kat. Your dad doesn't need to hear her whole history.'

But Katrina wasn't finished. 'I heard that she has formed a relationship with one of the men living in *The Haven*. There was an article about him in *The Echo*. He's a Vietnam veteran.'

'Hear that, Blair? You want to watch yourself. Seems like *The Haven* might be a nest of elderly women on the lookout for a man to sweeten their later years.' Brett chuckled.

Blair took another sip of beer and shuffled his feet. He wasn't worried about predatory women. He could handle that. But he'd forgotten about the gossip mill in small towns like Pelican Crossing, and how everyone knew everyone else's business and felt free to interfere in their lives. He determined to make sure he gave the other residents of *The Haven* and Pelican Crossing nothing to gossip about.

Seven

It was Halloween, and Lou had become caught up in the excitement of the activities Zoe had organised for the day. Not only had the children's section of the bookshop been transformed into a spooky cave with mock cobwebs, masks and a plastic skeleton her assistant had borrowed from somewhere, but the entire bookshop was decorated in orange and black, and there were pumpkin lanterns sitting in every corner. Even the book display was in keeping with the mood of the day, being composed of ghost stories and books featuring the supernatural. Zoe was dressed in a ghost costume which Lou hoped wouldn't frighten the younger children. Lou's concession to the occasion was to don a black, pointed hat which Zoe told her made her look like a magician, rather than a witch.

The bookshop was busier than usual for a Friday. It seemed children weren't the only ones eager to see the Halloween display, and it was rare for anyone to leave emptyhanded. With Zoe busy in the children's corner preparing for the influx of schoolchildren, Lou was kept occupied speaking to customers and ringing up sales, though she reasoned, you couldn't call it ringing up when almost everyone these days paid by card.

In a rare moment between customers, she took time to replenish the book display which had rapidly depleted, only to be interrupted by a young man and woman flashing ID cards proclaiming them to be from *The Echo*.

'We heard about your Halloween event and would love to cover it for *The Echo*,' the young woman said, brandishing a camera. 'Would that be okay?'

'Sure.' Any publicity was good publicity, and it was some time since *Books and Coffee* had been featured in the local paper. 'But the school groups haven't started to arrive yet.'

'No worries. We can take some shots here first, then…' She glanced towards the café from where there came an enticing aroma of coffee.

Lou laughed. 'Tell Ron the coffee's on me.'

'Thanks. It's Lou, isn't it?' the young man said.

'It is.' Lou had seen the pair before, but didn't know their names. They were new to the town, part of the surge of city folk seeking a sea change, though these two were younger than most.

After taking a few shots of the shop and the currently deserted children's corner, the pair disappeared into the café, and Lou carried on serving the growing flock of customers.

The shop door opened, and there was the loud chatter of excited voices as the first group of schoolchildren arrived, herded in by their teacher, a flustered woman in her late twenties. Lou smiled to see the variety of costumes which the parents had managed to come up with. There were the usual witches and ghostly figures, but also several dressed as their favourite book characters, the costumes no doubt left over from book week.

Lou was surprised when Rachel walked in. 'I hope I'm not too late,' she said. 'Are they here yet?'

It took Lou a moment to understand what she meant, then she realised that many of her customers had now moved into the children's corner where the kindergarten class was being urged to sit on the carpet ready for their story. 'You're here for story time?'

Rachel nodded. 'Verity insisted I come to see her all dressed up, and to hear her story. Gemma and Indie, too. Seems I might be here for most of the morning.' She attempted a grimace, but Lou knew she adored her three granddaughters and was most likely eager to see them and listen to Zoe reading to them.

'You're just in time, and you're not the only one.' She nodded to where the children's corner was fast becoming packed with adults. Perhaps they should have anticipated this and provided chairs, but there really wasn't room.

'Thanks. See you later.' Rachel drifted off.

Lou smiled with a tinge of regret. How nice it would be to have a granddaughter, even a grandniece to share special moments with. Her mind went again to her sister. If Fleur and Darren had children, they would be in their thirties now. It was a daunting thought.

*

Blair had spent the past two weeks finding his way around Pelican Crossing. He'd joined the library, signed on at the gym, and discovered a few favourite haunts. *The Blue Dolphin Café* was located across from the harbour and marina and provided a pleasant view across both. It was now his go-to spot for coffee and breakfast. And *The Grand*, which was aptly named, served a good selection of beer. From the outside, the grand old hotel looked as if it hadn't changed in the past fifty years, but inside, while dim, it had been brightly painted and renovated, and Blair was becoming addicted to the selection of craft beers brewed locally, he was told, by a couple of enterprising young men. He'd made a mental note to visit the brewery one day.

Today, he was looking forward to visiting a new venue. Both Noah and Harper had insisted he come to the bookshop which their respective classes were to visit for a special Halloween event. They were excited about getting dressed up and although they'd already paraded their costumes for him the previous evening, wanted him to come along to see them and their classmates and to hear the stories. He'd been happy to agree, not sure why he hadn't already made a visit to the bookshop which he'd learned from Katrina was actually a combined bookshop and café. Normally, a bookshop would have been high on his list of places to visit in a new town.

Blair pushed open the door to be greeted by the familiar smell of books, but this one was mixed with the delightful aroma of coffee. A quick glance around showed him it was a popular spot this morning, and the happy sounds coming from the back of the shop were a clear indication that the storytelling was well underway. He checked the time. He was early. He wondered if there was time for coffee. The aroma was so tempting. But the sound of children's voices grew louder, and a band of small children, accompanied by a harried-looking teacher filed past him.

A few minutes later, another group marched in, followed by a young man. Noah was in this group and waved madly at Blair as he passed him. The woman behind the counter grinned at Blair as he waved back. 'One of yours?' she asked, probably not expecting a reply, but, 'My grandson,' he said. 'Noah.'

'We have lots of parents and grandparents here this morning,' she said and, as if to confirm her words, a number of adults appeared from the back of the store where the children were headed.

Following Noah's class into what Blair could see was now the children's section of the bookshop, he heard gasps of surprise and perhaps a few of fear, as the class took their places on the mat, surrounded by myriad Halloween decorations including a realistic skeleton. But everyone soon settled down as a young woman who Blair assumed was a staff member in the shop, held up a book called *The Pomegranate Witch* and began to read the rhyming tale of a battle between the sly, plucky, young rascals and their wry, witchy neighbour.

Blair had never heard of the book, and enjoyed the story as much as the children, almost sorry when it was over, and the group filed out again.

It appeared the classes were arriving in rote, so it would be some time before it was Harper's turn. After a brief browse of the shelves, Blair decided he needed to return sometime when there was no Halloween event happening, no children noisily filing in and out, and no grandchildren to appease. Then checking the time again, figured he had time to sample the coffee in the adjoining café.

'Haven't seen you here before. New to town or here for the Halloween event next door?' the young man manning the counter asked.

'Both. I moved here a couple of weeks ago, and my grandchildren are involved in the event. The youngest's class has just left, the next one shouldn't start for an hour or so.'

The man nodded. 'We've had a few like you in this morning. I'm Ron.'

'Blair.'

'Pleased to meet you. Why don't you try one of our special caramel salted brownies? On the house since this is your first visit. I'm willing to bet it won't be your last.' He grinned.

'Thanks.' Blair liked him, his pride in the café and his generosity. And a salted caramel brownie did sound tempting.

'Take a seat, and Denny will bring your order over to you.'

'Thanks,' Blair said again, noticing for the first time the other young man who was ferrying orders to several tables, filled with a mixture of what looked like parents and grandparents, just as the woman in the bookshop had said. It seemed he wasn't the only one to head to the café, either. Seeing that many of the patrons had bags emblazoned with the *Books and Coffee* logo, it appeared the event was providing business for both the bookshop and café. Blair was no different. He had already planned to purchase copies of the books which Harper and Noah had heard read that morning.

The session for Harper's class proceeded in much the same way as the earlier one, apart from the story being read. In deference to the taste for horror of the class of ten-year-olds, the reading was of the first few chapters of *Night of the Hidden Mummy* from the Goosebumps House of Shivers series. Blair was amused to see how the girls huddled together while the boys in the group pushed on each other, pretending to be fearless. There were howls of disappointment when the reading ended.

The class returned to school, and Blair checked the display of children's books, finding the copies he wanted before taking them to the counter and waiting in the queue of others with the same idea. It was lunchtime, and it seemed the older woman he'd seen when he arrived was on a break. It was the young woman who'd been reading to the children who served him. She blushed when he complimented her on the way she'd managed to bring the books to life. He left with one of the bags he'd seen earlier in the café, pleased with his purchases.

He planned to wrap the books to present to Harper and Noah on Sunday when he'd made arrangements to treat them and their parents to breakfast at *The Blue Dolphin*. He wasn't ready to entertain in his villa just yet and wanted to thank them for their hospitality and kindness when he first arrived in town, even though Katrina said there was no need.

When he arrived home and took the books out of the bag, a leaflet fell to the floor. Picking it up, Blair saw that it was advertising future events at the bookshop, a couple of author talks, one of which was of interest to him, and something called a *Book Café*. Curious, he read further. He'd never been attracted to any of the book clubs that had proliferated back in Hobart, though Prue had enjoyed the one she belonged to and had encouraged him to join. He couldn't bear the thought of having to read a book chosen by others, then discuss it. This was different. If he understood correctly, the *Book Café* was a place where members brought along a book of their own, one which they had enjoyed, and shared it with the others. Now, that was something that appealed to him. He stuck the leaflet up on the fridge and made a note of the date in his phone.

Eight

Lou was glad when Sunday came around. It had been a hectic week and a particularly busy Saturday as many of the children who'd attended the Halloween event returned with their parents to buy copies of the books that had been read. It was lucky she'd had the foresight to order additional copies.

Today, she planned to take the morning off, leaving Zoe and Georgia to cope with customers. Sunday morning was normally a quiet time, most people either attending church or having a family breakfast. She'd go in around lunchtime and let them have a break.

She was enjoying a cup of lemon and ginger tea in her backyard, Tilly lying happily beside her in a puddle of sunshine, when her phone rang, making the cat look up with a start.

'I just wanted to compliment you on yesterday,' Rachel said. 'The girls all had a wonderful time. Jess says the twins haven't stopped talking about it and is sorry Emily missed out as she isn't in school yet. And Verity wants to know when the next one will be.'

'Thanks. It did go down well. I think we must have tripled our usual week's sales in two days. It's all thanks to Zoe. I'd never have thought of it myself.'

'Don't put yourself down. Anyway, we're all having breakfast at *The Blue Dolphin* this morning and I wanted to invite you to join us.' She paused. 'You are having the morning off, aren't you?'

'Yes, but I…' Lou bit her lip. It was kind of Rachel to invite her to join them for breakfast, and she did love the breakfasts at *The Blue*

Dolphin and didn't often get the opportunity to enjoy them. She was either working or too exhausted, and it was no fun to eat there on her own. 'Thanks, Rach. I'd love to,' she said.

*

The café was busy with the usual Sunday crowd when Lou walked in. Poppy was there with her partner, Cam, owner of *Pelican Marine*, seated at the same table they were every Sunday. Today, they were accompanied by their children and four grandchildren.

Poppy, Liz and Gill were all good friends with Rachel. All four had met when their first children were born and remained close ever since. All four had also found love a second time around after being widowed or divorced. They were all younger than Lou, and she sometimes envied them their close friendship. Even though she and Rachel were friends, and she often caught up with neighbours, it wasn't the same as having gone through all those years together.

It would have been different if Lou's best friend, Becky, had remained in Pelican Crossing, but she'd left when she married, moved to South Australia. It was then that she and Rachel had become friends, drawn together by their love of books. Becky had loved books too and would have loved *Books and Coffee*.

After greeting Poppy, and saying good morning to Liz and Finn, who were there with Liz's daughter Julie and teenage granddaughter, Tilly – not to be confused with Lou's cat of the same name – Lou headed for a table at the rear of the café.

'Here she is!' Rachel exclaimed, her voice resonating over the chatter of the others. There were so many of them around the table that it took Lou a few minutes to distinguish who was there. Smiling her greeting, she finally managed to recognise Rachel's partner, Luke, along with her friend's daughter, Jess, and husband, Paul, with their three girls. Then there was Rachel's son, Alexander, with his daughter, Verity, his new partner, Adele, and her son, Sandy. Lou hadn't realised there would be such a crowd. She'd only expected Rachel and Luke, though she should have known. Rachel always liked to be surrounded by her family.

By the time she was seated, some sort of order had been achieved, with the children all being relocated to a nearby table where they could be kept occupied with pencils and paper until breakfast was served, allowing the adults to converse without interruption.

Eventually their orders were placed. It was a relief to Lou when her coffee arrived – almost as good as that served by Ron – and she could draw breath. There were some downsides to a large family, she decided, but Rachel seemed to delight in the chaos.

During the meal, conversation revolved around the Halloween event the previous day and what plans Lou had for the bookshop over Christmas, with Jess declaring that Halloween would be a difficult event to top. 'The twins were so excited when they came home,' she said. 'They insisted we buy the book Zoe read to them, and of course Emily had to have one too. I bet your sales have gone through the roof.'

'Not exactly, but we did have a good couple of days.' Lou had noticed Jess come in with her three girls the previous day, though it had been Zoe who had served her. They were right, Christmas would be next. 'We always put on a good show for Christmas,' she said, wondering if perhaps they'd gone overboard this year with Halloween, and Christmas would be a poor follow-up.

'Of course you do,' Rachel said. 'I always enjoy bringing the girls in to see your tree and decorations… and all the Christmas books too, of course.'

'Of course.' But even as she spoke Lou's mind was working overtime. Maybe they could repeat the event with the school before they broke up for Christmas. She'd heard some teachers lamenting how difficult it was to maintain the children's attention as the holidays grew closer, and if they could come to the bookshop one day… if Zoe was prepared for a repeat performance. Lou was sure she would be.

'Lou?'

'Sorry.' Rachel had been speaking to her while her mind was elsewhere.

'I was asking if you had any plans for Christmas… for yourself.'

'Oh, just the usual. It's the only time of year when I manage a few days off. I fill the fridge and pantry with my favourite foods, ensure I have a plentiful supply of wine, and go into hibernation and catch up on my reading till everything opens up again.' She tried to sound upbeat. But clearly didn't succeed.

'Oh, Lou!' Rachel put a hand on her arm. 'You know you're always welcome at our place on Christmas Day. It's always a bit of a madhouse with all the kids, but…' Her eyes were so filled with concern, it made Lou cringe inside.

'Thanks, Rach, but I'll be fine. It's better I'm alone.'

'Have you never tried to find…' It was the second time Rachel had broached the subject recently, even if this time, she didn't mention Fleur's name.

Lou shook her head, glad their meals arrived at that point and there was more confusion as the plates were passed around, and the adults ensured the children were served. She gave a sigh of relief. Christmas and Fleur were two things she didn't want to talk about. It brought back too many happy memories, memories of times when *she* was part of a happy family too.

Nine

Blair had spent Saturday out on the water. He'd seen an ad in the local paper indicating there were several spots available on a fishing charter and called the number for *Whittaker Fishing Charters*. The guy who'd answered the phone, who gave his name as Jamie Whittaker, sounded pleasant. He explained that a group that had hired him for Saturday had lost a few members due to illness and were keen to make up the numbers. There was one spot left. It was Blair's lucky day.

It had been a long time since Blair had done any fishing, and that had been for trout during the Christmas holidays one year when the girls had been small. Prue had given him a licence for Christmas, knowing it was something he'd always wanted to do. He'd enjoyed it but had always been too busy to repeat the experience.

Ocean fishing was completely different. He hadn't expected to catch anything, but the lure of a day on the ocean was too tempting to resist, and it confirmed for him that he had made the right decision in moving here. Perhaps he'd even buy a boat, but that was in the future. For now, he was satisfied to let someone else do the work… and Jamie had been very informative about the shoreline and the ocean around the bay.

An unexpected bonus of the trip was that one of the others on the charter who'd also responded to the ad in *The Echo*, was a resident of *The Haven*. Stan was the Vietnam veteran Katrina had told him about, the one who had formed a relationship with Blair's nearest neighbour.

When the group progressed to *The Grand* for a beer at the end of the trip, Blair had time to talk with him further, pleased to discover the other man shared his love of books and history. As they made arrangements to meet again, Blair felt he'd made a new friend.

Now it was Sunday, and he couldn't wait to see Harper and Noah's faces when he handed them the books they'd heard read in the bookshop.

'Here's Grandad!'

Blair heard Noah's voice before he saw him. He and the rest of the family were seated at one of the tables outside the café, and the two youngsters came rushing to greet Blair, hanging onto his arms as if they were afraid he'd go off and leave them. 'Hey, you two,' he said, ruffling their hair with one hand – the other carrying the books which were in the bag he'd got from the bookshop.

'Dad.' Katrina rose to greet him with a hug, and Brett clapped him on the shoulder.

'Do you have something for us?' Noah asked, catching sight of the bag.

'Noah!' Katrina said.

'It's okay, Kat. These are for you.' Blair delved into the bag and took out the two books, handing them to the children.

'Ooh, thanks, Grandad,' Harper said, while Noah stared at his book. 'It's the one the lady read to us,' he said in awe.

'Dad, you shouldn't have…' Katrina said, but she was smiling.

'They're the only grandchildren I have – am likely to have, given your sister's current situation – so why shouldn't I spoil them? Though a couple of books is hardly spoiling them. It was fun to be at the story time in the bookshop. It's a beaut spot. I had a coffee there too.'

Brett appeared puzzled.

'*Books and Coffee*. It's where the kids went for the Halloween event,' Katrina said to him, adding, 'I thought you'd like it, Dad. I know what you're like with bookshops. Mum always said, if she ever lost you when you went shopping, she knew she'd find you in the nearest bookshop.'

'I did. I'm surprised I hadn't discovered it before. Now I have, I'll be back.' Blair thought of the leaflet on his fridge, the *Book Café*, but decided to say nothing about it. Katrina didn't need to know everything he did, even if he knew she'd like to.

This was borne out when after they'd ordered breakfast and been served with coffee, she asked, 'What did you do yesterday? I thought you might have dropped round.'

'I went on a fishing charter.'

'You what?' This was clearly the last thing she expected to hear. But Brett was interested. 'With Jamie Whittaker?' he asked.

Blair nodded.

'I've seen them advertised and often thought it might be fun.'

Katrina stared at him, as if seeing a side of her husband she hadn't known existed.

'And I met the guy you mentioned, Kat. Stan Ross. Seems like a good guy. He was telling me more about the local library. Seems it's a Family Search Affiliate Library which provides free access to record sets that are otherwise restricted. It'll really help with my research. We're going to catch up later in the week.'

'Oh, Dad, I'm glad you're making friends. I knew you'd like it at *The Haven*.'

It wasn't exactly what he'd said. Blair was still undecided about the over-fifties resort, and Stan was over ten years older than him. If he and Joan were typical of the residents, they were way over fifty.

Katrina's next comment floored him.

'You're not still thinking of writing about the family history, are you? I know Mum always said it was on your bucket list, but really, Dad. There are so many other things you could do in your retirement.'

Blair took a deep breath before replying. 'It's something I've always wanted to do, Kat. As you know, I've always been a history buff, ever since hearing stories from my grandmother who believed the first members of the family came to Australia on the second fleet. It was why I chose history as my major at uni, went on to lecture in it for my entire career. Now I'm retired and free from teaching commitments, I have the leisure to do the research I want to do.'

Katrina's lips tightened, and Harper and Noah, realising the mood had changed, looked from her to Blair and back again. 'If that's the way you feel, Dad.'

'It is, Kat. For once in my life, I have no one to please but myself. It doesn't mean I'll ignore your wishes on most things, but about this, I'm adamant.'

'Well said, Blair,' Brett said. 'Kat, you have to let your dad do his own thing, otherwise he might decide to leave us, go to live with your sister, or even back to Tassie.'

Katrina didn't reply, but Blair could see her mind working. His daughter hated it when she didn't get her own way, but while it was tempting to give in for the sake of peace, this was one matter on which he wasn't going to give way.

'Are you going to write a book, Grandad?' Harper, who had been trying to follow the conversation, asked.

'I am indeed, sweetheart. A book about people in our family who lived a long time ago, back when white men first came to Australia.'

'We've heard about that in school,' she said. 'About Captain Cook and the convicts. Were our family convicts?'

'That's what I aim to find out for sure.'

'Wow!' Noah said, suddenly aware of what they were talking about. 'Didn't they whip convicts?' He moved his arm up and down as if cracking a whip.

'That's enough about that for now. We're here for a lovely breakfast with Grandad.' Katrina glared at Blair as if he had been the one to start the conversation.

For the remainder of breakfast, the conversation was innocuous, revolving around Noah's sports ambitions – he was a keen footy player – and Harper's swimming prowess, about which the girl was modest, unlike her mother.

They were close to finishing breakfast when a group of people walked past. One smiling woman with short dark hair, nodded and said, 'Good morning,' to Katrina.

She looked familiar to Blair. 'Who was that?' he asked.

'Lou Chalmers. She's one of my clients, owns *Books and Coffee*. She…' Katrina continued talking, but Blair didn't hear what she was saying. That was where he'd seen the woman before, standing behind the counter of the bookshop when he walked in for the Halloween event.

'She's really nice,' Katrina said.

Blair found himself watching the woman as she walked away, chatting with her friends, the image of her disarming smile in his mind.

Ten

As Lou followed the others out of the café, she smiled and wished good morning to several people she knew, including the girl she occasionally went to for a massage when she wanted to pamper herself. She'd seen Katrina, who worked at the *Pelican Crossing Wellness Centre*, here before, with her husband and two children, and thought what a lovely young family they were. This morning, they were accompanied by an older man who Lou felt she'd seen somewhere before – she never forgot a face – who she assumed was either Katrina's or her husband's father. She was almost home when the penny dropped. He had come into the bookshop for the Halloween event and had said he was there to see his grandchildren. Having satisfied her curiosity, Lou continued on her way, to be greeted with disdain by Tilly when she arrived home.

'Did you miss me?' she asked the cat, picking her up and giving her a cuddle, despite knowing that her pet was fiercely independent and often eschewed any form of affection she didn't initiate. True to form, Tilly suffered Lou's hug for only a moment before wriggling out of her arms and dashing off to slip out the cat door.

With some time to spare before she needed to go to the bookshop, Lou settled at her computer. Over the years, she'd tried to find her sister on various social media forums, believing that Fleur, who was always more socially active than Lou, would have a presence there. To date, there had been no sign of her, but now Lou was determined to leave no stone unturned and social media was the obvious place to start.

An hour later, she was forced to give up. After searching Facebook, Twitter, now called X, Threads, Bluesky… and even in desperation, Goodreads, there was no Fleur Ross registered. Frustrated, she cursed the fact that, these days, it was almost impossible to search the white pages, even if she knew where her sister and Darren were living. When they'd left, it had been to go to Sydney but that had been over forty years ago. By now they could be anywhere.

'No luck today, puss,' she said to Tilly who'd returned to join her and was curled up in the nearby chair she'd commandeered as her own. 'But I'm not going to give up. Fleur is out there somewhere, and I intend to find her.'

It was a slow afternoon in the bookshop, giving Lou too much time to think. She was glad when closing time came and she could go home again, back to her little cottage where she could shut out the rest of the world. But tonight, she felt restless, unable to settle to the paperwork she'd brought home and promised herself she'd finish. Instead, she stepped outside, walked across the road and down to the beach.

Once there, she gazed out at the ocean, pulling her jacket around her as a slight breeze blew up, and watched the waves crashing to the shore.

'Hey!' a familiar voice interrupted her thoughts. Lou looked up to see Troy with his dog, and remembered her neighbour often walked his labrador here around this time. She'd often watched them from her window.

'Hi, Troy.'

'Don't often see you down here this time of day. Something worrying you?'

'No, not really.' Lou had no intention of sharing any troubles she might have, not with Troy or anyone else. They all knew what had happened, knew about her and Darren, about Fleur. It had been the talk of the town till some other scandal had replaced it in people's minds and the gossip mill had moved on.

'You sure?' Troy had always had a kindly nature, eager to help out anyone in trouble, to provide a helping hand, sometimes whether it was needed or not. But his heart was in the right place, and they'd known each other since primary school.

'I'm sure. Just one of those days.'

Troy nodded, while his dog ran in circles around them. 'Some days are like that,' he said. He paused, then said, 'Look, you can say no if you like, but Phil's coming round later, and we plan to throw a few steaks on the barbie. Want to join us?'

Did she? Lou wasn't sure. In her present mood she wouldn't be the best company, but she'd known Troy and Phil for ever and they'd seen her at her worst. 'Okay. Thanks. What can I bring?'

'If you have any of those desserts of Ron's…' Troy grinned.

Lou grinned back. 'I'll see what I can do. See you in a bit.'

Troy tipped his head with one finger in a mock salute and he and his dog walked on.

When they'd left, Lou turned to go back to her cottage. She knew she had some leftover brownies, and half a lemon meringue pie tucked away in the fridge. They'd be perfect.

*

Carrying the sweets in one hand and a bottle of chilled wine in the other, Lou made her way along the road to Troy's cottage, feeling brighter than she had earlier. A shower and change of clothes had helped, as had the prospect of spending the evening with old friends. It was so easy for her to hide herself away with Tilly instead of making the effort to socialise. Apart from the neighbourhood gatherings they held on the beach on a regular basis, she could spend every evening alone with Tilly.

'Hey, Lou. Come on in. You're just in time for a beer… or would you prefer wine?' Troy asked when Lou walked in and handed him the bottle of wine, before placing the sweets on the kitchen bench.

'Wine, please. Hi, Phil,' she said to the other man in the kitchen.

'Hi, Lou. Thanks for joining us. These look good,' Phil said, eyeing the two plates.

'Leftovers from the café. I often bring them home. That's why…' Lou gestured to her expanding waistline.

'Half your luck,' Phil said. 'The chef takes care of our leftovers at the club. One of his perks.'

'You're not working tonight?'

'I have good staff. They can manage without me.' But Phil seemed unusually out of sorts.

'Problems?'

He shook his head. 'Nothing a good steak and a beer with old friends won't fix.'

Lou was curious. There was something bothering him, but it was none of her business, and she was the last person to pry into someone else's life.

'Hey, you two. The barbie's ready. Come outside and help me keep Jacko from getting to the steaks before us.'

Once outside, the three of them stood around the barbecue, Lou with a glass of wine, while the two men had cans of beer. Troy cooked the steaks while the other two looked on, offering advice from time to time. Troy's labrador moved back and forth between their legs, determined not to miss out on the delicious-smelling meat.

When the steaks were cooked, and Jacko had been given a chunk of meat, they sat down at a stained wooden table in Troy's courtyard. It was almost identical to Lou's, the main difference being the trellis he'd erected and the profusion of bushes, a result of his years in the landscaping business.

'Why don't I make coffee?' Lou said, when they had finished eating, and Jacko, satisfied with his meal too, was lying at Troy's feet. No one objected, so she made her way inside.

While she was waiting for the coffee to brew, Lou gazed around the kitchen. She'd been here before, but never on her own like this. Her eyes were caught by a photo stuck onto the fridge. Moving closer, she could see that it was an old one, taken when they were all in their teens, three young couples grinning at the camera – Lou and Darren, Luke and Becky, and Troy and Carrie, who he subsequently married.

'Remember that day,' Troy said, walking in with the dirty plates and opening the fridge to get two more cans of beer. 'That was one of the last ones before…' He stopped, but Lou knew what he was about to say. It was one of the last photos before Luke went off to uni, three years before Darren left town with Fleur.

'It's okay, Troy. No need to sugarcoat it. I know when it was taken.' She paused, then, 'Ever hear from him?' She held her breath.

'Nah. Sent an invite to the reunion a few years back, but it was returned. *Not at this address*. No idea if they're still in Sydney. Maybe ask Luke. He's from down there.'

Luke! Of course. Why hadn't Lou thought of that before? He'd left before Darren and Fleur. Sydney was a big place. But maybe their paths had crossed. It was worth a try.

Eleven

Since moving to Pelican Crossing, Blair had been waking early and going for a swim before breakfast. He often arrived just as a group, comprised mainly of women, were leaving. They called themselves wild swimmers and set off before dawn to watch the sun come up over the ocean. While he had no desire to join them, he admired their dedication, suspecting that for him, it would feel more of a punishment than exercise.

Today, he had decided to spend the morning in the library before meeting Stan for lunch at *The Grand*, but first, he'd promised to drive Harper and Noah to school. He'd fallen into the habit of doing this several times a week. It helped Katrina, who always seemed flustered in the mornings, and the children loved his company. He loved theirs too, enjoying hearing their stories of school and their plans for the day.

But he was conscious of being too available, after Katrina had called several times to ask him to pick them up too, as she was caught up at work. He wondered how she had coped before he moved to Pelican Crossing. He had his own life to live and hadn't moved there to become a babysitter for his grandchildren, much as he loved them.

'What do you do all day when we're at school, Grandad?' Noah asked, when he and his sister were in Blair's car. 'Mum and Dad work, but you don't. Mum says you're retired and have a life of leisure.'

Blair chuckled. 'I keep busy. Today, for example, I'm going to spend the morning in the library, then have lunch with a new friend. Then, this afternoon, I have a man coming to see what he can do to help me in my garden.'

'Oh!' Noah sounded disappointed. Probably Blair's day didn't sound exciting to him.

'You had a nice garden in Hobart,' Harper said.

'I did. It was mostly your grandma's doing. She was the gardener, not me. That's why I need help with the one I have now.'

It had been his neighbour, Joan, who'd recommended the local landscaper. 'Troy Piper will see you right,' she'd said. 'He has his son running the business now, but if you give my name, I'm sure he'll fit you in.'

'Are you writing your book?' Harper asked. 'The one about the convicts?'

'That's why I'm going to the library, to find out more information, so I can write my book.'

Harper thought for a few moments. 'I'm going to write a book too, when I'm old like you.'

Blair had trouble supressing a laugh. 'You don't need to wait till you're my age before you write a book, sweetheart. You can start right now writing down the stories in your head. I wish I'd started sooner, but life got in the way.'

By this time, they'd reached the school, and the two children jumped out.

'Will you be picking us up today too?' Noah asked. 'Can we have ice cream?'

'I expect it will be your mum today, but next time I pick you up we can have ice cream.'

Noah beamed. 'Thanks, Grandad. I love you.'

'I love you too, mate.'

Blair watched as the pair ran into the playground to join their friends. Life was so simple at that age. Why couldn't it stay that way?

With a smile on his face at the memory of Noah's delight at the prospect of an ice cream sometime in the future, Blair headed to the library. Once there, he arranged to register for access to the relevant databases, before becoming lost in the search for his family.

'Still here?'

Blair looked up to see Stan peering over his shoulder. *What time was it?* He'd become so engrossed in what he was doing, he'd forgotten to check his watch. 'Sorry,' he said.

'No worries. It's only one. When you didn't appear in *The Grand*, I thought I'd find you here. Ready to go now?'

'Sure.' Embarrassed at his thoughtlessness, Blair closed down the computer and slid the pad he'd been making notes in into his backpack. He knew he could have brought along his laptop, but he was old school in some respects and had never lost the habit of using pen and paper for his notes.

After spending all morning seated in front of a computer, it was good to get out into the fresh air and stretch his legs. Blair fell into step beside Stan, and they made their way towards the marina and *The Grand*.

En route, Stan gave Blair a running commentary on the town, it's history and politics. As they neared the marina and passed a pod of pelicans, Blair asked, 'Are those where the town got its name?'

His companion laughed. 'I've heard various stories about that, one, that in days gone by, the pelicans crossed the road to be fed fish from the old fish shop – on the site where *Crossings* now stands. But it's more likely that it comes from the local river, the Boodalang, which is the Aboriginal name for pelican.'

'I should have thought of that. One of my former colleagues was an avid birdwatcher.'

By this time, they'd reached the hotel. Blair was hungry and ready for a beer and the pie and chips he knew was a speciality of the place.

'What'll you have? My shout,' Stan said as Blair reached into his pocket.

'Thanks. I'll have one of the craft beers. But I'm paying for lunch.'

'Have it your way.' Stan grinned.

Once the two men had placed their orders for lunch, they carried their beers to a table in the far corner of the bar.

'You said you lectured at university in Tassie,' Stan said. 'You must find living here a big change.'

'Yeah.' Blair took a sip of beer. It wasn't a bad drop. 'It was my daughter's idea. I lost my wife a few years back and the university became my life. It was a wrench to give it up, to give up the house we'd lived in together for so long, but...' he sighed, 'life has to go on, and it's what Prue would have wanted.'

'Prue was your wife?'

Blair nodded, suddenly beset with an aching sadness. It was as if he'd left Prue behind in Tasmania, along with everything else.

*

Back at the villa, Blair was still caught up in the past, thinking about Prue and how different this move would have been if she'd been with him, when Troy Piper arrived. The landscaper was around Blair's age but looked a lot fitter than Blair felt. There was a black labrador on the back of his ute, chained among the gardening implements.

'You must be Troy,' Blair said going out to greet him. 'I'm Blair. My neighbour recommended you.' He gestured to the villa next door where he could see Joan peering through the window.

Troy chuckled. 'Everyone knows Joan, but she's not so bad when you get to know her.'

Blair had already discovered that, and aware Stan and she were close friends, had revised his initial opinion of her.

'Hope you don't mind me bringing Jacko along. I can leave him on the ute if you like.'

Blair looked to where the dog was clearly anxious to be released, his tongue hanging out and his entire body trembling with excitement. 'No, fine by me. I like dogs.' In fact, he'd always wanted a dog. Prue hadn't, so they'd got a cat instead. One of the rare times they'd disagreed on something. He supposed that now she was gone he could get one, but it seemed a betrayal of her somehow. Anyway, something to think about. It might be nice to have a furry companion to take for walks, and to keep him company of an evening.

Troy unfastened the dog, and the animal leapt down to sniff around before approaching Blair and sniffing at his feet. Automatically, Blair's hand went down to ruffle the dog's ears, at which the creature pushed his head into his hand. It felt good.

'Hello, Jacko,' he said.

'He likes you,' Troy said. 'Now,' he surveyed the front garden, 'what would you like done?'

After providing a grateful Jacko with a bowl of water, the next half hour was taken up with Blair showing Troy the front and back gardens and discussing how they could be improved, closely observed by Jacko. To Blair's delight, Troy's views accorded with his own, and they soon came to an agreement of what needed doing to bring both areas up to scratch.

'I think this calls for a beer, if you have time,' Blair said, when he'd agreed to Troy's quote and signed a contract.

'Sure. I'm about to knock off for the day. A beer sounds good.'

They were already in Blair's kitchen, so he soon had two beers out of the fridge and topped up Jacko's water bowl.

Relaxing, the two men chatted and shared information about themselves. Blair learned that Troy was widowed too and had a son, who worked in his landscaping business, two daughters who tried to look after him and a swag of teenage grandchildren. 'Kids, today!' He shook his head. 'Not like we were, with all their devices and talk of making a difference.'

In return, Blair shared the loss of his own wife, information about his two daughters and his two grandchildren who fortunately, had still to reach their teens. It sounded as if Troy's daughters were not unlike Katrina in their efforts to keep tabs on their dad. It was something the two men had in common.

'Thanks, Troy. Good to meet you,' Blair said, when Troy and his dog were finally ready to leave. 'I look forward to seeing the result of your efforts.'

'No problem. Good to meet you too. We need more people like you in Pelican Crossing. And not everyone is in our children's age group, or like Joan and Stan. There are a few of us in our sixties, still fit and with plenty of life in us. Okay if I give you a call when a few of us next get together?'

'Sure.' Blair felt a surge of anticipation. Since moving here, he'd missed his old friends, missed the companionship of men who shared memories of growing up in the nineteen-sixties. It would help make up for leaving them and Tasmania if he could make a new group of friends here in Pelican Crossing.

Twelve

Lou wasn't able to catch up with Rachel and Luke until the weekend. She'd invited them to dinner saying that she was always going to their place, and it was time she returned their hospitality. Rachel had been surprised, but readily agreed, offering to bring dessert. But Lou had refused, telling her there were always plenty of leftovers from the café that needed to be eaten.

It was another busy Saturday in the bookshop and as always, the enticing aroma of coffee filtering through from the café encouraged customers to extend their visit. There were several familiar faces interspersed with the tourists now the holiday season was drawing closer. Lou had already placed her orders for Christmas releases, expecting a bumper season.

Life was strange, both Darren and Luke ending up with the younger sister of the girls they'd dated through high school. At least Rachel hadn't stolen her sister's boyfriend. Both she and Luke had married other people, only reconnecting when both had been widowed for some time.

Lou thought back to the photo on Troy's fridge. It had brought it all back, the bitterness, the sadness. She'd missed Darren. She'd missed her sister too. Despite their quarrels – and there had been many – she'd loved Fleur. But it had been years before she could bear to hear or speak her sister's name.

She was pulled back to the present by a flurry of customers, and the shop remained busy till closing time.

'You wanted these?' Denny appeared carrying a box of goodies.

'Thanks.' Lou was planning to serve a quiche with salad, followed by whatever she could take home from the café.

'There's almost a whole strawberry flan there, and half a dozen friands,' Denny said. 'Expecting guests?'

'Rachel and Luke. Thanks. That'll be great, Denny. I hope you and Ron have some too.'

'Don't worry about us. We never go short.' He patted his flat stomach, making Lou laugh.

'I wish I could eat your cakes and stay as slim as you and Ron.'

'Willpower… and I guess the exercise helps.' Denny chuckled. 'Well, have a good one.'

'Thanks. I'm sure we will. You, too.'

'Thanks.'

*

Back home, after giving Tilly the attention she demanded after being left alone all day, and feeding her, Lou prepared the quiche and salad. Then, popping the salad into the fridge and turning on the oven, she showered and changed into a fresh pair of pants and a brightly coloured tunic she'd bought on a recent visit to *Birds of a Feather* in Bellbird Bay. It was a boutique Rachel had introduced her to and which she now loved.

By the time Rachel and Luke arrived, everything was ready. The table in the dining area was set with Lou's best dinnerware, the quiche was in the oven and the cottage was redolent with the fragrance of the bergamot, jasmine and cherry blossom candle Lou had lit. As usual, she hadn't turned on the main light, preferring the more subdued lighting from a couple of lamps which, combined with the light from the moon and stars shining through the window, gave the room a delightful ambiance.

As soon as the visitors walked through the door, there was a flash of ginger as Tilly rushed past them. Rachel laughed. 'Cats are so different from dogs. Our two would be all over us by now. They'll probably smell Tilly on us when we get back and go mad.'

'Hmm.' Lou didn't think she could cope with a dog, and now Rachel and Luke had two between them – his boxer and Rachel's little Westie. She'd always been a cat person, preferring the independent nature of felines to the overt affection of their counterparts.

'For you,' Luke handed Lou a bottle of wine. It was already chilled, so she took out three glasses and poured them all a drink.

'This is nice.' Luke wandered around the room and gazed out of the window. 'You have a slightly different aspect from Joe, though your cottages are similar.'

'It was a row of old fishermen's shacks,' Lou said, realising this was the first time Luke had been here. 'Back in the eighteen-hundreds. They've seen a lot of change and renovation since then but have lasted well. They were soundly built in the first place.'

'Not like my modern monstrosity,' Rachel said with a smile.

'Don't be silly. You don't mean it. It's a lovely house,' Lou said.

'Yes. You're right. And I'd be lost without it. I'm glad Luke was happy to move in, given I'd lived there with Kirk.' She threw him an affectionate glance.

'It's your family home,' he said. 'I understood.' He met her gaze.

Feeling excluded from what had become an intimate conversation, Lou said, 'Why don't you both have a seat. Dinner will be ready soon.'

They did, and soon the conversation was on an even keel again as Rachel revealed Alexander and Adele's plans to marry in the spring. 'I'm so glad to have him back home. I thought he was in the UK for good. Then when he brought Verity home and left her with me...' She shook her head. 'Who would have thought Verity and Sandy would prove to be matchmakers,' she said, referring to the fact that Alexander had fallen in love with the mother of his daughter's friend.

'And she's almost family,' Lou said. Adele's father was Finn whose partner was Rachel's good friend, Liz. 'It's as if it was meant to be.'

'It really is,' Rachel said. 'Like Luke and me.' She smiled at him again. 'Though I knew he dated Becky first... then we were both married. But we found each other in the end. It's time you found someone too, Lou.'

Lou stared at her friend. Where had that come from? It was the first time... since Darren left... that anyone had dared to suggest such a thing. But it gave her the excuse she needed. 'Once was enough for me. I don't suppose you ever came across Darren in Sydney, Luke?'

'Darren? Darren Ross?' Luke shook his head. 'The last time I saw him was here in Pelican Crossing before I went to uni. Didn't he…?' His words died away as he no doubt recalled hearing about Darren and Fleur running off together. 'Sorry,' he said weakly.

'Why are you asking about him now? Has something happened?' Rachel asked, her eyes filled with concern.

Lou shifted uncomfortably in her seat, now wishing she hadn't mentioned Darren. 'It's not him. I've been thinking about Fleur, wondering what happened to her. It's been a long time, Rach, too long. I think I may be ready to make amends, to forgive her.'

'Oh, Lou. I did wonder. You seemed… odd… when I mentioned her.'

'I felt odd. I'd just been thinking about her. It was a shock when you said her name. But it got me thinking even more. I want to try to find her before it's too late.'

'Too late? Oh, you mean… Well, I guess none of us are getting any younger.'

Lou was about to reply when she heard the oven beep. 'I need to see to that,' she said, rising with a sense of relief. She hadn't intended to get into this conversation, to share her need to find Fleur. But Rachel did have a habit of being able to worm things out of a person, and *she* had started it by asking Luke about Darren.

No more was said about Fleur and Darren, and they enjoyed a nice meal together, Luke relating some amusing anecdotes about his time as a vet, Rachel sharing stories of her four granddaughters, and Lou incidents which had occurred in the bookshop.

By the time Rachel and Luke were leaving, Lou was feeling more relaxed, sure neither of them would repeat what she had said. It was a shock when, as she hugged Rachel goodbye, her friend whispered into her ear, 'I'm still in touch with a few of our year. Let me know if you want me to ask them about Fleur. I won't mention your name.'

Lou stared after Rachel and Luke, her stomach churning with a mix of fear and exhilaration. *Why hadn't she thought of Fleur's schoolmates?*

Thirteen

Blair was feeling good. He'd spent the day in the library and his research was coming along so well he'd made a start on his novel. He'd picked up Harper and Noah from school, taken them home via the gelato shop, and enjoyed an ice cream with them. And tonight, he was planning to attend the *Book Café* at *Books and Coffee*.

Eating dinner out in his backyard, he stared around, amazed at what Troy had been able to achieve in just over a week. The place had been transformed into something even Prue would approve of. The front yard was next. And Troy had kept his promise. On Sunday Blair had been invited to Troy's home where he and his mates were getting together for a barbecue. Things were really looking up. Perhaps moving here hadn't been such a bad decision after all.

Dinner over, he picked up the book which had been keeping him awake for the past week. Despite his love of history, he was a sucker for a good crime story and a big fan of Michael Connelly's Bosch series. This last book *The Waiting*, was a cracker, involving not only Harry Bosch but Connelly's new character, Renée Ballard, and Bosch's daughter, Maddie. He was looking forward to sharing it with the others tonight.

As he drove into town, Blair wondered about the group he was about to meet, and what sort of books would be discussed. He hoped he might discover some new authors and perhaps meet some new friends. This business of making new friends in Pelican Crossing was something he hadn't considered when he agreed to move here. He should have thought about it. But Katrina had been so insistent. She'd brushed aside all his objections and, almost before he knew it, he'd put his house on the market and put down a deposit on a villa in *The Haven*.

The lights of *Books and Coffee* shone out to greet Blair as he walked along the street, having parked some distance away, and a hum of conversation greeted him as he pushed open the door. Once inside, he could see that the interior of the bookshop had been rearranged to accommodate a circle of chairs. The sounds he had heard came from a group of people congregated around a table, helping themselves to tea and coffee and plates of the sweet concoctions he'd seen on display in the café. The aroma of coffee competed with the familiar scent of books.

Blair helped himself to coffee and one of the brownies he'd had in the café and joined the others as they took their seats in the circle.

'Welcome everyone.' The woman who spoke was the one he'd seen on his first visit to the bookshop, when he'd come to the Halloween event. It seemed a long time ago, but it had only been a couple of weeks. 'This is the second meeting of the *Book Café*, and I'm pleased to see so many familiar faces… and a few new ones.'

It seemed to Blair that she looked directly at him. He glanced around, wondering who else was new to the group. He hadn't realised the group had been created so recently.

'For those of you who don't know me, I'm Lou,' she said, 'and I'm the owner of *Books and Coffee* and a longtime resident of Pelican Crossing. I've lived here all my life and would never want to leave.'

There were a few laughs and murmurs of agreement. Blair wondered what it would be like to have spent your entire life in this small coastal town. He'd spent many years in Hobart but had left Tasmania to attend university on the mainland and had taught in schools in Melbourne while studying for his doctorate. It was there he'd met Prue, another teacher.

Lou was speaking again and holding up a book. 'Next month, I'll expect one of you to start off,' she said with a smile, 'but for now… This is the book I want to share with you this month. It's by an author whose writing I've come to love and admire. The research underpinning each of her books is outstanding, and I've learnt so much about the early days of settlement in Australia.'

Blair stared at the copy of *The Governor, his Wife and his Mistress* by Sue Williams. He'd read all of her books and, like Lou, admired her grasp of history and the research involved in each of them. He wished he could emulate her, but knew it was a forlorn hope. For a start, his own family history wasn't as interesting as the governors she portrayed, but he was enjoying ferreting out what he could about his ancestors and fashioning it into a story.

Lou gave a very brief outline of the book which Blair thought was cleverly done, just enough to whet the appetite of anyone in the group who was interested in historical fiction based on fact, but not too involved for those with no interest at all. This was followed by a few questions – one person who wanted to know the titles of the author's other books and a couple who had also read this one.

Next, it was the turn of members of the group to share their books, and Blair listened with interest as some proved eloquent while others stumbled to say much. But what was clear was that everyone in the group enjoyed being there and sharing what they had read with others.

When it came to his turn, Blair discovered he was feeling unsure of himself. Most of the other books mentioned had been by Australian authors, a mixture of crime, romance and literary fiction. Should he have chosen something else? He had plenty of crime books by Australian authors on his bookshelf. Taking a deep breath, he held up the Michael Connelly book; there were a few muffled comments from the male members of the group. Undeterred, Blair gave a brief description of the novel, then proceeded to outline what he liked best about Connelly's writing. He finished with a couple of anecdotes from the one time he'd been fortunate enough to hear the author speak at an event, and how impressed he'd been with Connelly's admission that, if he'd known the Bosch series was going to be so popular, he wouldn't have aged him so quickly. This generated a few laughs and, as he was the last of the group to speak, a discussion of the preferred ages of protagonists ensued with many of the older women in the group expressing a preference for heroines of a mature age and outlook.

'Thanks, everyone,' Lou said, as people began to gather their belongings and rise to their feet. 'I hope to see you all again next month. Those of you who aren't in a hurry to leave are welcome to have another cup of tea or coffee and help finish off the delicacies Denny kindly brought along.' She gestured to where one of the men Blair had met in the café was by the table ready to dispense more drinks.

He'd been there all the time, Blair realised, quietly listening without taking part.

Tempted by the prospect of another cup of the delicious coffee and with nothing to go home to, Blair accepted the offer. As he turned back to the others, he was surprised to find himself alone with Denny and Lou. Denny was unobtrusively collecting the used cups and mugs.

'Blair, Blair Stevens,' Blair held out a hand.

'Hello, Blair.' Lou shook his hand, a firm grip. 'I've seen you before, haven't I?' she said, helping herself to one of the two remaining brownies. 'I can't resist these.' She grinned.

'I have been in the bookshop a couple of times.'

'Yes, but not here, in *The Blue Dolphin*. You were there with Katrina.'

'My daughter.'

'Ah! You're new to Pelican Crossing?'

'Yes. My daughter's idea. I'm widowed, recently retired, and she thought it would be a good idea.'

'You don't?'

Surprised by Lou getting immediately to the point in a way that reminded him of Prue, Blair chuckled. 'I didn't at first, but I'm coming round to it. I've bought a villa in *The Haven* and…'

'Oh!' There was a wealth of meaning in that one syllable.

'You're not a fan?'

'I don't know much about the place. A friend's mother lives there. She seems to like it. But I can't see myself living with a bunch of old people. Sorry.'

Blair chuckled again. Lou was nothing if not blunt. It was refreshing. He liked it. 'We're not all old fogies. It's an over-fifties resort.' Though, so far, he hadn't met anyone under seventy.

'So, retired from…?'

'I lectured in Australian history at the university in Hobart.'

'You must find life here very different.'

'To an extent. But there's a good library. I can still engage in research. I was interested in the book you chose to share.'

'I don't think many of the others were. But that's what the *Book Café* is all about, exposing people to new authors and genres… among other things.'

Blair raised an eyebrow.

'I've discovered that a lot of people are lonely. The *Book Café* gives them an opportunity to mix with other likeminded folk, an excuse for some to get out of the house.'

'So, you're providing a community service.'

'Something like that. And it does bring in custom to the bookshop. I can guarantee several of those who were here tonight will be back in the next couple of days looking for copies of one or more of the books we discussed.'

So, she was an astute businesswoman too. 'Sounds like you have it all worked out.'

'Not really. The extra sales are a serendipity. I really started this as an alternative to all the other book clubs in town, for people who don't want to be told what to read.'

'It's a great idea. It's what appealed to me.'

'Thanks.' Lou smiled, that smile he remembered as she'd walked past the café.

'Thank *you*. I guess I should be going.'

'Hope to see you next month.'

'Oh, you'll no doubt see me before that. My late wife used to tell me I'd live in a bookshop if I could.'

On his way home, Blair reflected that the evening had been pleasanter than he expected. The group had been a mixed bunch, several around his own age or older, but others younger, even a couple in their twenties. But they all had one thing in common – their love of books.

Fourteen

Lou stretched lazily, and Tilly purred her annoyance at being disturbed. Recently, the cat had taken to sleeping at the foot of Lou's bed. She knew she should shoo her out, insist she sleep in the laundry where her own bed was, but the animal's weight on her feet was comforting, made her feel less alone. It was only at times like this, when Tilly intimated she was not happy at being disturbed, that Lou regretted her failure to show her pet who was in in charge. *Or was she?* Sometimes it seemed that Tilly was the one in charge of everything that happened in the cottage, and Lou was merely her servant.

With that thought, she gently pushed the cat off the bed, only for her to land on the floor then leap up onto the bed again, mewling her displeasure. But by this time, Lou was on her way to the shower.

As she let the water flow over her and rubbed the shampoo into her hair, Lou thought about the previous evening. The second meeting of *The Book Café* had been as successful as the first, if not more so. The extra chairs she and Denny had set out had been filled, as not only those who had attended the first meeting arrived, but several new members, including the man she'd seen with Katrina in the café. She'd been right about him. He *was* her masseuse's father. Now she knew for sure, she could see the resemblance. On Blair, Katrina's auburn hair had faded, and his nose was more prominent, but they shared the same high cheek bones and deep blue eyes and whereas on Katrina it looked elegant, on Blair it was distinguished.

And he was living in *The Haven*. She hadn't been joking when she said it wasn't for her. The very thought of living in a community of older people made her shudder. And he didn't seem the type to want to be involved in all the social events that were on offer there. But what did she know? She'd only met the man – Blair – briefly. All she knew about him was that he was a retired university professor from Tasmania with a penchant for crime novels. She had no idea why he was on her mind, perhaps because he'd stayed behind when the others had left. She washed the shampoo out of her hair, laughing as she remembered the song from the movie, *South Pacific*. As if she could wash the memory of their conversation away.

It was Saturday, and the bookshop would be busy again. Now they were halfway through November, people were beginning to do their Christmas shopping. The town Christmas tree would soon appear in Pelican Plaza, and Lou had already ordered one for the bookshop from the local Christmas tree farm which both delivered and picked up their trees. But not just yet. She'd wait till the beginning of December to put up the Christmas decorations.

Zoe had agreed to arrange another set of story-times with the local primary school, and Lou had ordered extra copies of the books she'd chosen. She knew from her experience at Halloween that there would be a demand for them, and any not sold by Christmas could go into the sale at the start of the new year. She didn't want to think of that just yet, either. There was the rest of November and Christmas to get through first.

'Good morning, Lou.' Zoe greeted her cheerily when she walked in carrying her takeaway coffee from the café.

Lou's assistant was always bright in the mornings and, with her hair swinging in a ponytail, her skintight jeans, and her multicoloured tops, she reminded Lou of herself at that age. She drew her fingers through her own short locks and looked down at the outfit she was wearing – it was like every one she'd worn to the shop for years. It might be time for another trip to Bellbird Bay, to the boutique there to replenish her wardrobe. Maybe she could fit in a trip before the Christmas rush.

There was no time for further thought as the bookshop became busy. Lou had been right again. Many of those who'd attended the *Book Café* returned, eager to purchase one or more of the books that had been discussed, and to Lou's surprise, some even asking for other books by Sue Williams.

Lunchtime came and went, with little time to breathe. It was only when Zoe said, 'You need a break,' that Lou realised she was hungry. She hadn't eaten since breakfast which had only been a slice of toast and marmalade, and it had been hours ago. She really needed to take more care of herself. She'd intended to pick up something from the café when she arrived at work but had become sidetracked. Now it was almost two o'clock.

'Off you go. Georgia and I can cope here for a bit. Get yourself a coffee and something to eat,' Zoe said.

Lou looked at the bright faces of the two young women, who still had the energy they'd had when they arrived at work six hours earlier, while she was flagging. Zoe was right. She needed something to keep her going till closing time. 'Thanks,' she said.

In the café, Ron greeted her with a grin. 'Denny says it was another success last night. Expected to see you in here earlier.'

'Busy day, Ron. I expect it is for you too,' she said, glancing around at the tables filled with customers. 'I'll have my usual coffee and a ham and cheese panini.'

'No problem. Take a seat if you can find one, and Denny will bring it out to you.'

'Thanks.' Lou found an empty table and sat down, glad to give her feet and back a rest. She needed to make another appointment with Katrina. While she told her friends her visits to the masseuse were because she liked to pamper herself, it was really a way of relieving the back pain she often suffered from. Katrina had suggested the physiotherapist in the wellness centre might be of more help, but Lou had rejected her suggestion, feeling it would be making too much of what was just a sign she was getting older.

Waiting for her coffee and panini, Lou had time to think, and Blair's face once again intruded into her thoughts. She'd expected him to be one of the book café patrons to visit the bookshop this morning, but there had been no sign of him. She'd remembered him mentioning he came from Tasmania and had wanted to ask if he'd read the historical novels by Mary-Lou Stephens which were set there. She was still thinking about him when a familiar voice greeted her.

'Taking a well-earned break?'

Looking up, Lou saw it was her neighbour, Livvy Grace, accompanied by two little girls. Lou smiled. Livvy's daughter and family had moved back from England the previous Easter, much to her delight. Both girls were carrying bags from the bookshop.

'I am. A late lunch. Looks like you've been busy. Join me?'

'Thanks. Yes, I have Nancy and family visiting for the weekend, and these two and I have been spending time together to give their mum a break.'

'How lovely for you.' Lou knew how much Livvy had wanted to have all her family together. Nancy and her husband hadn't settled in Pelican Crossing, but Brisbane wasn't too far away.

'Isn't it? I still can't believe it.'

'And you and Dan?'

Livvy blushed. She and the physiotherapist Lou had avoided seeing were in a relationship, and Lou had heard he was planning to move into Livvy's cottage.

'You've heard?'

Lou nodded. It was difficult to keep anything secret in this small town.

'Now Dan's daughter is studying in Sydney, he's been rattling around in that big house on his own. It makes sense… and there's plenty of room for Kim when she comes back home.'

'Of course. I'm happy for you.'

'Thanks, Lou. You've always been a good friend.'

Lou smiled at Livvy, then at Denny as he delivered her order, along with colouring-in sheets and pencils for the two little girls. 'Yours is coming up,' he said to Livvy.

'Go ahead. Don't wait for me. I know you'll need to get back to the bookshop,' Livvy said, much to Lou's relief, adding, as Lou took a sip of coffee and a bite of her panini, 'Katrina's dad has moved to Pelican Crossing. She said he's addicted to bookshops, so you may see him.'

Lou should have remembered that Livvy worked at the wellness centre too and would be well-acquainted with all Katrina's news. 'I already have. He came to the *Book Café* last night. Seems like a nice guy.'

'Katrina said he's been a bit lost since her mum died, threw himself into his work. She's hoping moving here will help him develop some new interests and move on with his life.'

Not for the first time, Lou was glad she had no family, no children to try to organise her, to *know* what was best for her. She remembered Blair saying that his move was his daughter's idea. She wondered if *The Haven* had been her idea too, an attempt to force him into socialising, and felt a tinge of sympathy for him.

Fifteen

Blair had spent the day with Katrina, Brett and the grandkids. They'd had breakfast at *The Blue Dolphin* again, then gone to the beach where the others went for a swim while he remained under the shelter of their cabana with a book. He'd had his swim before breakfast and didn't enjoy being in the ocean when the UV factor was high, even slathered with sunscreen and wearing a rashie as they were. He'd had enough sunspots and skin cancers removed to last him a lifetime, after spending too much time out in the sun as a young man. He'd tried to remonstrate with Katrina, but she assured him they were careful.

Now, after a picnic by the river for lunch, during which they were visited by a pair of pelicans, and a walk along the beach, he was back in his villa, enjoying a much-needed rest before preparing for the barbecue at his new friend Troy's.

Troy had sent him a text with directions to his cottage which he had said was one in a row of cottages, which had originally been fishermen's shacks, on the far side of the harbour. It was a part of Pelican Crossing which Blair hadn't visited, and he was interested to see the cottages as well as looking forward to the barbecue and to meeting a few others of his own vintage who might share his interests.

Blair found the place easily, the historian in him visualising what the cottages might have looked like when they were first built, when Pelican Crossing was a small village, when the main occupation was fishing. As if to confirm his imaginings, a couple of pelicans strode across in front of the car as he was trying to park.

Before he reached the door, Blair could hear Jacko barking and the sound of voices. Carrying a six-pack of beer in one hand, he knocked on the door with the other. There was no reply. He knocked again, louder, and a faint voice yelled, 'Coming!'

Troy opened the door, his dog pushing past him to sniff at Blair's feet, before turning back into the house.

'Come in. We're out in the backyard. You're just in time.' Troy slapped Blair on the shoulder and led him through to a backyard which showed off his landscaping skills to good advantage with a trellis extending across a paved courtyard and a garden anyone would be proud of. A group of people were gathered next to a state-of-the-art barbecue, two men and a woman.

Blair blinked. He'd thought this was to be an all-male event.

'Let me introduce you,' Troy said. 'Everyone, this is Blair. He's a newcomer to Pelican Crossing, moved here from Tassie and living in *The Haven*. I did some landscaping work for him and thought he might like to meet a few locals. Blair, this is Phil, who lives three doors down and owns the yacht club, and Luke, retired like you but does some work for the local vet. The member of the fair sex is Rachel, Luke's partner. We all went to school together, though Rachel was a few years younger. Still is,' he laughed.

'Hello, Blair. Welcome to Pelican Crossing. We're not all as crazy as Troy,' Rachel said while the two men nodded.

'Hello everyone. Nice to meet you all. It was good of Troy to invite me.' He was interested to hear that one of the men owned the yacht club. He hadn't eaten there yet but had walked past it on several occasions and it was on his to-do list to have a meal there, perhaps take the family. He handed over the beer, flipping off one can, and had just taken his first sip, when he heard a voice he recognised calling, 'Sorry I'm late,' and the woman from the bookshop walked out from the house.

Blair's breath caught at the sight of the tall, elegant, dark-haired woman. She was almost as tall as he was, the silver streaks in her dark hair the only indication that she was a contemporary of the others and, he suspected, close to his age. She was elegant rather than pretty, her high forehead giving her a somewhat forbidding appearance. But there was something about her that aroused his curiosity. She was someone he'd like to get to know better.

*

Lou was running late. Troy had invited her to another barbecue, telling her Rachel would be there too, but she'd been kept late at the bookshop when a customer dithered about which books would suit her niece, then left without buying anything. Then, she'd arrived home to discover Tilly had been sick over the rug in the bedroom, and she'd had to take it up, scrape it, rinse and wash it and hang it up to dry. The cat seemed none the worse for being sick and was lying happily in her usual spot.

Changing quickly and pulling a comb through her hair, Lou renewed her lipstick, grabbed a bottle of wine from the fridge and hurried along the road. She pushed open Troy's front door and calling, 'Sorry I'm late!' made her way through to the backyard, stopping on the way to pop the wine into the fridge.

'Here she is!' Troy said, 'Better late than never.'

'Sorry, I got held up at the bookshop, then found Tilly had been sick and…' Her eyes widened. She was surprised to see Blair among her friends.

'This is Blair Stevens,' Troy said. 'He's new to town. I did some work for him and invited him. Blair, this is Lou. She…'

'We've already met,' Lou said. 'Blair attended the *Book Café* on Friday. Good to see you again,' she said to the man who seemed as surprised to see her as she was to see him.

'You look as if you need a drink,' Rachel said, pouring Lou a glass of wine and handing it to her.

'Thanks, Rach.' Lou accepted the wine and Rachel's one-armed hug.

'So?' Rachel raised an eyebrow and nodded to where Blair was chatting with the other three men.

Lou took a sip of wine and shook her head. Rachel was incorrigible. Just because she'd become involved in a new relationship when she was close to sixty didn't mean Lou was about to do the same. She was four years older for a start… and had never been as attractive as either Becky or Rachel. Darren was the only man who'd ever shown an interest in her and look what had happened there. 'I'm happy as I am, Rach.' And she was. It was only really at Christmas that she wished for family around her.

When Lou and Rachel joined the men at the barbecue, where Jacko was hovering around, attracted by the smell of steak cooking, they were discussing the future of the yacht club.

'What's the problem, Phil?' Lou asked. 'You own it, right?'

'Yeah, but that's only the start of it. With the increased popularity of Pelican Crossing with retirees – no offence, Blair – and sea changers, house prices and rents have soared. It's making it difficult to attract staff, when they can't find anywhere to live that they can afford. I know some establishments down the coast at Bellbird Bay have either closed up altogether or are operating on reduced hours. I'm not sure how long I can keep going as we've been doing.'

'Oh, I had no idea. Is there anything we can do to help?'

'Not unless you can find me some cheap accommodation. Otherwise, I may have to make some changes if I don't want to close.'

'No! That would be a disaster. The yacht club's been there for as long as I can remember. Have you talked to Joe about it?' she asked, referring to the local mayor.

'I'm seeing him next week, but I'm not hopeful. At least we'll be able to stay open through the holidays,' he said with a wry smile. 'After that, who knows.' He spread his arms wide.

'It's happening everywhere,' Blair said. 'Just before I left Tasmania, my favourite café changed to opening only Wednesday to Sunday, and one of the local restaurants stopped serving breakfast. I hope that doesn't happen here. I've been enjoying the breakfasts at *The Blue Dolphin Café.*'

'It's a great spot,' Rachel agreed. 'No staff problems for you, Lou?'

'Not so far. But I only have two assistants. Zoe grew up here and lives with her parents, and Georgia is still at school and only works weekends and holidays. The guys in the café are established residents too.' She was lucky, she realised.

Troy had just announced, 'Steaks are ready!' when the heavens opened, and heavy rain began to fall. He quickly slipped the steaks onto a platter and rushed inside, the others following carrying salads, beer, wine, plates and cutlery, and Jacko managing to get under everyone's feet.

'Wow,' Rachel said, shaking out her hair when they were all in the kitchen, and the food had been placed on the kitchen table. 'I didn't expect that.'

'First rain I've seen since I arrived,' Blair said.

'We get quite a bit,' Troy said, 'but I'm with Rachel. I didn't expect it tonight. Everyone happy to eat here?'

There was a combined murmur of agreement, and they all took their places around Troy's kitchen table. It was a tight fit. The kitchen hadn't been designed to hold so many people. Lou would have moved them to the dining area, but it was Troy's home, not hers.

'More wine?' Troy asked Lou and Rachel when they had finished eating and the men were still drinking beer.

Lou nodded. 'I put a bottle in the fridge earlier.'

'I'll get it.' Rachel said, pushing herself up from the table, and almost tripping over Jacko who was lying at her feet.

'Jacko!' Troy called.

'It's okay, Troy. I'm used to it with my Angus and Luke's Nelson. We fall over dogs all the time.'

She seemed about to open the fridge when she stopped and stared at the door, at the photo Lou had noticed on her last visit. 'I haven't seen that one before,' she said. 'You all look so happy.' She drew her finger over her sister's photo. 'Becky looks…' Her voice broke. 'Sorry. It was just the shock of seeing her like that.' She wiped her eyes.

'They were good times,' Troy said, while Luke rose to join Rachel, putting an arm around her shoulder.

'We were all so young,' Luke said. 'Troy, me and Darren Ross. And look at us now.'

'And we're all here but Darren,' Phil said. 'Wonder what happened to him after…' He glanced over at Lou. 'Sorry, Lou.'

'It's okay, Phil. It was a long time ago. Forgiven and forgotten.' That wasn't exactly true, but Lou had no intention of giving her old friend any need to feel sympathy for her.

'Ross,' Blair said. 'I've met a guy called Ross at *The Haven*. Stan Ross. Any relation?'

Lou stared at him, her eyes widening in surprise.

'Of course, there was an article in the local paper about him a few years back. Vietnam vet, isn't he?' Troy said.

'That's right. Seems like a regular guy.'

'I forgot all about him when you asked about Darren, Lou. Sorry. You must have read the article too.'

'I don't think so.' Lou often didn't take time to read the local paper. It could lie on her kitchen table for weeks, before being tossed out unread.

'Is he related to Darren?' Rachel asked.

'Darren had an older brother, half-brother, I think. He was a lot older. He wasn't around,' Lou said. *Could this be the link she was looking for? Had he been here all this time?*

Sixteen

That photo! It was all Lou could think about on her way home. And to think that Darren's older brother might have been living in Pelican Crossing all this time. Well, perhaps not since Darren and Fleur left. There had been no sign of him then. She didn't remember him, only that Darren had an older brother. She thought he'd been in the army, which tallied with him being a Vietnam vet.

When Lou walked into the cottage, Tilly greeted her with her usual disdain before weaving between her feet – her way of telling Lou she wasn't forgiven, but some food would help. Laughing, Lou filled the cat's food bowl and checked that there was water for her to drink. Then she made herself a coffee. She wasn't sure how many glasses of wine she and Rachel had consumed, but there had been that second bottle…

It had been a surprise to see Blair there, but it shouldn't have been. Troy was always picking up strays he met during his landscaping work. Most didn't last past the first week. But there had been something about Blair, about the way he seemed to fit in with everyone, that made Lou think he might prove to be the exception.

She took her coffee into the living room, turned on one of the lamps and took a seat in her favourite armchair. As soon as she sat down, Tilly appeared and leapt into her lap, curling up and purring as if to say, 'All is forgiven'.

As Lou automatically began to stroke the cat, her thoughts turned again to the photo on Troy's fridge. She wondered why he had kept it. Probably to remind him of those days when they were all so carefree.

It had been taken on a Sunday afternoon in January. Luke was about to go off to university, and Troy and Carrie had just become engaged. All three couples were in high spirits, having recently finished school, and were looking forward to a bright future ahead of them. While there had been no mention of marriage between Lou and Darren, she'd thought they had an understanding. Over the next few years, they were inseparable. Troy and Carrie married, and Lou was sure she and Darren would be next. Everyone else thought so too, or so she imagined.

Luke hadn't returned to Pelican Crossing, and Becky had met someone else – a guy called Andy – and had moved to South Australia. But Lou and Darren were still together. She had started working in the library and loved spending every day surrounded by books. She'd become friends with Becky's younger sister, Rachel, discovering they shared a love of books and reading. Everything had been going so well until one evening when she and Darren were walking along the beach together.

She sensed there was something wrong, but it never occurred to her that he was about to break her heart, to tell her that he was in love with Fleur, her younger sister, the sister in whom she'd confided all her hopes and dreams.

Lou had been a wreck. She'd wept for days, ranted and raved about Fleur, who she blamed for her broken heart, sure she had set out to steal Darren away. Rachel had helped her in those dark days, days when all she wanted to do was curl up in bed and try to forget.

It had taken weeks, but finally, Rachel's words had made sense. Lou didn't need a man in her life. Instead, she'd focus on her career. She enrolled in a Diploma in Information and Library Services at TAFE, then, almost twenty years later, opened *Books and Coffee*.

She'd done all right and had forgotten the hurt she'd suffered. Seeing the photo again had reminded her, but now there was no pain, only regret, regret that she'd allowed a youthful romance to destroy her relationship with her sister.

As if reading her mind, Tilly stretched and dug her claws into Lou's leg. 'Ow!' She took hold of the cat's paw. 'But you're right, Tilly. There's no sense in thinking about it. I need to do something. Maybe I need to talk to this Stan Ross.'

*

Next day was Monday, and Lou had arranged to stay home and finish some of the paperwork that had piled up. She wasn't a details person, preferring to deal with customers, but it had to be done, and Monday was always a slow day in the bookshop. Zoe would be able to manage on her own.

Lou settled down comfortably at her laptop, a mug of peppermint tea beside her, the force of the rain pelting against the window making her glad she didn't need to leave the house. Sensing her mistress intended to spend the day at home, Tilly squirrelled her way into Lou's lap and curled up, as if determined to stay there all day and to ensure Lou didn't move.

She worked steadily for a couple of hours, managing to make more headway than she'd expected, when she was disturbed by a knock on the door. The noise startled Tilly who leapt from her lap and disappeared.

Lou made her way to the door, wondering who could be calling on such a wet day. Most sensible people would be safely tucked up at home. She was surprised to see Rachel, the rain dripping from her rain jacket and umbrella.

'Rachel! What are you doing here? Come in out of the rain.'

Once she was inside, and Lou had helped her hang up her jacket and place her open umbrella just inside the door, the two women hugged.

'Tea? I was about to make another cup. And I might have some muffins I brought home yesterday.'

'Sounds lovely.'

By this time, they were in the kitchen, and Tilly reappeared to press herself against Lou's ankles. 'Not now, Tilly,' Lou said. The cat gave a howl of annoyance and jumped up onto an empty chair where she proceeded to groom herself.

'It's lovely to see you, but I didn't expect to see you today,' Lou said when she had made tea and set a couple of blueberry muffins on a plate. 'How did you know I was here?'

'Blueberry, yum.' Rachel picked one up and took a bite. 'I went into the bookshop to see you, and Zoe said you were working at home today.' Rachel took a sip of tea. 'I wanted to catch up with you after yesterday. I felt... I thought... you seemed upset.'

'No,' Lou picked up the other muffin and put it down again.

'Are you sure? I know you've been talking about trying to find Fleur and I thought maybe the talk about the photo, about Darren… Sorry if I was wrong.'

'Oh, Rach!' It was good of her friend to be concerned. Rachel was like that, but… 'As I said, it was all a long time ago.'

'Time doesn't heal all wounds.'

Rachel was right, but she was wrong about Lou. 'What I feel now is more regret than anything else, Rach. Regret that I allowed myself to ignore Fleur's letters, to cut myself off from my only sister. Regardless of what she did, she's still my sister. But I was young, hurt and pigheaded. Then when I did try to find her, I couldn't. Maybe, if this guy they were talking about *is* Darren's brother, he'll know where they are. I hope it's not too late to put things right.'

'I know who he is.'

Lou's eyes lit up. 'You do?'

'I don't know if he's Darren's brother, but I do know he's Liz's mother's new man friend.' She smiled.

Lou smiled too. 'I'd heard Joan was seeing someone.' She'd been surprised. Liz's mother was at least ten years older than her.

'I can ask Liz.'

'No, please don't. I know she's a friend of yours, but I also know about her reputation.' Liz Phillips was well known to be one of Pelican Crossing's biggest gossips.

'It's not all true. She just tries to keep people informed.'

'Well, I don't want the entire town to know that I'm trying to find Fleur. There was enough gossip when she and Darren left, and I'm sure there are many people around who haven't forgotten.' Lou shivered. She'd been the butt of gossip for months. She didn't want to go through that again. 'And this Stan guy might be no relation.'

'True. So, what do you want to do?'

'I'm not sure, but I'll find some way of contacting him.' Blair Stevens' face floated behind her eyes. Maybe she could ask him to help.

Seventeen

Blair had enjoyed the barbecue on Sunday. It had been good to see Troy again and to meet his friends. They reminded him of the ones he'd left behind in Hobart. And the steaks had been good too. The big surprise of the evening had been to see Lou, the woman from the bookshop, and to learn that she lived in one of the cottages. He'd love to learn more about the history of these cottages. Maybe she'd know.

It had been a fun evening, apart from that awkward moment when the other woman – Rachel – commented on a photo on the door of the fridge. Blair had taken a look at it later, and it was of three teenage couples. It seemed that they were Troy, Luke and another guy and Lou was one of the girls – the one with the other guy who might be related to his new friend, Stan.

He wasn't sure what the issue was, but it had seemed to upset Lou. It had sounded as if she had lost touch with the guy. She should speak to Stan. If they were related, he'd know how to contact him. It didn't seem difficult. But maybe there was more to it. The others seemed to go very quiet afterwards.

An unexpected outcome of the evening for Blair was his decision to visit the bookshop as soon as he could. He'd intended to do it after the Halloween event but had got caught up with spending time on the library computer and with Harper and Noah. Then at the *Book Café*, he vowed to go in again next day, but Katrina had insisted he spend the day with them.

Next morning, the rain which had sent them inside at Troy's had set in, forcing Blair to abandon his plans for a morning swim. But it was still too early to visit the bookshop, so after breakfast, he decided to drive to the beach. Once there the sight of the grey of the ocean and the white-tipped waves crashing to the shore made him glad he'd decided to forego his swim. He wondered if any of the wild swimmers had been foolish enough to brave the rough seas. He hoped not, sure anyone mad enough to try to swim in those waters would have been swept out to sea.

He checked the time. The bookshop should be open by now. The rain was still pelting down when he parked, and he pulled up the hood of his rain jacket and made a dash for it, a blast of warm, dry air hitting him when he pushed open the door.

The bookshop wasn't busy this morning but, when Blair glanced over at the counter, there was no sign of Lou. Her assistant was there alone, serving a customer. He assumed Lou was elsewhere in the bookshop or in the café. Meanwhile, he'd take time to browse the shelves.

Time flew by as Blair moved around the shop, taking one book after another off the shelves and reading the back matter before replacing some, and adding others to the pile he intended to purchase. He chuckled to himself at the thought of what Prue would say if she could see him now, his amusement stalling at the reminder that Prue would never see him again. Or perhaps she could. Maybe in some form of the afterlife, about which no one really knew, she was chuckling about him too.

By the time his arms were full of books, Blair knew it was time to stop. He carried the bundle to the counter, but there was still no sign of Lou.

'Lou not here today?' he asked the young woman who served him, seemingly surprised at his large purchase which was a mixture of crime novels and historical fiction. He'd discovered three books set in Tasmania by an author who wasn't familiar to him, but it seemed that Mary-Lou Stephens had thoroughly researched the apple, chocolate and jam industries of the apple isle. He was looking forward to reading them.

'She's working at home today,' Zoe said. 'Is there something I can help you with?'

'No, thanks.'

'She'll be back tomorrow.' She gave him an odd look.

'Thanks.' Blair picked up the two bags containing his purchases. He'd return next day. He could talk with Lou then, maybe even have coffee with her, he thought daringly. He barely knew the woman, but they now had friends in common, and perhaps he could introduce her to Stan.

Eighteen

Next morning the sun was shining brightly. It was difficult to believe it had been so wet the previous day. Lou ate breakfast at her kitchen table with the sun streaming in through the window, and Tilly lying stretched out in a patch of sunlight.

She was feeling optimistic as she drove to work. Perhaps this guy living at *The Haven* had the answer she was looking for, perhaps he could help her find Fleur. Her heart raced at the thought that maybe, just maybe, she could find her before Christmas, and they could spend it together.

'You're looking cheerful this morning,' Ron said, when she collected her morning cup of coffee from him, before going into the bookshop.

'Life's good, Ron,' she replied with a grin.

But once she was behind the counter, dealing with some early customers, Lou began to wonder how she was going to meet Stan Ross. If she was to ask Blair to introduce them, she'd need to see Blair again. Would she have to wait till the next *Book Café* in the hope he'd come along again, or could she ask Troy for his contact details? Troy would want to know why she wanted them. He might get the wrong idea, think she was interested in Blair. She wasn't sure why that notion sent a shiver down her spine.

She was still thinking about this when the door of the bookshop opened, and Blair walked in.

'Good morning,' she said.

'Good morning. Nice to see the sun again. I enjoyed the barbecue on Sunday. It was good to meet you again. A lovely group of people. It was kind of Troy to invite me.'

'Yes. It was good to meet you again too.'

The conversation stalled, and Lou served another customer. When she had finished, Blair was still standing there.

'Is there something I can help you with?' she asked him.

'Actually, I wondered if we could have a chat.' He glanced around. 'Can you get free for coffee?'

Lou checked the shop. There were only a few customers browsing the shelves, and Zoe was helping a woman and her daughter choose a book in the children's section. 'It should be okay. Zoe,' she called. 'I'm just going for a coffee. Call me if we get busy.'

A few minutes later, Lou was seated opposite Blair in the café with a cappuccino. There was a plate on the table containing two of Ron's salted caramel brownies.

'I'm afraid I've become addicted to these,' he said. 'I'm not sure what it's doing to my waistline.' He patted the slight bulge on his midriff.

'Don't I know it. I've been eating them for years… and all of Ron's other creations.'

They both laughed, before lapsing into a comfortable silence while they ate the brownies and sipped their coffee. Lou was surprised how relaxed she felt in his company. It was like being with an old friend. 'You wanted a chat?' she asked eventually.

'I did. Please tell me if I'm overstepping the mark, but after the barbecue, the talk about Stan, I wondered if it might be appropriate for me to arrange an introduction.'

Lou felt a sense of relief. He'd just answered her question of how she was going to meet Stan Ross. 'Not at all. In fact, I'd welcome it.' She paused, then continued. 'You're probably wondering why I want to get in touch with an old boyfriend. It's complicated. It's not Darren I want to find. He and my sister ran off together over forty years ago, and I haven't spoken to her since. I've tried to find her before now without success, but this might be the connection I've been looking for.'

'Wow! That's some story. I don't have any siblings, so I can't imagine…' He shook his head. 'I'm happy to do what I can. Do you want me to talk to Stan or…?'

'I'm not sure. You know him. What do you think?'

'Hmm.' Blair pulled on one ear. 'It's a bit odd. I could ask him if he has a brother called… Darren, wasn't it? Or I could arrange for you to meet him. Which would you prefer?'

'I'd like to ask him myself.' That way, she could see his reaction, and maybe if she saw him, there would be a family resemblance.

'Okay.' Blair fell silent, clearly trying to work out how it could be arranged. 'I'm not sure how flexible your time is, with having the bookshop, but maybe you could come to my place for coffee one morning, and I could invite Stan too.'

'To your villa… in *The Haven?*'

'Ye…es, unless… Would you prefer to meet here? He glanced around the café which was filling up with customers, a typical morning.

'Probably not.' But his villa, next door to Joan Ellis, who was as big a gossip as her daughter? What the hell. 'Okay, your villa it is.'

'If you let me know what day suits, I'll text you directions.'

'I know where *The Haven* is.'

'To my villa.'

'Oh, sorry.'

'This is my number.' Blair handed Lou an embossed card. 'It still has the university details, but my mobile hasn't changed.'

'Thanks.' Lou stared at the university logo and Blair's impressive title – Professor of Australian History – before tucking it into her pocket. She'd check with Zoe when she got back. She needed to get this done as soon as she could, the possibility of finding Fleur again taking precedence over everything else in her life. Now she was on her trail, she couldn't wait to find her.

'I don't suppose you've time for another coffee?'

Lou knew she should get back to the bookshop but was strangely loath to leave. Blair was surprisingly good company, and they'd just made arrangements to meet again, for her to meet Stan Ross. It would be rude to leave immediately. 'Why not?' she said. 'But I can't stay much longer.'

Denny winked as he served their next coffees, and to her annoyance, Lou blushed. To cover her embarrassment, she said, 'Given your interest in Australian history, I wanted to ask if you'd read Mary-Lou Stephens' books set in Tasmania. What?' she asked, seeing Blair laugh.

'I bought them yesterday when I was in the bookshop. I'd hoped to see you then and spent ages browsing your amazing collection.'

'Oh!' Lou laughed too.

'Tell me about yourself,' he said. 'You've lived in Pelican Crossing all your life?'

'Why would I want to live anywhere else? But yes, I have. I never saw any reason to move. As you've no doubt gathered, there are quite a group of us who've spent our lives right here.'

'I'm beginning to understand why. This place gets under your skin. Katrina certainly loves it. She mentioned you're one of her clients?'

'I often like to pamper myself. She's an excellent masseuse.' There was no need to admit her occasional back pain to him, though he'd no doubt understand, perhaps even sympathise. From what he'd said, he was older than her, but he seemed too fit to suffer from the aches of encroaching age.

They chatted for a bit longer, just as long as it took Lou to drink another cup of coffee. She learned he'd been widowed three years earlier and, in addition to Katrina, had another daughter who lived in Brisbane and owned a photography business. He had initially been unsure about moving to Pelican Crossing but was coming to like it and enjoyed spending time with his grandchildren. In return, she shared how she'd been the local librarian before opening *Books and Coffee* and how she loved what she did so much, she couldn't contemplate retiring, but knew that, one day, she'd be forced to give it up.

'Now, I need to get back,' she said. 'Thanks for agreeing to help me meet Stan Ross.'

'No worries Just let me know which day suits.'

'I will.'

Lou left the café with a smile on her face and more hope in her heart than ever.

Nineteen

Blair had enjoyed talking with Lou in the café, learning more about her and making arrangements for her to meet Stan. He'd been shocked to hear about her sister and former boyfriend and was flattered she'd confided in him. But he supposed it wasn't a secret. In a small place like Pelican Crossing, everyone would know. It must have been quite a scandal at the time.

He could understand her desire to contact her sister after all this time. Life was too short to hold grudges, and it was when you reached your sixties that it hit home and made you want to get your life in order. He knew that too well. He'd thought he and Prue had many more years together and since her death had wondered what they might have done differently if they'd known her life was going to be cut short.

The beach was empty when he arrived for his morning swim. He was a little later than usual. The wild swimmers had gone home, and the young families were yet to arrive. There were only a few surfers sitting out on the ocean waiting for the wave that would bring them in to shore. He loved it when it was like this, just him, the ocean and the endless stretch of blue sky.

Arriving back at *The Haven*, Blair waved to Joan who was in her garden, surprised her presence no longer annoyed him. Since meeting Stan, he'd learned a little about her and had become more understanding of her ways, and Stan seemed fond of her. Both had been widowed and seemed to have found companionship with each other. Blair couldn't imagine anyone taking Prue's place in his life, but he guessed everyone was different, and, unlike Stan, he had a daughter and grandchildren in Pelican Crossing. Though he had to admit, it wasn't the same as having a loved one with him all the time. The evenings were the worst, when he was home alone, or returned from visiting Katrina and her family. It was then that the villa seemed so empty, when he yearned for Prue's soothing company, for someone to talk to, to share his day with.

After breakfast, he took his coffee into the courtyard with one of his new books and was soon lost in the world of Hobart in the eighteen hundreds, the life of Henry Jones and the history of the Tasmanian jam industry.

When he heard someone at his front door, Blair put down his book with reluctance.

'Morning, Blair. A few of us are going to have a game of pickleball, and I wondered if you'd like to join us,' Stan said.

About to decline, Blair hesitated. Prue would have accepted, would have told him he needed to make friends, try new things. But pickleball? He didn't even know what it was. 'I've never played,' he said, 'but I'm willing to give it a try.'

'Good man,' Stan said. 'I'm going over to the court now. Just come as you are,' he added, his eyes taking in the shorts, tee-shirt and pair of Converse All-Stars Blair had changed into when he returned from the beach.

Blair locked up and accompanied Stan to a section of *The Haven* he hadn't visited before. There was a pool, a barbecue area, a building which Stan told him housed a small library, movie theatre and meeting room, and what looked like a small tennis court. He remembered how he'd enjoyed playing tennis in his teens and early twenties. He and Prue had even won a competition. But, like many other things he'd enjoyed in his youth, tennis had given way to work pursuits as his career had taken off.

'This is us,' Stan said, stopping by the court where two other men were clearly preparing to play. They were holding smooth-faced paddles and chatting. They fell silent when Blair and Stan approached. 'This is Blair, the guy I told you about who's moved in next to Joan. Meet Fred and Ewan, Blair. They're old hands here,' he said.

'Hi,' Blair said. The two men looked closer to his age than to Stan's.

'Have you played tennis before, Blair?' Stan asked.

'Not for a long time.'

'Well, you'll find this is pretty similar. It's a slower game, easier on the old body. We play with these paddles and a perforated, hollow, plastic ball, sending it over the net till one side is unable to return it or breaks a rule. You'll soon pick it up.'

'There are only five rules,' Fred said, listing them. 'We'll keep you right. As it's your first time, we won't be too hard on you.'

'Right.' It didn't look too difficult. He might even enjoy it.

Less than half an hour later, the game was over. Blair and Stan had played against Fred and Ewan, and the other two men had won.

'Another?' Fred asked.

'Not today, thanks. But I enjoyed it. Perhaps another time.' Much to his surprise, Blair had enjoyed the game. He remembered how he'd mentally ridiculed his friends back in Tassie for raving about it. He'd been too quick to knock something he didn't understand… or had he changed? Had coming to Pelican Crossing changed him, turned him into someone his old friends wouldn't recognise?

'We're all going to the yacht club for lunch,' Stan said. 'Join us?'

'Thanks. I've been meaning to go there.' And he could check it out before taking the family there for dinner.

Blair was on his way to pick up his car, having declined Stan's offer of a lift, when his phone pinged with a text. It was from Lou.

I can get away tomorrow around ten. Let me know if that works for you. Lou.

Blair smiled. He'd check with Stan over lunch.

When Blair walked into the yacht club, he was greeted by Phil. 'Good to see you again,' he said. 'So, you decided to give us a try?'

'As you see.' Blair grinned. 'I'm meeting some friends here.' He glanced round the restaurant. It was busy for a weekday lunchtime, a mixture of older couples and some younger ones, clearly on holiday. He spied the guys he was looking for in the far corner. 'There they are,' he said.

'Oh, you're with the group from *The Haven*. They're regulars on Wednesdays and Fridays. Enjoy your meal.'

'Thanks.' Blair headed towards the table where Stan and the other two were sitting. He wondered what it would be like to have your life so regulated that you were known as regulars for lunch at the yacht club on Wednesdays and Fridays – or anywhere else for that matter. Was this what his life was going to be like from now on?

'You made it,' Stan said, pulling out a chair for Blair. 'We've ordered wine. Okay for you?'

Blair nodded. Wine wasn't his usual lunchtime tipple, but he supposed he could make an exception. 'Sure,' he said, picking up a menu.

The meal was delicious. Blair had followed the others' lead and ordered the grilled barramundi and chips which went well with the wine. They followed it with a shared cheese platter and coffee which finished off the meal nicely.

While they were eating, Fred and Ewan revealed they were in a relationship and had lived at *The Haven* for five years. Stan, it appeared, was a newer resident having lived in the town before moving into the complex. 'The old family home became too difficult to maintain,' Stan said. 'I was sad to see it go. It had been in the family since my parents married. But I had only been back since I retired, and the oldies had let things go. Then my wife died. *The Haven* works better for me, now I'm on my own.'

'You grew up here?' Blair asked, thinking he could at least test the water for Lou.

'Until I was eighteen. I joined the army in search of adventure. I got it all right, was sent to Vietnam. When Whitlam brought the troops home in seventy-two, it had got into my blood, and I signed up for another stretch. Kept doing it. As I was moved around the world, the army became my family, much to my wife's dismay. But I always knew I'd end up back here. These two are incomers like yourself.' He nodded to Fred and Ewan.

'We used to come to Pelican Crossing for holidays,' Ewan said, 'So when we retired, it was a no-brainer to move here. We've never regretted it. You won't either. Stan says you have family here?'

The rest of lunch was taken up by Blair telling them about Katrina, Harper and Noah, and Chelsea in Brisbane. He didn't touch on his research or his writing. They didn't need to know about that. Some things he preferred to keep to himself, and he was never sure how strangers would react. Even Katrina thought he was mad and was wasting his time.

As they were leaving, he managed to have a quiet word with Stan to invite him to coffee the following morning as a thank you for today and, 'There's someone I want you to meet,' he added.

'Sounds mysterious, but I'll be there. See you then.'

Blair smiled to himself as he drove home, having texted Lou that Stan would be there. It had been a pleasant morning, better than he'd expected when Stan suggested pickleball, and he was impressed with the yacht club.

Twenty

Lou hadn't slept. In the past hour her stomach had been doing cartwheels, and she'd thought she was going to be sick. Now it was time to leave the bookshop.

The drive to *The Haven* seemed to take for ever, but at last she was driving through the entrance, along an avenue bordered by palm trees, past a beautiful old sandstone building. There were a lot of villas, all with tidy gardens. She followed Blair's directions to pull up and park opposite the one which must be his. The garden looked amazing. Troy had done a good job.

Still feeling nervous, Lou took a deep breath, got out of the car, walked across and knocked on Blair's door, conscious of someone peering out through the next-door window. *It must be Liz's mother*, Lou thought, stifling the urge to wave.

It was a relief when Blair opened the door, and she could go in. The villa was different to what she'd expected, smaller than her cottage, but well-designed, the large living/dining area having a kitchen at one end. No doubt the bedrooms were through the hallway she could see stretching back from where they were standing. It was tastefully furnished, a large bookshelf taking up one wall, opposite which was a sofa, two armchairs and a coffee table. At right angles to the bookshelf a wide-screen television sat on a low shelving unit, and between this area and the kitchen, was a small round dining table and chairs.

'Why don't I make you a coffee?' Blair asked, as if sensing her nervousness. 'Take a seat. Stan should be here shortly.'

'Thanks.' Lou sat down warily on the edge of one of the armchairs. 'It's a nice place, *The Haven* and your villa. I haven't been here before.' It wasn't for her, but Lou could see the appeal of the modern building, the low maintenance. She preferred her little cottage with her view of the sea which changed with the seasons.

'It's not bad.' Blair seemed as if he was about to say something more when there was a knock at the door. 'That'll be Stan.'

'What did you tell him?' Lou asked anxiously.

'Only that I had someone I wanted him to meet.'

'Oh! I hope he didn't get the wrong idea.'

'I didn't think of that.' Blair chuckled. 'Well, too late now.' He went to the door, returning with a tall, burly man with thinning white hair and wearing a curious expression. His eyes widened when he saw Lou.

'It's not what you think, Stan. This is Lou Chalmers from *Books and Coffee* in town. She has something she wants to ask you. Let me get us all coffee, then she can tell you what she wants to know.'

Stan still appeared puzzled, but he took a seat on the other armchair, calling through to Blair as he made coffee, and waiting till the coffee was served, before asking, 'What's all this about?'

Lou shifted nervously in her seat and took a sip of coffee before speaking. 'I've been trying to find my sister, Fleur. We lost touch a long time ago, and I'm not getting any younger, so I've decided to try to find her and…' She stopped. There was no need for Stan to know the whole story, or was there? If he was Darren's brother, he probably knew it already. She wished she had sat on the sofa where she would have had Blair's support, though if she had, perhaps he'd have sat on the armchair. She tried to stem her thoughts and get to the point. 'Are you Darren Ross's brother?' she asked.

There was silence for a moment, broken only by the hum of the refrigerator and a car driving past outside. Then Stan spoke. 'Darren's my half-brother. What does he have to do with it?'

A wave of excitement filled Lou, threatening to overwhelm her. 'Over forty years ago he and my sister left Pelican Crossing together. We lost touch and… I'm hoping you might be able to help me contact her.'

Stan stared at her. 'Over forty years ago? What makes you think they're still together?'

Lou's heart sank. That possibility had never occurred to her. Surely she hadn't suffered all that hurt only for Darren and Fleur to break up? All those years she'd envisaged them living happily together, creating a family somewhere far away from Pelican Crossing.

Stan was speaking again. 'Anyway, I'm sorry I can't help you. Darren was only ten when I enlisted. I hardly knew the kid. I was overseas when what you're talking about occurred. I seem to recall my mother writing me that he'd run off with a local girl, then that they were living in Melbourne. I don't know any more than that. He didn't come back for Mother's funeral, or Dad's. I don't have an address. I can't help you. I'm sorry,' he repeated.

'Oh!' Lou sagged against the back of the armchair. She felt sick. She'd been so close, or thought she had. But she was one step further forward. Melbourne. She clutched at the straw. 'Do you know which part of Melbourne?'

'Sorry.' Stan shook his head. 'I wish I could be of more help. If Mum and Dad had any information, it would have been thrown out when I sold the house. There were a lot of old papers… Sorry,' he repeated.

'Thanks, Stan.' It was Blair who spoke.

Lou was too distraught. She picked up her coffee to take a sip, her hand shaking so much she almost dropped the cup.

'Careful,' Blair said. 'It was worth a try, Lou. Now we know your sister went to Melbourne, I have a few ideas. Maybe I can help you locate her.'

Lou stared at Blair in surprise. How could he help and why would he? They barely knew each other. But he seemed to be a kind man, and she felt comfortable with him. 'Thanks,' she muttered. 'I should go now.' She knew she was being rude, leaving so abruptly, but she had to get out of there, breathe some fresh air. And she had to get back to the bookshop. Maybe in its familiar surroundings, she could come to terms with the fact that she was really no further forward in her search for Fleur.

*

'Are you all right?'

Lou only nodded to Zoe in reply when she returned to the bookshop. She knew her disappointment must be obvious in her expression, but she didn't want to talk about it. It was going to be difficult enough to deal with customers for the rest of the day. Somehow, she got through it, smiling politely and saying as little as possible. Then when it was almost closing time, and she was looking forward to going home, curling up with Tilly and having a good cry, Blair walked in. He was the last person she wanted to see, a reminder of her disappointment.

'I had to come to see you,' he said. 'I could see how letdown you felt when Stan couldn't help. I'm sorry I couldn't get here sooner.'

'It's okay. I'm no worse off. I had just hoped...'

'I'm sorry I raised your hopes. But at least now we know where to start.'

We? There was no *we*. This was *her* problem, *her* search which had come up against a brick wall.

'Melbourne,' Blair said. 'We know your sister went to Melbourne. We can search marriages, births... deaths. Then there are electoral rolls.'

Lou stared at him in surprise.

'It's what I do... in my research. I've been searching my family history going back to the eighteen hundreds, but it works for more recent history too.'

'Really?' Lou felt a lightening of the despair that had been weighing on her since she heard Stan's words. *But why would he help her?*

As if in response to her unspoken question, Blair said, 'I'd like to help if I can. I have a lot of spare time, and your search interests me. Although we've only just met, I consider you a friend, and it would be a pleasure to be of some assistance. What can I say? I'm a sucker for ferreting things out. May be why I love reading crime novels.' He chuckled.

Lou attempted to smile, but was aware it fell flat.

'You look as if you need something to cheer you up,' he said. 'Why don't you join me for dinner. I ate at the yacht club for the first time yesterday and was impressed.'

'The yacht club. Oh, I don't know...' Lou had never eaten there with a man, alone, but the idea appealed to her. If she went home, she knew she'd spend the evening rehashing what Stan had said, wallowing in her disappointment and frustration. 'Okay,' she said, 'but I'll pay for my own meal.'

'There's no need,' he said, then, clearly seeing Lou's determined expression, added, 'but if you insist.'

'I do.' Lou didn't want to be beholden to him. It was enough he'd arranged for her to meet with Stan. *She* should pay for *his* meal to thank him. *Why hadn't she thought of that?*

'I'll make a booking for seven. Can I pick you up?'

'I… why not? You know where I live. My cottage is five down from Troy's.'

'Okay, see you then.'

Lou stared after Blair, wondering what had possessed her to accept his invitation to dinner. But she did enjoy the meals at the yacht club and didn't get there often enough. It was ages since she'd had dinner there with Rachel and Olivia. And, so far, Blair had proven to be good company.

Twenty-one

Back home, Blair made himself a cup of coffee and took it into the courtyard with the book he was reading. He was enjoying learning about the history of jam making in Tasmania and the origin of the IXL brand. But today he found it hard to concentrate.

He wasn't sure why he'd invited Lou to dinner. It was out of character, something he'd never done before, not since he'd invited Prue to dinner all those years ago. Although he had women friends back in Hobart, most were wives of friends or colleagues, and it would never have occurred to him to invite any of them to dinner without their husbands.

He'd decided to drop into the bookshop on impulse, knowing how upset Lou had been, how she'd left so abruptly. He'd felt guilty for having set up the meeting, having raised her hopes. He'd wanted to apologise, offer to help. And he had to admit, her story, her search for her sister, had aroused his curiosity. But when they got talking, his guilt increased, and he found himself inviting her to dine with him at the yacht club.

What would Katrina think, he wondered, knowing his daughter would most likely be delighted he was making more friends. But was Lou the sort of friend she meant when she said he needed to make more of an effort socially? He knew Chelsea would be thrilled. She'd often told him that Prue wouldn't want him to spend the rest of his life grieving.

But it was only dinner, and Lou was far from being a femme fatale.

She was more like a mate, like Troy or Stan. She just happened to be a woman, and one who had presented him with a project that was just up his alley. He'd enjoy helping her discover what had happened to her sister, where she was living, and any other nuggets of information he could glean.

Blair knew Melbourne well. It was where he and Prue had met and spent the first years of their married life. For him it would be like a trip down memory lane. Whereas Lou had spent all her life in Pelican Crossing. For her, Melbourne was as foreign as Paris or London would be.

Prue, dear Prue. How he wished she hadn't been taken from him, and so suddenly, giving him no opportunity to say goodbye. He missed her every day, but life had to go on. For a few moments he sat, lost in thought, remembering those early years, images flitting through his mind as if it was yesterday when he and Prue were in their twenties, before the girls were born.

Blair pulled himself back to the present. He wasn't in Melbourne, or even in Hobart. He was in Pelican Crossing and had arranged to take Lou to dinner. With a sigh, he closed his book. He picked up his cup. The coffee had gone cold. It was time to change and get ready to head out.

*

Tilly watched on disdainfully as Lou changed into one of the dresses she rarely wore. Was it too much? But it was the yacht club. It had been kind of Blair to invite her. And she wanted to make an effort. She thought back to his offer to help her find Fleur. It was true he was experienced in researching family history, and he certainly had more time available than she did – the bookshop was getting busier every day as summer tourists arrived, and the locals did early Christmas shopping. But did she want him getting involved in her family?

Deciding any help was better than none, he did seem to genuinely want to be of assistance, and he was Katrina's father, not a complete stranger, Lou stifled her reservations. She'd be a pleasant dinner companion and accept his help as gracefully as she could, ignoring her lifetime habit of refusing to be dependent on anyone. Fleur and Darren's behaviour had cured her of any shred of reliance on others. It was probably what had made her such a successful businesswoman, that and her pigheadedness, her determination to succeed in anything she chose to do.

She picked up the photo of Fleur she'd unearthed the previous evening, the only one she still had. It showed Lou with her sister. They were standing arm-in-arm, their faces wreathed in smiles. Lou remembered the day so well. It had been taken on Fleur's eighteenth birthday, and they were celebrating. To think that only a year later… Lou dropped the photo down on the bedside table. Some things were best forgotten. Hadn't she decided to forget and forgive? But deciding was very different from acting on it.

Tilly leapt from her perch on Lou's bed when she heard a knock at the door and scurried into the kitchen and out the cat door. Lou made her way to the front door with a wry smile. The cat rarely stayed around to meet visitors, Rachel having been the exception last time she was there.

Lou experienced an unexpected tingle of excitement at the sight of Blair. Tonight, he was dressed more formally than she'd seen him, in a pair of grey pants and a pale blue short-sleeved shirt. She was glad she was wearing a dress.

'Ready?'

'Yes. I'll just get my bag.' She was unsure whether to invite him in or not, so decided against it.

Thursday night at the yacht club was busier than Lou had anticipated. She smiled and nodded to several of her customers before she and Blair were seated at a table overlooking the marina.

'You seem popular,' Blair commented when they'd been handed menus. 'Come here a lot?'

'Not as often as I'd like. Those were mostly customers.' Lou glanced around again, relieved not to see any of her friends. 'I sometimes come here with Rachel and my friend, Livvy, but it's been a while.' Not since Rachel started seeing Luke, and Livvy went overseas. 'You said you'd been here yesterday?'

'Yes, for lunch, with Stan and a couple of other residents from *The Haven*. We'd been playing pickleball, and it seems they make a habit of lunching here afterwards.'

Lou stared at Blair in surprise. 'You don't strike me as someone who plays pickleball.'

Blair chuckled. 'In my defence, it was my first time, but I enjoyed it more than I expected. It's a bit like tennis, and Prue and I used to play. I may even play again.'

'Wow! I've never been into sports, apart from swimming, and I don't do much of that either these days. I suppose I should. It would help keep the weight down. Spending every day next to the café has its drawbacks… then there are the boxes of leftovers I take home…' She gave a wry smile.

'You've no need to worry about your weight. You look fine to me.' Blair drew a finger around the inside of his collar as if embarrassed by his comment.

'Thanks.' Lou picked up her menu to hide her blushes. She couldn't remember the last time a man had paid her a compliment. *Was it a compliment, or was he just being polite?* 'What do you recommend?' she asked to hide her confusion.

'I had the barramundi and chips yesterday and I couldn't fault it.'

'Sounds good.' It saved Lou thinking what to order and she knew the fish would have been freshly caught that morning.

'Wine?'

'Yes, please. You choose.' Thinking of the cask wine in her fridge, Lou guessed Blair would be more of a wine buff than she was.

Blair was still perusing the wine list when Phil appeared to take their order. Lou glanced up at him in surprise. He didn't normally serve customers himself. 'Short-staffed tonight,' he said. 'Good to see you both. Are you ready to order?'

When Blair had placed their order, Phil turned away, but not before he had winked at Lou. She flinched, reminded of Denny doing the same when she'd had coffee with Blair. They couldn't think… could they? She was past all that sort of thing… though Blair was pleasant company.

Twenty-two

Blair enjoyed the evening more than he'd expected. He'd issued the invitation to dinner on impulse, as a way of trying to make amends for the fact Stan couldn't help Lou in her search for her sister. But he'd found it was good to have some female companionship again. It was something he'd missed since Prue's passing. Spending time with Chelsea or Katrina wasn't the same as with someone of his own age, and he'd never been alone with the wives of any of his friends back home.

Home. He still thought of Hobart as home. Probably not surprising since he'd spent most of his life there, and no matter how well he was settling in here in Pelican Crossing, he still felt as if he was on an extended holiday.

He hadn't made any arrangements to meet Lou again, but it would be easy to catch up with her. He only needed to go into *Books and Coffee*, and he knew he'd be back to enjoy the coffee and brownies in the café. Meantime, he could get started on researching her sister. Now he knew she had gone to Melbourne, it shouldn't be too difficult.

Planning to spend the day in the library, Blair set off early, only to be thwarted by a message from Katrina. 'Can you come round, Dad? Noah's feeling sick this morning, and I have a full day of clients.'

Heaving a sigh and wondering yet again how Katrina had managed before he moved to Pelican Crossing, he agreed, turning the car around and heading to his daughter's home.

'Thanks, Dad,' Katrina said as soon as he arrived. 'You're a lifesaver.

I don't know what I'd do without you. Noah's in his room. I've given him a Panadol, so he may sleep for a bit, but if you could look in on him from time to time. I'll call between clients.'

'Can't I stay home with Grandad?' Harper asked. 'I could help him look after Noah.'

'No, honey. You need to go to school. Will you be okay, Dad? There's plenty of food in the fridge for your lunch, and…'

'I'll be fine. This isn't my first rodeo. Your mum and I brought up you and Chels and saw you through lots of childhood illnesses. You go off to work and don't worry about me… or Noah.'

'Thanks, Dad,' she said again, giving him a hug.

When Katrina and Harper had left, Blair went upstairs to check on Noah. He was asleep, one hand tucked under his chin. After watching him for a moment, Blair tiptoed out, leaving the door ajar, so he'd hear if Noah awoke and called out.

Back downstairs, he was at a loss as to what to do. Since he'd intended to work on the library computer, he'd left his laptop at home. He didn't have his book with him either. Nor did he have the password for Katrina and Brett's computer he realised, after trying to access it.

Blair made himself a cup of coffee and picked up a copy of the local paper which was lying on the coffee table. He could at least check out the local news. His own copy was lying, still unopened, on his kitchen table. He flicked through the paper as he sipped his coffee and nibbled on a Tim Tam.

A couple of articles interested him. One was a report on the opening of a palliative care centre named *Barbara Harris House*. It was apparently named after the former lady mayoress, who had passed away after a long illness, and had been well-loved and popular. The article finished with a potted history of the mayor and praise for him and his new partner who was a local family and divorce lawyer. It reminded Blair of the conversation at Troy's, and Phil's reference to the mayor. It appeared that Joe Harris was another of those who'd grown up in the town and spent his entire life here.

The other article also referred to Harris, this one being a summary of the latest council meeting. The writer reported that there had been some discussion of the need for affordable housing and the rental crisis which had the potential to devastate the hospitality industry. It was exactly what Phil had been worried about. Blair was surprised he'd been able to get into the mayor's ear and onto the agenda for the council meeting so speedily. Noting that all meetings were livestreamed, he made a note to check one out when he had access to a computer again, perhaps even attend the next one. They sounded more interesting than those he'd heard about back home. He and his friends had often despaired of their local councillors' ability to get things done.

Blair had laid the paper down and was flicking through the television channels in search of something to watch. He was trying to decide between a cooking programme featuring someone who'd won Master Chef, The Antiques Roadshow and a repeat of The Movie Show, leaning towards the latter when there was a cry from upstairs.

Dropping the remote, Blair made his way up to Noah's bedroom.

'Grandad, what are you doing here?'

'Mum asked me to stay with you while she went to work.' Blair put his hand on his grandson's forehead. It was cool to the touch, no fever. 'How are you feeling?'

'I'm hungry.'

Blair smiled, remembering from when Katrina and Chelsea were little, how quickly they could recover from childhood illnesses. 'Let me see what I can find. How about a nice, boiled egg with soldiers?' It was what Prue had always made the girls when they were sick.

'Yes, please. And can I get up?'

'Best stay where you are for a bit longer.' Blair checked his watch. It was lunchtime. 'I'll bring it up to you, along with some lunch for me and we can have a picnic right here. How does that sound?'

'Ooh, yes, please.' Noah slid down under the covers again, and Blair suspected that despite him saying he felt better, he still hadn't fully recovered.

They ate lunch, then played a game of checkers which Noah won, before his eyes started to close again. Blair packed up the game, tucked a blanket around Noah, then dropped a kiss on his forehead before going back downstairs.

Now he'd read the paper, and given up on the television, Blair was at a loose end again. Katrina hadn't called as promised, so he hadn't been able to ask her for the password for the computer, and he hadn't wanted to disturb her at work, and worry her about Noah.

Seeing a library book on the coffee table, he picked it up. He recognised the author. Katrina obviously shared her mother's taste in reading. It wasn't his. He prowled around the house, ending up in Brett's study where the unavailable computer taunted him. Turning away, his eyes fell on a bookcase he hadn't noticed earlier. He was mildly surprised to see a complete collection of Agatha Christie. He hadn't known Brett was a fan. Below them was a line of the Jack Irish books by Peter Temple. Now that was something he could read. Temple was one of Blair's favourite Australian authors. He'd enjoyed the books, and the television series based on them. He picked one from the shelf and settled himself in Brett's comfortable office chair.

The book was set in Melbourne, and the mention of familiar locations in what was often called The Garden City reminded Blair of the years spent there, happy times in the early years of his and Prue's marriage and when Katrina and Chelsea were only small. But it also got him thinking about Lou and her sister, and he vowed once again to do everything in his power to help her find Fleur, not sure why the prospect felt so thrilling.

Twenty-three

As the days rolled into December, the bookshop became increasingly busy. The weather had become hot and humid, and Lou was grateful she was able to spend each day in the airconditioned comfort of her shop. The tree had arrived and after closing on the first of the month, she, Zoe and Georgia had spent the evening decorating it. Now, its lights twinkling, the tree sat proudly just inside the door, providing a focal point for everyone who entered.

Zoe and Georgia had decorated the rest of the bookshop too, with garlands of tinsel, fake snow and artificial holly, turning it into a Christmas wonderland. And, of course, there was a seasonal display of Christmas books. At Zoe's incentive, the children's corner had even more tinsel and glitter than the rest of the bookshop, transforming it into a magical grotto prompting many oohs and aahs from its young visitors.

Over the past couple of weeks, Blair had fallen into the habit of dropping into the café for his morning coffee, and on most days, Lou managed to join him. She tried to tell herself it was only because she was eager to hear the results of his research, but if she was honest with herself, she knew it was more than that. She enjoyed his company, and he seemed to enjoy hers too, though he pretended it was Ron's coffee and caramel salted brownies that were the attraction.

At ten o'clock, Blair pushed open the door and walked into the bookshop as he did at that time every morning – Lou could almost set her watch by him – smiling at Lou as he passed through on his way to the café. This morning, there was something about him, a jauntiness to his walk, a particular sparkle to his smile that made her think he'd found something. Lou's heart raced. Was this the day she was going to discover where Fleur was? Checking Zoe could handle the customers, she hurried to join him in the café.

Lou managed to contain her patience until Denny had served them with coffee and the inevitable brownies – she really must go on a diet after Christmas – before asking. 'Well? Is there news? You look particularly cheerful this morning.'

Blair took a sip of coffee before replying. Then he smiled. 'I do have some news. I'm sorry it's taken me so long. Katrina… Anyway, when I finally managed to access the Victorian website for Births, Deaths and Marriages, I did find Darren Ross and Fleur Chalmers.'

'Yes?' Lou could barely wait.

'I found that they did marry and had a child – a girl.'

'Oh!' Lou felt a warm glow. She had a niece. She was an aunt. Though that niece would now be in her thirties or forties. 'Anything else?'

'I'm sorry to say that Darren passed away several years ago.'

'Oh,' Lou said again, this time her voice dropped. It was sad to think that the boy she'd once loved to distraction, the cause of all her unhappiness, was no more. 'And Fleur?' she asked, impatient to learn more.

'There was no record of her death, so we can assume she's still alive.'

Lou's body tingled with excitement at the prospect that her sister could still be living in Melbourne, that they could be reunited, that… 'What's next?'

Blair took another sip of coffee and a bite of his brownie. 'Next, I'll access the electoral roll. As long as your sister has registered to vote, I should be able to find her address.'

'Wow!' Lou picked up her cup in both hands. She was trembling so much, she was afraid of dropping it. 'How soon can you do that?'

Blair smiled, his lips curling in a way she had become familiar with. It was strange, she thought, how he had become such a close friend. They had known each other for less than two months, but she felt she'd known him for years. From regarding him as a stranger she was unwilling to share her family history with, she now trusted him implicitly. 'I'll do it as soon as I can, but first, I think we ought to celebrate. I've heard *Crossings* is the best restaurant in town. Why don't I book a table there for tomorrow evening?'

'What a good idea.' Lou's spirits rose at the prospect. She hadn't eaten at *Crossings* since the Melbourne Cup Luncheon last year. It was one of the town's major social occasions, when Poppy and her staff went all out to provide a superb meal.

'Good.' Blair smiled again, a warm smile that seemed to Lou to hold a promise of something more than dinner at *Crossings*.

*

Lou wasn't sure why she felt so excited. She'd had dinner with Blair before, eaten at *Crossings* before, but there had been something in his expression... 'I'm probably imagining it, Tilly,' she said to the cat who, as usual was watching her get ready with a jaundiced expression. *What was it about cats that could make you feel they disapproved of you,* Lou thought, as she twisted this way and that in front of the mirror. Tonight, she'd steered away from a dress and was wearing a pair of black wide-legged pants and a brightly coloured tunic she'd bought at the boutique in Bellbird Bay on a trip with Rachel earlier in the year. She still hadn't found time for the return trip she'd promised herself, perhaps after Christmas...

When she opened the door to Blair, Lou had to stifle the sudden thrill she felt at the warmth of his closeness as he gave her the now customary peck on the cheek. She quickly moved away lest he might think... 'Good timing. I'm just ready,' she said as Tilly flew past them to take up position at the edge of the garden.

'Will she be all right?' Blair asked.

'Mmm. As soon as we've left, she'll be back in through the cat door. She doesn't go out much at night, ever since she was caught up in a fight with another cat. She only wants to annoy me. Don't you, Tilly?' she said to the cat who let out a loud meow of agreement before disappearing around the side of the cottage.

'I've never seen the inside of your cottage,' Blair said as he helped her into his car.

'Maybe one day.' Should she invite him back for coffee… to dinner? Lou was completely unaware of what the protocol was with male friends these days. Rachel and Livvy were the only two friends she entertained, and then only rarely. For the most part, she preferred to keep herself to herself. But Blair had invited her to his villa, and he had expressed an interest in the row of cottages. 'It's much the same as Troy's,' she said, 'apart from the décor.'

'I think I mentioned my interest in the history of the cottages. These old buildings fascinate me.'

'You should check the heritage collection in the library. When I worked there, the heritage librarian was developing a collection of historical archives of the town to include all sorts of resources – timelines, town histories, oral histories, historical images, books, maps, newspaper cuttings, magazines, films and sound recordings, pamphlets, and organisational records. I'm pretty sure it will be fairly advanced by now.'

'Wow, that sounds impressive. Thanks. One more thing to add to my to-do list. And I thought retirement was going to be boring.' Blair chuckled.

Lou felt guilty. Blair was a busy man, and he was spending time helping her. 'If the search for Fleur is taking up too much of your time…'

'Not at all. I'm enjoying it. I only hope I can get the result you're hoping for. What will you do once we have your sister's address?'

Lou didn't reply immediately. She hadn't dared to figure that out. 'I'm not sure. I haven't thought that far ahead. Write to her, I suppose.' But what if Fleur treated her letter the way Lou had treated hers all those years ago? 'Or I could go to Melbourne, visit her, turn up at her door. But it would have to be after Christmas, after the New Year sale, after the tourists have left, which means after the school holidays.' She sighed.

By this time, they had reached the restaurant. 'Wow!' Blair whistled. 'This is nice. I'd read about *Crossings*, saw it featured on television when we were visiting Katrina one time, but we never made it inside.' He glanced around. 'This could be in the city.'

'Not bad for a small town like Pelican Crossing?' A short, blonde, curvy woman approached them.

'Poppy!' Lou said. 'I didn't think you were working any longer.'

'Oh, I like to keep my hand in from time to time. Cam and I are having dinner here, and I thought I'd pop over early to make sure everyone was on the ball. And this is…?' she raised an eyebrow.

'This is Blair Stevens, he's…'

'I know who he is.' Poppy snapped her fingers and turned to face Blair. 'You're the new resident at *The Haven,* Joan Phillips' neighbour. You should know you can't keep anything secret in this town, Lou.'

Lou blushed.

'Hi Blair, I'm Poppy.'

'The owner of this lovely restaurant,' Blair said. 'I'm delighted to meet you.'

'Let me show you both to a table,' Poppy said, giving Lou a knowing look.

Lou sighed inwardly. She knew Poppy would be in the bookshop next day, and by lunchtime, Rachel, Gill and Liz would know she'd had dinner here with Blair. The local gossip mill had never concerned her, never had anything to report since Darren and Fleur ran off together – and it had taken Lou weeks to show her face in town after that. But now, as soon as the gossipmongers heard about her being here with Blair, they would be putting two and two together and making five. And she knew if she protested to Poppy that she and Blair were only friends, it would make things worse. 'Thanks, Poppy,' she said, lifting her head and forcing a smile.

'Problem?' Blair asked when they were seated with menus, and Poppy had walked away.

'Not really,' Lou sighed, 'but now Poppy has seen us here together, it'll be common knowledge among her friends… and mine.'

'Ah!' The penny seemed to drop for Blair. 'And that worries you?'

'I remember only too well what it was like to be the butt of gossip.'

'But surely, having dinner together doesn't signify anything untoward. Isn't it something friends do?'

'I suppose, but…' Lou looked across the table at Blair's kindly face. He could have no idea how the gossip mill worked in a place like Pelican Crossing. But he was right about one thing. There was no sense in worrying about it. What was done was done. Poppy had seen them together. Lou might as well forget it and enjoy her meal. 'Sorry, I'm being foolish.' She picked up her menu.

Twenty-four

Blair glanced across at Lou who was now studying the menu intently. Although he could understand her concern, he thought it was misplaced. As he'd said, they were two friends enjoying a meal together in the best restaurant in town. So what if the owner was a friend of Lou's and likely to mention it to her other friends? Blair knew how the gossip mill worked. The suburb where he had lived in Hobart wasn't too different, and as for the university… it was a hotbed of gossip. But there was nothing to gossip about with him and Lou. They couldn't imagine they were anything more than good friends, could they?

Blair wasn't sure why the idea sent a shiver down his spine. Lou was an attractive woman, good company, but it had never occurred to him to think of her as anything other than a good friend, a mate… not till now. Suddenly, he was aware of the curve of her cheeks, the way her hair flattered her heart-shaped face, her normally placid nature, her… He swallowed hard.

'Have you decided?' he asked to cover his confusion, the realisation that, for the first time since Prue's death, he was attracted to a woman. It was something he'd never thought would happen to him, even though he and Prue had often talked about what might happen when one of them died… to the one who was left. She'd said, if she went first, she hoped Blair wouldn't spend the rest of his life alone, while he couldn't countenance her with someone else.

Lou was completely different from Prue, but Prue would have liked her, admired her independence, her zest for life, what she'd achieved with *Books and Coffee*, her desire to find her sister and make amends.

'I think I'd like the pepper and herb crusted salmon with roast potatoes and salad.'

'Sounds good.' Blair had been staring at the menu without taking anything in. 'Wine?'

'Yes, please.'

'How about prosecco since we are celebrating?'

Lou smiled her agreement, her worry seemingly forgotten.

'So, who are those people you're so worried about?' he asked, when they had toasted each other and were enjoying their first glass of prosecco.

Lou toyed with the stem of her glass. 'Poppy has three good friends. They regularly lunch together, and one of them, Liz, is quite a gossip.'

The name rang a bell for Blair. 'Liz? You've mentioned her before. Isn't she…?'

'Her mother is your neighbour, Joan Phillips.'

'Oh!' Somehow, Blair found this amusing. He stifled the urge to smile.

'My best friend, Rachel, is one of them too. So, before long…'

'I see.' Blair tentatively reached across the table to cover Lou's hand with his. 'And would it be so bad?'

'But… we…' Lou blushed. She was pretty when she blushed. 'What about your daughter?'

'Kat?' Blair thought for a moment. 'I have no idea. It probably wouldn't occur to her that at my age I might…'

'Here we are, two crusted salmon. Enjoy your meal.' A waiter placed the two plates on the table interrupting their conversation. Probably just as well, Blair thought. They were getting into difficult territory. *How had a simple meal out morphed into this?*

*

Lou was relieved when their meals arrived. She had no idea where this conversation was going. What had started out as a celebratory meal between friends had turned into… what exactly? It should have occurred to her they might run into Poppy. But she wasn't in the habit of dining here, and she had thought Poppy had given up her days overseeing the restaurant staff. Now, it would be all over town that she and Blair… And he was suggesting…?

Lou was trembling so much she had trouble holding her glass, then… when he put his hand on hers, her whole body began to tingle, just like it had when he'd arrived at her door to take her to the yacht club. She'd never felt like this before, not even when Darren… No, she didn't want to think about Darren. Darren was dead. She still couldn't believe it. But Blair had seen the notice of his death. It must be true.

As she ate, Lou surreptitiously studied Blair. For a man of his age, he was attractive. She'd noted that before, before he suggested… But what had he suggested? He hadn't said anything in as many words, only that it might not be so bad if the local gossips suggested they might be more than friends. Maybe he hadn't meant… perhaps she'd been too quick to ask about his daughter, the daughter who was also her masseuse. Lou's heart shrank. Now she wished their meals hadn't arrived when they did, that Blair had had time to finish what he was saying.

The salmon was delicious, and Lou decided to say nothing more about their earlier conversation unless Blair brought it up.

Neither spoke on the drive back to Lou's. Lou was feeling pleasantly satisfied after another enjoyable evening in Blair's company. She had no idea what Blair was thinking. She soon found out. When they parked outside Lou's cottage, he turned to face her. But instead of the peck on the cheek she'd expected, Blair said, 'May I come in? We need to talk. I think we have a conversation to finish.'

For a moment Lou stared at him, her insides churning. Then, almost against her will, she said, 'Sure. I can make coffee.'

'That would be grand.' Blair sounded strange, as if he wasn't sure, as if he was already regretting his request.

As soon as they walked in, Tilly ran up to Lou, weaving around her feet as usual, expecting to be picked up and cuddled. Then, she suddenly stopped, clearly aware Lou wasn't alone. To Lou's surprise, the cat didn't immediately disappear but sidled towards Blair, who bent down to scratch her ears. Tilly pushed her head into his hand, purring loudly.

Lou stared in amazement. 'How did you do that?'

'What? Cats like me. Prue and I had one till he finally passed away. We couldn't face replacing him.'

'Tilly doesn't normally like people… other than me. Though she has been known to tolerate Rachel on occasion.'

'But you like me, don't you, Tilly?' Blair asked the cat who was still rubbing herself against him. He picked her up, and she cuddled into him.

'Well!' Lou shook her head. 'Coffee,' she said, galvanised into action, leaving Blair and Tilly together and heading into the kitchen

They followed, Tilly's purrs growing louder.

'You wanted to talk.'

They were seated at Lou's kitchen table. Tilly had become tired of being petted and had retired to curl up in her bed, keeping a wary eye on the two humans.

'Yes.' Now the time had come, Blair seemed lost for words. After a few moments of silence, he began. 'At the restaurant, when you mentioned the gossip mill, it suddenly occurred to me how much I've come to rely on your company. Not just that. You're a very attractive woman Lou and… I believe… I think… No, I know, I'd like to know you better, to find out what makes you tick, to… Hell, I'm no good at this. I've been on my own since Prue died. I'd never thought of having another woman in my life, but since meeting you, I've come to realise what I've been missing, the companionship that only a woman can provide, a woman like you. Forgive me. I'm probably putting this badly.'

Stunned, her heart beating so loudly she thought Blair must be able to hear it, Lou said, 'No… I mean yes, you probably are.'

They both laughed and the tension was broken.

'What I mean is this. I realised that once I find an address for your sister, there will be no real need for us to meet again, and I couldn't bear that. Seeing you each day, having coffee together in the café, it's helped me adjust to living here in Pelican Crossing. I know I have family here and I love them dearly, but it's not the same as having a companion of my own age.'

Lou liked Blair's use of the term companion rather than anything more intimate. That's what they were, companions. That she could cope with and if, in the future… But she wouldn't, couldn't, think of that now.

'I'd miss it too.' It was only now that Lou realised how much she'd come to look forward to seeing Blair walk into the bookshop each morning, to spending those few minutes, stolen from her busy day, having coffee with him.

'Good, so we're agreed?' Blair seemed relieved.

'We are.'

'By the way, I like what you've done with your cottage. It's quite different from Troy's.'

'Thanks. You must come again and see it in daylight.'

'I'd like that. Now, I guess I should go, leave you and Tilly together.'

'Mmm.'

At the door, they stood, indecisive, then Blair reached out and hugged Lou. 'Goodnight, friend,' he said.

It felt good. It was a long time since Lou had felt a man's arms around her. She breathed in his musky scent, a mixture of sandalwood and something else. 'Goodnight, friend,' she said. Then, after a peck on her cheek which seemed to last longer than normal, he was gone.

Twenty-five

In a hospital room in an outer suburb of Melbourne, Iris sat vigil, listening for her mother's last breath, as the older woman lay in that liminal zone between life and death. In the days since the diagnosis of her terminal illness, there had been a conga line of visitors to her bedside, weeping and voicing their goodbyes. She was popular and well-liked in their small community, an active member of her local church, a volunteer with the library and Meals on Wheels, and always ready to offer a helping hand to anyone in need. Now there was only Iris and her mother, the silence broken only by the hum of the equipment designed to maintain life for just a little longer.

Iris didn't know what she was going to do when her mother was gone. They'd been close all of her life, becoming even closer when Iris's dad died ten years earlier, two weeks after the birth of his granddaughter. It had been an easy decision for Iris to move in with her mother, and for the two women to bring up Violet together. The child's father had disappeared as soon as Iris revealed she was pregnant, and she'd later heard he was seeing the girl who had been her best friend. 'Good riddance,' her mother had said. She'd never liked Scott.

A tear rolled down Iris's cheek. Her mother was only sixty-three, too young to die. She should have lived to see her granddaughter grow up, marry…

A sound came from the bed. Iris looked up, startled. *Was this the end?* Her mother stretched out a skeletal hand. Her lips were moving. Iris leant closer.

'Tell Lou I'm sorry,' the older woman whispered. 'I didn't mean to hurt her. We fell in love. I should have…'

Iris's eyes widened. 'Who's Lou?'

The hand in hers tightened ever so slightly. 'In my bedroom. There's a box with papers. My sister. Go to see her. Tell her…' Her voice faded away, and the grip on Iris's hand loosened.

'Mum! What do you mean? Your sister?' Iris had never known her mother had a sister. Where was she, this sister? Why hadn't she been part of her mother's life, of Iris's life? She had always thought both her parents had been only children, their parents long dead. Growing up, she'd often envied her friends with their big families, the family get-togethers on weekends and holidays, the Christmas celebrations. *Why hadn't she known, been told? Were there other family members out there somewhere? Did they know about her, about Violet?*

But it was too late. It was as if these words had taken the last vestige of life from the woman in the bed. Her mother was gone.

*

It wasn't till some weeks later, when the funeral was over, and Iris plucked up the courage to go through her mother's belongings, that she remembered Fleur's last words. A sister. Her mother had a sister. She had an aunt.

She tried to recall exactly what her mother had said, but those last hours were a blur, overlain with her actual death, her and Violet's grief, and the business of arranging a funeral. She'd taken time off work to take care of her mother's estate, the manager at the local library proving to be very understanding and telling her to take as long as she needed. She was due leave. It would soon be Christmas, and the library would be closed for a couple of weeks.

Violet would be on holiday too. At ten, she was having trouble coping with her grandmother's death, waking in the night and coming into Iris's bed to cuddle up with her, while Iris lay awake till the first few glimmers of dawn filtered through the window.

Today, she'd decided to tackle her mother's bedroom. She'd left it to last as it was the one room in the house where Fleur's presence could be most strongly felt. As she pushed open the door to be greeted by the familiar fragrance of her mother's perfume, she wondered for the first time how her mother had coped with her dad's death. At that time, Iris, as a new mother, so caught up in her own life, was only grateful to move into the family home. She hadn't given a thought to how her mother must feel at the loss of her lifetime companion, at sleeping in the room, and the bed, that had once held them both.

As she glanced across the room at the old-fashioned wardrobe, her mother's words came back to her. Something about a box, a sister. And a request to go to tell this sister she was sorry.

Her breath coming in gasps, her stomach churning, Iris opened the wardrobe to be assailed once again by her mother's perfume. At first, her eyes were so blurred by tears she couldn't see properly. There were her mother's clothes, all carefully hung in place and colour coded. Her mother had always looked good and been proud of her fashion sense. When her eyes cleared, Iris looked up. There, above the dresses, pants and shirts, was a high shelf on which were several boxes, one of which was taped up and from the layer of dust on it, looked as if it had been like that for years.

Reaching up, Iris lifted it down and laid it on the bed. She sat there with it for a long time, afraid to open it, wary of what she might find. Then she gave herself a shake. It had been her mother's wish that she open it and read what was inside. Taking a deep breath, she pulled off the tape and lifted the lid.

Peering inside, Iris gave a sigh of relief. It seemed to be filled with photographs, photos taken when Fleur was young, some of her with another, slightly older girl. Was this the sister she'd mentioned? Iris turned one of the photos over. It showed the two girls standing on a beach, grinning at the camera. There was writing on the back. *Lou and Fleur, Christmas 1970*. Iris's stomach churned. Her mother and her sister. She flipped through the rest of the photos, coming across one of her dad and the sister. It must have been taken quite a few years later. They looked like they were in their teens. They appeared happy. Her dad looked so young. He was handsome. *Had her mother taken this one?*

Iris put the photos aside. Underneath was a bundle of newspaper clippings. These looked old too. They all referred to a town in Queensland called Pelican Crossing, the most recent dated twenty years earlier and reporting on the opening of a new shop, a combined bookshop and café called *Books and Coffee*.

Puzzled, Iris set those aside too. The only other item in the box was a bundle of letters tied with a ribbon. They were addressed to a Lou Chalmers at an address in Pelican Crossing, and all were marked *Return to Sender*.

Iris didn't know how long she sat there, trying to make sense of it all. She was still staring at the bundle of letters when she heard the front door open and bang shut, then Violet calling, 'Where are you, Mum?'

'I'm here, in Grandma's room.'

Violet bounced in, her hair flying, her face red with the exertion of having ridden her bike home from school on the hot December day. 'What are you doing?' She flopped down on the bed beside Iris and picked up the bundle of photos. 'Oh, who are they? Is that Grandma?' she turned one over and read, *'Lou and Fleur, Christmas 1970.* Who's Lou?' She gazed up at her mother.

Iris swallowed. Violet would have to know sometime. 'It seems your grandma had a sister.'

Violet's eyes widened. 'A sister? This is Grandma's sister?' She picked up the photo which she'd dropped. 'Did you know about her?'

Iris shook her head. 'Your grandma said something just before she died. She wanted me to go to see her.' As soon as the words were out of her mouth, Iris regretted them, but it was too late. She couldn't take them back.

'Where does she live? Why didn't we know about her? Why…?'

Iris shook her head again. 'I don't know, Vi. I always thought Mum was an only child, like me… and you. This is as much of a surprise to me as it is to you.'

'But where is she?' Violet began to sift through the newspaper clippings, reading them quickly then casting them aside, all except one, the one which reported on the opening of *Books and Coffee*. 'Does she live in this Pelican Crossing place? Can we go there? Please, Mum. It would be fun. We could visit this place, this *Books and Coffee*.' She waved the newspaper clipping in the air. 'You know how much you love bookshops. And we don't have any other plans for Christmas.'

Iris hesitated. Violet was right. They didn't have any plans. Her mother's death had knocked her for six and put all thought of a Christmas celebration out of her head. Maybe they could go to Pelican Crossing, check out the bookshop, maybe even find this Lou Chalmers and fulfil her mother's last wish.

Twenty-six

Lou hadn't slept well. She'd tossed and turned for most of the night, trying to work out what had changed between her and Blair, and what people would read into their having dinner at *Crossings*. It was too much to hope for that Poppy would keep it to herself.

Over the past few years, not only Poppy, but her three friends had found love a second time around and were blissfully happy, sickeningly so, Lou sometimes thought. Then, there was her other friend Livvy… and *her* friend, Erica. One could be excused for thinking Pelican Crossing was a town straight out of a Hallmark movie. Only Lou and another of Livvy's friends, Rhana, who lived outside of town and bred spaniels, remained single. They were the exceptions. And likely to remain so. Lou had no idea why her thoughts were travelling along this path. Nothing Blair had said had implied… he hadn't said anything about love. So why was she thinking about these happy couples? Was there a small part of her that envied them, wished she could be as lucky as they'd been? Surely not.

Tilly pushed open the bedroom door and leapt onto the bed, her loud meow indicating it was time for Lou to get up and feed her.

'Okay, Tilly.' Lou slid her legs out of bed and padded through to the kitchen to fill Tilly's bowls before returning to shower and dress. It was going to be a busy day at the bookshop. She didn't have time to worry about anything else.

Lou was right. There was a continuous stream of customers giving her little time to think about anything other than serving them. Ten o'clock came and went with no sign of Blair. Was he regretting their conversation? Lou tried to stifle her disappointment. She'd become so accustomed to seeing his cheerful face, to their daily chats over coffee.

Instead, it was Rachel who arrived in the bookshop, her expression telling Lou that Poppy hadn't been idle. 'Don't!' she said, holding up her hand. 'I don't want to hear what Poppy is saying about me. We were only having dinner. Can't a person have dinner with a friend without the whole town knowing and making something of it?'

'Well, good morning to you, too. But how did you know? Poppy only said…'

'Poppy should mind her own business.' Lou realised she didn't know what Poppy had actually said, but she could imagine.

'Don't be like that, Lou. We're all happy if you've found…'

'Blair and I are friends. He's been helping me with some family business and invited me to dinner. There's nothing more to it, and I'd be grateful if you can tell that to Poppy, and to anyone else who is making assumptions about what was an innocent dinner between two friends.'

'Don't get your knickers in a knot. Can't we be happy for you? Poppy said the "friend" you were with is Joan Phillips' new neighbour. Liz was talking about him when we had lunch last week. He sounds nice, exactly what…' Rachel stopped as if seeing Lou's expression. 'Anyway, as you say, it's your business. But we're your friends and we just want you to be happy.'

'Thanks, Rach, but we don't all need a man to make us happy. Now…' Lou gestured to the line of customers waiting to be served.

'Sorry. I'll let you get on.' Rachel moved away, but Lou had the impression that her friend hadn't given up.

*

The bookshop was closing when Blair walked in, the last customer leaving with a bag full of books, a small girl trailing behind her. Lou appeared surprised to see him.

'Sorry,' he said. 'I couldn't make it earlier. You'll understand when I tell you what I've discovered.'

Lou barely looked up from the computer where she seemed to be checking the day's takings. Zoe was already on her way out and had put the *Closed* sign on the door.

Blair waited patiently till Lou was finished, browsing through the book display on the nearby table.

'You're here.' Lou looked up.

'Sorry,' he said again. 'Look, we can't talk here. Can I take you for a drink, a meal, something?' He tried to suppress his excitement, but it spilled over, forcing Lou to take notice.

Her eyes lit up. 'You've found her?'

Blair nodded. 'Can we go somewhere?' he repeated.

'I have to go home and feed Tilly. We can have a drink there, and maybe something to eat. You can follow me.'

'Okay.'

They left the shop together, and Blair followed Lou home, where Tilly greeted her with her tail in the air, before weaving around Blair's ankles.

'There's wine and beer in the fridge, glasses in the cupboard,' Lou said. 'I'll be with you as soon as I see to Tilly.'

Chuckling to himself, Blair took a bottle of Pinot Grigio out of the fridge, found two glasses, and went to where a small table and two chairs sat on a paved courtyard.

'Right,' Lou said when she joined him. 'You found Fleur? Why the drama? Why couldn't you tell me in the bookshop?'

'I could have, but I thought you'd prefer to hear it in more congenial surroundings. I checked the Victorian Electoral Roll today and I have your sister's address for you. Not only that. I found another Ross living at the same address – Iris – presumably her daughter.'

Lou leant forward, her wine forgotten.

'Out of curiosity, I checked back several years. She was still there. I kept going to discover that she only appeared at the same address as your sister after Darren Ross died. Prior to that, only Darren and Fleur were listed.'

Lou took a sip of wine. She seemed to be thinking. 'So, Fleur's daughter moved in with her after Darren died. I wonder why.' She took another sip of wine.

'I was curious too. It's why it took me so long, why I didn't come in this morning. I decided to check out Iris Ross…'

'And?'

'It seems she never married, but has a daughter, who was born the same year Darren died.' Blair gazed at Lou to see tears trickling down her cheeks. 'I'm sorry, Lou. I didn't mean to upset you. I thought you'd be pleased.'

'I am, I am,' she said through her tears.

'Here, take this.' Blair handed her a handkerchief. He always kept one in his pocket – for emergencies, he always told Prue who had laughed at the habit.

'Thanks.' Lou wiped her eyes then folded the handkerchief carefully and handed it back to him. 'Sorry,' she said again. 'It's all too much. How can I thank you.'

'There's no need. It was a pleasure.' Blair felt his own eyes moisten. He blinked. He wasn't used to feeling so emotional. It had been a long time since he'd had feelings like this, not since Prue…

They sat in silence for a few minutes, then Lou said. 'You'll stay for something to eat? It's the least I can do after all your trouble.'

'As I said, it was no trouble. But, yes, I'd like to eat with you.'

'I was only going to have a chicken salad. I don't normally feel like cooking after a busy day.'

'Chicken salad is okay with me, or I could order a takeaway. I've discovered the local Thai does a good meal.'

'No, I'm happy to make salad. It will give me something to do while I digest what you've told me.' Lou filled Blair's glass, before disappearing into the kitchen.

It would give Blair time to pull himself together too, but he wasn't alone for long. Almost as soon as Lou left, Tilly appeared and leapt into his lap. 'Hello, there,' he said, scratching the cat's ears, whereupon she purred contentedly.

The rest of the evening passed uneventfully. Blair could tell Lou was distracted, thinking about her sister, her sister's daughter and granddaughter. It was a lot to take in. He had no idea how he'd feel to suddenly discover a family he hadn't known about.

When he finally rose to go, Blair could see Lou was exhausted. 'Sorry, I shouldn't have taken up so much of your time,' he said.

'No, I was glad of the company. It stopped me obsessing about Fleur… though I doubt if I'll get much sleep.'

'What will you do now?'

'I'll write to her, hope she replies. If not, I'll go to Melbourne to see her.'

'Good plan. And…' Blair hesitated for a moment, '… if you want company, I'd be happy to go with you.'

To his surprise, Lou threw her arms around his neck and hugged him. 'Thank you, Blair. You really are a very good friend.'

Twenty-seven

As she'd predicted, Lou didn't get much sleep, thoughts about Fleur whirling round and round in her head. Not only did her sister have a daughter, but also a granddaughter. And her daughter was called Iris. Lou smiled at that. Fleur had always loved the fact that her name was the French word for flower. It was no surprise she'd continued the floral theme with her own daughter.

There was so much Lou still wanted to know; first and foremost, had Fleur and Darren been happy? She hoped they had, that her heartbreak hadn't been in vain, a fleeting desire on Fleur's part to score points over her older sister. It had hurt a lot at the time, when Lou had been flooded with bitterness. But, as the years passed, so did the bitterness. Now it was like the story in a book she'd read, one she'd shed a few tears over.

Then there was her daughter, Lou's niece, Iris. What was she like? Did she resemble Fleur or Darren? How old was Fleur's granddaughter? Lou couldn't wait to meet them. Surely, after all this time, Fleur would agree to meet her, to share her family with Lou.

Lou must have slept, because when she heard the sound of the resident kookaburras, the sky was beginning to lighten. But Fleur, and what Blair had told her, was still at the forefront of her mind, and she knew she had to write to her sister before she went to work.

After feeding Tilly, who communicated her surprise at Lou being awake so early by a high-pitched meow, and making herself a cup of strong coffee, Lou pulled out a sheet of writing paper and pen.

It was strange to be writing a letter. Letter-writing had gone out of vogue, overtaken by emails, text and messages on WhatsApp. But an address was all she had for her sister. Lou thought of the letters she used to write to penpals, waiting eagerly for their replies, the notes penned on scraps of paper and surreptitiously passed across desks in the classroom, or slipped equally surreptitiously when passing in the school corridor. How times had changed, now everyone relied on technology to do what Australia Post had done for years.

Lou picked up her pen to communicate with her sister for the first time in over forty years.

Dear Fleur,

I expect you'll be surprised to hear from me after all this time. I can only hope that you're reading this and haven't returned it, as I did your letters, or consigned it to the bin.

The fact is, that I've been thinking about you a lot and regretting how I allowed my bitterness about you and Darren to ruin our relationship. You're my sister, and I love you. I never stopped loving you, but I was so hurt when you ran off with Darren, it took me a long time to forgive you.

It's been over forty years, Fleur, and I don't want to die without us being reconciled. It's only in the past weeks that I've learned you are living in Melbourne and that Darren has died. Please accept my deepest sympathy. I forgave both of you long ago, but wasn't able to contact you until now, when I met Darren's half-brother. He told me you and Darren had gone to Melbourne. Thanks to another friend, I've been able to find your address.

A lot has happened in the years since you left. Mum and Dad have both passed away, and I'm still living in Pelican Crossing which hasn't changed very much. You'll be surprised to learn I now own a bookshop and café, and I know you have a daughter and granddaughter.

I would dearly love to see you again, to meet your daughter. I don't know anything about your life, whether it would be possible for you to come to Pelican Crossing, but I'd be happy to visit you in Melbourne once Christmas is over.

I look forward to hearing from you.

Your loving sister, Lou.

Lou read over the letter. It wasn't perfect. There was so much else she wanted to say, but it would be better said face-to-face. She could only hope it would have the result she was hoping for. She added her address to the back of the letter and, if Fleur hadn't replied by the end of the school holidays, she'd go to Melbourne and knock on her door. It had been kind of Blair to offer to accompany her, but this was something she knew she had to do alone.

Feeling relieved at having written the letter, Lou made herself a cup of peppermint tea and fixed breakfast, eating the toast topped with banana in the courtyard before going back inside to shower and dress, ready for the day.

On the way to the bookshop, Lou stopped at the post office to mail her letter to Fleur, hesitating for a moment before pushing it through the slot in the mailbox. It was done. Now all she could do was wait.

*

As she went about her daily routine and served customers, Lou tried not to think of the letter, which was even now wending its way to Melbourne. But it was always on the edge of her consciousness. It was a relief when at ten o'clock, Blair walked in as usual, and she was able to join him in the café.

'Everything okay?' he asked when Denny had served their coffees with a brownie for Blair – Lou had refused one this morning.

'I've written to Fleur.'

'Already?'

'I couldn't sleep, so I got up at the crack of dawn. I mailed it on my way here.'

'Well done! I guess it wasn't an easy letter to write.'

'No.' Lou smiled. Blair understood. There wasn't anyone else she could tell. 'But it's done now.'

'Another cause for celebration?'

'Perhaps, but I have an appointment with your daughter after work today, so it would have to be later.'

'I could bring round a takeaway… unless you'd rather not have my company?'

'No, of course I'd enjoy your company. I always do, but…' Lou didn't know why she was being so hesitant. Blair was a comfortable person to be with, and the only person with whom she could talk about Fleur.

'Why don't you text me if you're too tired, if you'd rather I didn't come round. Otherwise, I'll bring round a takeaway at eight. Will that give you enough time?'

'Thanks.'

The prospect of seeing Blair that evening helped Lou get through the rest of the day. He was a nice man, a good man. She knew if she was to spend the evening alone, she'd only worry about the letter, wonder if she'd said the right thing, wonder if Fleur would even open it, and, worst of all, wonder if Fleur hated her for returning all *her* letters and mark hers as "return to sender".

Lou felt a sense of relief when she closed the bookshop door behind her. She gazed into the shop one last time, as she always did these days, enjoying the sight of the lights on the Christmas tree glowing in the darkened shop, turning it into a fairy grotto. Then she turned away, already looking forward to her massage. Her back had been paining her more than usual in the past few days. She'd put it down to the increased hustle and bustle in the shop in the lead-up to Christmas, but knew it was partly due to stress which always affected her this way. An hour of Katrina's tender care should help. She was glad the masseuse chose to stay open one evening each week to cater for people like her who found it difficult to get to the wellness centre during the working day.

Arriving at the wellness centre, Lou greeted Katrina, then changed into a gown behind the screen, before lying on the massage bed face down and pulling a towel over her, the familiar actions helping her relax for the first time since she'd dropped the letter to Fleur into the mailbox.

As she had on all of Lou's previous visits, Katrina had dimmed the lights, and a delicate aroma of lavender, geranium and bergamot filled the air. Some soft music was playing.

As Lou lay there, Katrina's firm but gentle hands working their magic, Lou felt the tension of the past few weeks leave her body, and her mind began to wander. But this time, it was positive thoughts that filled it, the possibility of seeing Fleur again, what she might look like after over forty years. Had she aged much, or had she managed to retain her youthful prettiness? It was that prettiness and Fleur's charming ways that had captured Darren and taken him away from

Lou. That was silly, Lou thought. Darren hadn't belonged to her. He'd been a vulnerable young man, easily led, willing to be seduced by a pretty face. Now she could see that he'd never been strong, not strong enough to withstand her sister, not like… Blair's face floated behind her eyelids. Lou gave a groan.

'Was I being too firm?'

'No, sorry. I just thought of something. You're good, as always.'

'Almost done. I heard you and my dad had dinner together.' Katrina's tone was chatty, but Lou thought she could hear an underlying note of concern. *Had she read Lou's mind?*

Lou decided not to reply, hoping Katrina might forget her question. But when she sat up, and was drinking the glass of water Katrina handed her, the masseuse said again, 'You had dinner with my dad… at *Crossings?*'

'Ye…es. We met at my *Book Café*. We got talking. He's been helping me with some family research.' Lou wasn't sure why she was glossing over their friendship, why Blair hadn't mentioned her to his daughter. But if he wanted to keep their friendship secret, it was up to him.

'That's Dad all over!' Katrina sounded as if she found Blair's interest in researching family history something to condemn, rather than be fascinated by. 'I hope he hasn't been boring you with all his stories. I don't know how Mum put up with him. Now, he says he wants to write a book about it.' She rolled her eyes.

Unsure how to react, Lou laughed, stopping when she saw the expression on Katrina's face. 'Sorry. I guess I'm the last person to be surprised or shocked about someone wanting to write a book. If there were no books, I'd be out of business.'

'Of course, you own *Books and Coffee*. I should have thought. We all imagined it was just a pipe dream of Dad's, that he wasn't really serious about it, but now…' She shook her head. 'Well, I suppose it gives him something to do when he's not helping out with Harper and Noah.'

'Your children? Blair has spoken about them. He seems glad to be able to spend time with them.'

Katrina gave Lou a suspicious look. 'How well do you know my dad?'

'We've become friends, but if he hasn't mentioned me to you, perhaps you should ask him.'

'I will.'

Lou couldn't determine from Katrina's tone whether she was pleased, annoyed, or simply curious. She paid for her massage and left, without making another appointment. Maybe she would see the physio next time. Oh, why had her life suddenly become so complicated?

Twenty-eight

Lou seemed particularly subdued when Blair arrived with the Thai takeaway and a bottle of wine. He put it down to her worry about her letter to Fleur. It was a big deal, to write to a sister you hadn't seen or heard of for over forty years. Blair had no idea how he'd feel if he were in Lou's position.

'You look as if you need a drink,' he said, when he had given her the hug that was now a regular feature of their meetings.

'Thanks, it's been quite a day.' Lou took two glasses out of the cupboard and held them out while Blair poured the wine. Then she took a gulp, almost choking. 'Sorry. I'll be fine.'

But Blair could see she wasn't fine. Had something else happened to disturb her? 'We should eat before it gets cold,' he said, deciding to say nothing and hoping she'd tell him what was wrong.

'Where's Tilly?' he asked, wondering if something had happened to the cat. There was no sign of her.

'She slipped out. She'll be back soon. That cat has an unerring way of knowing when there's food around, even if it's something she wouldn't eat.'

Sure enough, they had just started to eat, when Tilly appeared and made her presence felt by meowing loudly before settling down to watch them.

Lou still seemed rattled. Blair remembered she'd had an appointment for a massage with Katrina. Surely she should be feeling relaxed, unless... He changed his mind about speaking out. 'Did something happen when you were with Katrina?'

Lou forked up some noodles before replying, 'Not exactly.'

Blair dragged a hand through his hair. He knew Katrina too well, how abrasive she could be at times. But Lou was her client… He sighed. 'What did she say?'

'She'd heard we had dinner together. I tried to brush it off, said you were helping me with research into my family history.'

'Which I am.'

'Yes. Then… she wanted to know how well I knew you. I couldn't work out what she was thinking, but I'm not sure I can face her again.'

'What did you tell her… about us?' Blair felt a rush of anger that Katrina had interrogated Lou.

'I told her she should speak with you. You hadn't mentioned me – or the *Book Café* – to her?'

'I had no reason to. My daughter doesn't run my life.' *Though she'd like to.* 'She doesn't need to know everything I do, everywhere I go, everyone I speak to… or have dinner with.'

'She's your daughter, Blair. It's only natural for her to be concerned about you.'

Blair felt a wave of guilt. It was his fault that Lou had been put in a difficult position. If only he'd mentioned her to Katrina, said he'd become friends with the bookshop owner, perhaps none of this would have happened.

'I'm sorry, Lou. I guess I should have told her about you. It's just… Katrina… she's not like her sister. Chelsea has been telling me for ages that I need to move on with my life, find someone to…' He coughed. 'Katrina was close to her mother, I wasn't sure how she'd react, so I took the coward's way out.'

Blair saw Lou's eyes widen. *Had he said too much?* While he'd told her he wanted to get to know her better, and they were now on hugging terms, he had been careful to avoid saying anything that might scare her off. He already knew she was a very private person. He suspected he might be the first man she'd been to dinner with since Darren, the first man to be invited into her cottage.

The problem was, Blair suspected he was falling for Lou, and he had no idea how she felt about him.

*

Lou stared at Blair. What was he saying? That he had feelings for her? Lou picked up her glass and took a sip of wine, then put it down again, trying to subdue the tingling in the pit of her stomach. This was different from the tingling she'd experienced in his presence before This was accompanied by a warm glow. Her hands automatically went to her cheeks which she knew must be bright red.

Blair was speaking again. 'I didn't mean to offend you. It's just that… I'm sorry. I should have told Katrina we were friends,' he repeated.

To Lou's relief, Tilly chose that moment to leap onto the table and sniff at the empty food containers, effectively diffusing her awkwardness and making them both laugh as Lou shooed her off.

As Blair picked up the empty containers and dropped them into the bin, Lou decided she'd been wrong. He hadn't been talking about anything other than friendship. So, instead of feeling relieved, why was she filled with a sense of… disappointment? It wasn't as if she wanted or needed a man in her life. Ever since Darren's betrayal, she'd been careful to avoid any sort of entanglement with anyone of the opposite sex. Not that there had been many opportunities in a town the size of Pelican Crossing, where she'd been at school with most of the men of her age. And she'd always lived by the motto, *once bitten, twice shy*, and shied away from any sort of commitment. She'd become Lou, bookshop owner and good mate, and was happy to keep it that way.

So why did she suddenly have this desire for more?

'I'm having dinner at Katrina's tomorrow. I'll talk with her then,' Blair said. 'I'd hate to think my failure to share our friendship with her has ruined your future massages.'

'It's okay.' Lou felt embarrassed to have allowed her feelings to show. 'I should probably be seeing the physio anyway. I've been too afraid to admit it.'

'Physio?'

Lou put her hand on her lower back. 'A bit of back pain sometimes.'

'Hmm.'

Lou could tell Blair didn't believe her.

When Blair left that evening, their farewell hug felt more awkward than usual. *Had Lou spoiled things between them? She should have kept her mouth shut.*

Twenty-nine

Blair was still feeling awkward when he entered the bookshop next morning, but he was determined not to allow anything to get in the way of his morning coffee with Lou. He hoped she felt the same, and they could continue as before.

The bookshop was busy. Although Harper and Noah still had classes, some schools were already on holiday. There seemed to be children everywhere, running around, pulling books off the shelves and generally making a nuisance of themselves. Despite what seemed to Blair to be chaos, Lou stood behind the counter looking as calm as usual. Maybe she'd forgotten that awkward hug which had kept him awake most of the night.

'Coffee?' he mouthed, nodding towards the café, the noise of the children, overlaid by the sound of Christmas carols, made speech difficult.

To his relief, Lou smiled and nodded back.

Going through to the café, Blair ordered coffee for them both, choosing the day's special of strawberry and white chocolate muffins instead of brownies as a peace offering. The café was busy too, but he managed to find an empty table which had been squeezed into a corner.

It wasn't long before Lou joined him. 'I can't stay long today,' she said as soon as she sat down. 'You saw what it's like through there. And there are still weeks to go till Christmas.'

'What do you plan to do… for Christmas?' Lou had no family here. Blair wondered if she spent the day with friends.

'What I always do,' she said with a wry smile. 'I hibernate, just me and Tilly. It's the one day of the year when there are no demands on me… apart from one crazy cat, that is. We snuggle down together till it's all over, and I catch up on all the books I didn't make time to read.' She laughed. 'You?'

'Family. Chelsea is coming up from Brisbane. There are Harper and Noah. Christmas is all about the kids.' Blair remembered Christmases past, when Katrina and Chelsea were the ages Harper and Noah were now, how he and Prue went all out to make them days to remember. It would be the same this year, with Katrina trying to copy her mother, to replicate the Christmases of her youth, while Brett would go along with her, anything for peace – just as he had.

'Nice.'

There was a fleeting expression in Lou's eyes, there for a moment, then gone. Was it envy? Envy of the chaos which would undoubtedly ensue, leaving all the adults exhausted and vowing never to repeat it… till next year when they'd do it all over again.

'Maybe you'll have heard from Fleur by then.'

'Maybe.' Lou didn't sound hopeful.

Blair wished there was something more he could do, something to bring a smile to her face – she looked so pretty when she smiled. But he couldn't think of anything and before he could find words, she rose.

'I really should get back. See you tomorrow?'

'Of course.' By then he'd have spoken to Katrina about Lou, something he wasn't looking forward to, but it had to be done. He should have done it before now.

*

The sky was turning dark when Blair made his way to Katrina's that evening, the sound of a flock of lorikeets flying overhead failing to raise his spirits as it normally did.

'Do you have something for me, Grandad?' Noah asked as soon as Blair walked in, undeterred by his mother's attempt to silence him.

'Where's your sister?' Blair asked, when he'd hugged both Noah and Katrina. 'I have something for both of you and this…' he handed Katrina a bottle of wine, '… is for Mum and Dad.'

'I'm here, Grandad.' Harper flew downstairs and threw herself into his arms, almost knocking him over. 'I was watching for you from my bedroom window.'

'Hi, sweetie. Gosh, you're almost getting too heavy for your old grandad.' Blair pretended to groan, while the two children laughed.

'These are for you.' He handed each of them the books he'd bought in the bookshop that morning, a *Captain Underpants* for Noah which he was sure he'd enjoy, and for Harper, the latest book in the *Nevermoor* series which she was currently devouring.

'Ooh, thanks, Grandad,' they chorused, just as Brett appeared with a glass of wine.

'Why don't you two make yourselves scarce till dinner's ready, and let your grandad relax?' he said with a grin. 'Come and have a seat, Blair. Don't let these two tire you out.'

'They're fine, Brett. I'm not in my dotage yet.' *Was this how Brett and Katrina saw him – as an old man past his prime? Was it how Lou saw him?* His heart dropped. Then he remembered he still had to tell Katrina about her – if she didn't bring the subject up first.

Dinner was as chaotic as it usually was at Katrina's with the two children squabbling and talking over each other, and Katrina trying to keep the peace. Blair loved it but was relieved when they had all finished, and the children had been banished to watch television.

Brett was quizzing Blair about pickleball, when Katrina brought in coffee. Blair took a sip. It was exactly to his liking.

'I have something to…'

'Dad…'

They both spoke at once.

Blair sighed. 'You go first, Kat.'

'You didn't tell us you had a woman friend.'

Brett appeared surprised.

So, she hadn't mentioned it to him. But *woman friend* made it sound more than it was. He took a deep breath. 'I was about to. Lou said you'd spoken to her when she had a massage.'

'Who's Lou?' Brett asked.

'The woman who owns *Books and Coffee*. She's one of my clients, and I had to hear from someone else that Dad has been seeing her. Dad?'

'You're making it sound more than it is. As you know, I love bookshops. When I went to the Halloween event Harper and Noah were involved in, I discovered the shop hosted a *Book Café*. It sounded interesting, so I went along and got talking to Lou. We bumped into each other again at a barbecue. The guy who did my garden and she are neighbours. We talked about my research into family history, and she told me she was trying to find her sister. I offered to help. We became friends. That's all there is to it.' He spread his hands. 'I didn't think I needed to tell you about every person I talk to.'

'It's more than talk, Dad. You had dinner at *Crossings*.' Katrina sounded as if she was accusing him of something underhand.

'It's a good restaurant.'

'What's your problem, Kat?' Brett asked. 'Your dad's free to make whatever friends he likes. I thought that was the plan when he moved here. You should be pleased he's settling in and making friends.'

'I am. It's just…'

'Is it the fact Lou's a woman?' Blair asked, determined to get it out into the open. He hated subterfuge.

'Nooo.' She sounded doubtful. 'I know you must get lonely at times, and I know Mum wouldn't want you to spend the rest of your life on your own. But I thought we'd be enough for you.'

'Give your dad a break, Kat. What's she like, this Lou woman?' Brett turned to Blair.

Blair thought for a moment. 'She's a bit younger than me, lives alone in a cottage on the other side of the harbour, has owned the bookshop and café for around twenty years. We share an interest in books and, as I said, I've been able to help her track down her sister.'

'And you're just friends?' Katrina asked.

'As I said. I have some men friends too. Do you want to know about *them?*'

'No.' Katrina reddened. 'Chelsea said I was worrying about nothing, that it was time you moved on, but Mum…'

She'd spoken to Chelsea about Lou? He should have guessed.

'Your mum's been gone for three years, Kat,' Brett said. 'It's natural for your dad to want some female company. Good on you, I'd say. Blair.' He winked.

Blair felt his cheeks warming. 'It's not… We're not… We're just friends. I doubt Lou would want anything more. She's a single lady, never been married.'

'All the more reason…' Brett grinned, his grin fading as he saw Katrina's irate expression.

'What more do you want me to say?' Blair was becoming impatient with his daughter.

'Why don't we meet her?'

'You already know her.'

'But as a client. I don't really know her. Why don't we invite her to dinner?'

'Oh, I don't think that's a good idea.' Blair had no idea how Lou would react to such an invitation.

'Why not? I'm not averse to the idea that you have a woman friend, Dad… or a woman as a friend. I'd just like to get to know her better.'

So would I.

But would dinner with his daughter and her family help Blair get to know Lou better, or would it ruin the friendship and trust they were building? But he knew his daughter. Once she got an idea into her head, there was no shifting it. She was like her mother in that regard. It was why he was here in Pelican Crossing instead of enjoying his retirement in Hobart.

'Okay,' he said. 'When did you have in mind?'

Thirty

Lou was busy with customers when Blair arrived and gestured to the café. She knew he'd had dinner with Katrina the night before and wanted to know how it had gone, but her customers had to come first.

There was still a line of people waiting to be served when Blair appeared again, this time on his way out. 'Tonight,' he mouthed as he made his way past the counter, miming putting a phone to his ear.

Lou nodded, wishing she could magically find time to speak with him now. But she knew she'd have to wait.

The rush continued till closing time, only slowing mid-afternoon to allow Zoe, then Lou, time to grab a few bites of a sandwich and a mouthful of coffee before returning to the fray. If it continued like this, it would be a bumper season for both the bookshop and the café.

When Zoe had left, Lou placed the *Closed* sign on the door, slipped off her shoes and rubbed her back. She really should make that appointment with Dan, the physiotherapist in the wellness centre. After Christmas, she decided, as she did with most things these days.

Lou peered out the window. It was still raining, the lights from the shop reflected in the puddles on the pavement outside. Perhaps that was why they'd been so busy today – everyone wanting to get inside out of the rain. But she hoped the weather would clear. The tourists who came to Pelican Crossing came to spend time on the beach. They expected sunshine.

Lou was wet and tired by the time she got home to find a hungry cat waiting for her, upset at having spent the day inside. 'I can't control the weather, Tilly,' Lou said as she filled her pet's food and water bowls. 'I hate the rain just as much as you do.'

Undecided as to what to have for dinner, Lou headed to the shower in the hope it would make her feel better. It wasn't till she'd showered and changed into a pair of comfortable pants and a tee-shirt that she remembered Blair's mime and checked her phone. She smiled as she read his text.

Saw you were busy. You still need to eat. Fish and chips at eight, your place?

The message was finished with a funny emoji.

This was exactly what she needed to cheer her up. She'd also been feeling despondent at the realisation that it would be some time before she could expect to hear from Fleur. She quickly sent off a thumbs-up emoji in reply, then checked herself in the mirror. If Blair was coming round, she didn't want him to find her dressed in her oldest clothes, with her hair all over the place. She hurriedly changed into a pair of smarter pants with a blue linen shirt she always felt good in, brushed her hair, applied a smear of lipstick then, after only a moment's hesitation added a spritz of perfume. While she didn't want to appear as if she'd made an effort, she did want to look and smell good.

By the time Blair arrived with containers of piping hot fish and chips, Lou had opened a bottle of wine and had two glasses ready. Having felt shamed by Blair's superior knowledge about wine after their meal at *Crossings*, she'd visited the local bottle shop and asked for advice before stocking up on several bottles and hiding her cask wine at the back of the fridge.

'Hey,' he said, the rain dripping from his hair and collar. 'Boy, it's wet out there.'

'Let me get you a towel,' Lou said, hurrying to the bathroom. When she returned, Blair was in the kitchen and had placed the containers he'd been carrying on the benchtop.

'Thanks,' he said, taking the towel and rubbing his hair. 'Didn't think I'd need the umbrella between the car and the cottage.' He gave a wry grin. 'I'll soon dry off.'

Lou grinned too. Blair looked different with his hair plastered to his head. She could imagine him as a small boy… or exiting the shower. Stop right there, she told herself as she felt a rush of heat envelop her.

'No, Tilly,' Lou said, as the cat, attracted by the scent of fish looked ready to leap onto the benchtop. 'We should eat this before Tilly gets to it first. The wine's chilled.'

'Good stuff. Plates?'

'Sorry.' In the heat of the moment, Lou had completely forgotten about plates and cutlery. 'Shall we eat here?' she asked, rueing the fact that the rain had prevented their customary hug.

'Perfect.' Blair poured two glasses of wine then helped Lou transfer the food onto plates, while Tilly retired to her bed beside the door to glare at them both.

Lou waited till they were seated before asking what she was desperate to know. 'What did Katrina have to say?'

Blair chuckled. 'She was her usual self. At first, she was annoyed I hadn't told her I had a *woman friend*. He made quote marks with his fingers as he said the last two words.

Lou gasped.

'Brett calmed her down, and I explained you were just a friend who happened to be a woman, and that I'd helped you track down your sister.'

'And?' Lou had the feeling there was more to this.

'And… she wants you to come to dinner on Saturday.'

Lou nearly choked. 'Dinner? At her home?'

'Where else?' Blair appeared embarrassed. 'I'm sorry. I had no idea she'd react like this. It's over the top, even for her. Don't feel you have to come. She'd been talking to her sister too.'

Lou felt her chest tighten. This was what she'd been afraid of, why she'd eschewed anything resembling a relationship for all these years. She'd learned the hard way how people would talk, how… Blair was speaking again.

'Chelsea told her not to be stupid. She's been telling me to move on for over a year now. I don't mean…' Blair reddened, as if suddenly realising what he'd said… admitted.

'Was Katrina right?' Lou said before she could stop herself. She held her breath, waiting for his reply.

Thirty-one

Blair didn't know what to say. He hadn't intended to reveal to Lou his growing affection for her, aware how fiercely independent she was. She'd avoided any entanglement for over forty years. How could he expect her to change the habit of almost a lifetime after meeting him? He was nothing special. A retired academic. A widower with two daughters. An incomer to Pelican Crossing. Someone who'd walked into Lou's bookshop and helped her solve a family problem. Nothing more.

The problem was… Katrina had been partly right. He did want Lou to be his *woman friend*. The challenge was… Lou herself. And now he'd put his foot in it.

Lou was staring at him, waiting for his reply. Even Tilly seemed to be holding her breath, ready to pounce if he said the wrong thing.

'Would it be so dreadful if she was?' Blair tried to sound casual, but he was dreading her reply. What if she was shocked? Annoyed? What if this was the end of their friendship? Because Blair knew that, regardless of his growing feelings for Lou, he valued her friendship above everything.

Instead of replying, Lou rose and carried her plate over to scrape the remains of her fish into Tilly's bowl, before placing it in the sink and returning to the table, The delighted cat ran to feast on the unexpected treat, while Blair watched in nervous anticipation. Was this it? Was he going to be shown the door?

Lou still didn't speak.

Somewhat reassured by her silence, Blair said, 'I don't want to rush you into anything. If you don't want anything more than my friendship, it's okay by me. I value our chats. I was glad to be able to help you locate Fleur, and my offer to accompany you to Melbourne is still valid. But I have to be honest with you, Lou. If by any chance, you could have feelings for me, feelings that go beyond simple friendship, I'd be thrilled to take things further.' He picked up his glass and drained it, wishing it was something stronger than wine.

Finally, Lou did speak. 'I'd be happy to have dinner at Katrina's,' she said. 'About the rest. You've taken me by surprise. I never expected this, not at my age.' She gave a derisive laugh. 'It's been a long time since anyone…' She took a gulp of wine. 'I'm sorry. I can't think straight. I value your friendship too. As for anything else… I need time. There's so much…' Her voice trailed off.

'It's okay. There's no rush. I know you have a lot on your mind at the moment, and this is a lot to process. But you asked, and I wanted to be honest with you.'

'Thanks for that.' She smiled, and to Blair's relief, it was her usual lovely smile, not the forced one he'd expected. 'So, Katrina's on Saturday. Should I be worried, expect an interrogation?'

'No. I'm sure Brett will keep her in line. And the kids will be there, Harper and Noah.'

'Your grandchildren.' Lou nodded. 'It'll be lovely to meet them properly.'

'They're good kids, though they can sometimes be a bit boisterous.'

'Like all children their age. I see them every day in the bookshop.'

'Of course you do.' Blair was glad they seemed to be on the same footing again. For a few moments he'd been worried.

'More wine?' she asked, gesturing to his empty glass.

'Thanks.'

*

Lou's hand shook as she replenished their glasses. Blair's announcement that he had feelings for her was the last thing she'd expected, even though her feelings for him were growing too. While she'd imagined…

even hoped… what practically amounted to a declaration was a lot to cope with. Especially with her letter to Fleur, and Christmas approaching with the usual festive buzz in the bookshop and the time when she felt especially alone.

She'd accept the invitation to dinner, as she'd said. Dinner with his daughter wasn't any sort of acceptance of anything else, was it? Lou had no idea how these things worked nowadays. And what did she mean by these things?

Blair had said there was no rush, but he was a man. She shivered, more in fear than anticipation. There had been no one since Darren, and then… The memory of the one time they'd made love was something she'd tried to forget, the one time she'd allowed her heart – or her desire for him – to rule her head, to forget everything her mother had warned her of. Had he and Fleur made love back then too? Had he preferred her to Lou? Was that what had happened? Had her younger sister been a better lover, perhaps more practiced? That invidious thought had kept her awake, fuelled her bitterness.

Blair was different. He was a kind man. But he'd been married, was experienced in those matters whereas she… It might be better to remain *just friends* and avoid disappointing him.

'Are you okay?' he asked, solicitous as ever.

'Yes, thanks. You just surprised me.' Lou took a sip of wine, glad he couldn't read her mind, glad too that Tilly chose that moment to leap into her lap, looking for more fish. It helped her compose herself.

'Maybe I should go. Tilly can finish my fish.'

'There's no need…' But Lou would be glad to be alone. She needed time, time to process what he'd said, to consider if she could risk her heart again, or if she was too old to become involved in a romantic relationship that might have no future. She'd made a life for herself, become successful, independent. It was a lot to give up for what might be a collection of ephemeral emotions.

'Nevertheless. I should get home, anyway, in case…'

As he spoke there was a loud peal of thunder.

Lou jumped, and startled, Tilly leapt off her lap to cower under the table. Lou had always hated thunder. When she was little, she would climb into her sister's bed during a thunderstorm, and the two girls would huddle together, the younger comforting the older, till the storm had passed.

Blair calmly gazed out the window. 'We're getting the tail end of the storm they've been having up north. And there are reports of a cyclone on the way.'

'Luckily we don't get them this far south,' Lou said. The thunder was bad enough.

'Good to know. But I should go before it gets any worse.'

'Mmm.' For a moment she wished he could stay, that she could hide from the thunder in his arms, that he could comfort her and protect her from her fear. But common sense prevailed. She had Tilly. Tilly didn't like thunder either. They could cuddle up together and pull the covers over themselves till the storm blew through. It would probably be a lovely day tomorrow. It often was, after a storm.' Good idea,' she said.

As they stood in the doorway, there was a flash of lightning, then another peal of thunder. Startled, Lou grabbed hold of Blair's arm, only to find herself enveloped in a warm hug as both his arms folded around her. 'Sorry,' she said, pulling away, embarrassed at having shown herself to be so weak.

'It's okay to be scared of thunder.' Blair's calm voice soothed her. 'Are you sure you don't want me to stay?'

'No, I have Tilly. We'll be fine.'

'Okay. See you tomorrow.' Blair pulled Lou into a hug again, his lips brushing her forehead before he walked away.

Thirty-two

'Mum, we're here!' Violet yelled, bouncing in her seat as the sign for Pelican Crossing came into view. It had been a long trip, the flight to Brisbane, then the drive up the coast, but at last they had arrived.

Iris peered through the windscreen spattered with the rain which had been getting heavier all the way up the coast. Not an auspicious start to their visit, but she couldn't help feeling excited at what lay ahead.

She'd googled bookshops in Pelican Crossing to discover there was only one. Then she'd checked out the website and Facebook page for *Books and Coffee* and been surprised. For a small town, the combined bookshop and café seemed to be doing well. The café menu was impressive – as were the reviews – and the bookshop appeared to host a variety of events. There were photos of a Halloween event and the Christmas decorations which seemed to have turned the shop into something resembling an Aladdin's cave or fairy grotto, reports of author talks, and something called a *Book Café* which sounded intriguing.

And it was owned and managed by this person who was her aunt! Iris couldn't wait to visit the shop and to meet her. But she intended to be cautious. Her mother's last words had given no indication of why she'd never spoken of her sister. What was Iris to apologise for? Then there were the letters… Tempted though she'd been, Iris hadn't opened them. Though she had brought the bundle with her. Perhaps she'd return them… perhaps not. She'd wait and see what this aunt of hers was like. It was quite possible she'd want nothing to do with Iris and her daughter.

If that was the case, Iris would be disappointed, but at least she and Violet could enjoy a nice holiday, spend Christmas on the Queensland coast, before returning to Melbourne for the start of school and for Iris to go back to the library.

'Sit still, Vi!' she said to her daughter who was still bouncing around in her seat.

'How can I? Look, there's the beach, and the ocean and… pelicans!' She pointed to where three of the large birds were making their ungainly way across the road. 'Is that why this place is called Pelican Crossing?'

'Probably.' Until now, Iris hadn't given any thought to the name. To think this was where her mother had grown up. She wondered what it had been like all those years ago. From what she could see of the main street, she suspected not much had changed since then.

'Can we go and see Aunt Lou now?'

'Not yet. We need to book into our motel, unpack and get something to eat. Then I expect it'll be time for bed.' She peered at the rain which was becoming heavier. 'Hopefully, it'll be sunny tomorrow.' Iris hadn't worked out how to approach her aunt. She'd been too busy organising their trip. But now they were here, she needed to figure out what she was going to do.

*

The sun was shining next morning when Iris peered out the window. Violet stirred behind her in the bed.

'Is it morning? Can we go to the beach?'

Iris turned away from the window to face her daughter. 'Maybe not this morning, but we can go out and have a look around, find somewhere to have breakfast, then…'

'Go to meet Aunt Lou,' Violet finished for her.

'We may go to the bookshop, but I think we should perhaps hold off on meeting her. If what Mum said was right, she may not even know we exist. She'll be older than your gran, remember. It would be a shock for her.' *It might even kill her,* Iris thought, *then she'd never learn what it was all about.*

'Okay!' Violet jumped out of bed, making Iris wonder, not for the first time, how she'd managed to give birth to someone who was so bright first thing in the morning. It always took Iris some time, a hot shower and a cup of coffee, before she felt ready to face the day. She examined the coffee provided in their motel room, before deciding the packets of the instant variety wouldn't cut it. Sighing, she headed for the shower.

An hour later, Iris and Violet left the motel.

'This is ace,' Violet said as with the help of a map they'd picked up in the motel, they made their way towards the marina and the harbour where the motel receptionist had assured them they'd find the perfect spot to have breakfast.

The marina was filled with boats of all descriptions from small yachts to large motor launches and at this time in the morning, there seemed to be a lot of action going on. Farther along, Iris could see what she guessed was the harbour where the vessels appeared to be of a more commercial nature. And there, on the opposite side of the road, was the welcome sight of *The Blue Dolphin Café*, the one she'd been told about.

'Is that where we're having breakfast?' Violet pointed to the café, skipping along at Iris's side.

'It is.' All Iris wanted was a cup of decent coffee. Living in Melbourne which was renowned for its vibrant and serious coffee culture, she doubted a café in this small Queensland town could compete, but she had no choice. At least it would be hot and wet, and better than the packets of instant stuff in their motel room.

Walking past the outside tables, at one of which sat a man with a chocolate labrador, Iris led Violet inside to be greeted by the fragrant aroma of coffee. This was more like it. She inhaled it, taking comfort from the familiar nutty scent. She ordered coffee with eggs benedict for herself, and a banana smoothie along with pancakes for Violet.

The coffee, when it arrived, was delicious, equal to anything she'd had at home. As soon as she'd taken her first sip, Iris felt much better. While she was waiting for their meals to arrive, and Violet was busy, noisily slurping her smoothie, Iris stared out the window. The man with the dog had been joined by another man, and they appeared to be engaged in a serious discussion. She idly wondered what could be so important that they'd sit outside instead of the airconditioned comfort of the café, if dogs were allowed inside. But there was no accounting for taste. She'd learned that the hard way when Scott… No, she wouldn't go there. All that was best forgotten, though she sometimes felt guilty at having deprived Violet of a father. Although he'd known she was pregnant, she'd never contacted him, never told him he had a daughter.

Breakfast proved to be as good as anything she could have eaten back home, Iris vowing to come there again.

'Are we going to the bookshop now?' Violet asked impatiently.

Iris flinched. Now the time had come, she wondered if it had been a mistake to come here, to seek out the woman who was her aunt. It had been her mother's last wish, but would it really matter if Iris didn't make her mother's apology? She didn't even know what her mother was sorry for. She looked at her daughter's face, at her eager expression and knew she couldn't disappoint her or fail to do as her mother asked. 'We'll just take a look today,' she said. 'We're here for another four weeks. We have plenty of time.'

Using their map to guide them, *Books and Coffee* was easy to find.

'Wow!' Violet said as they stood looking through the window at the large Christmas tree, the gaily decorated shop, the children running around and the line of customers waiting to be served.

Wow indeed, Iris thought. The bookshop looked even better in real life than it had online. She was still trying to summon up the courage to go in, when Violet pushed open the door.

Thirty-three

The sun was shining when Blair pulled open the curtains. As he prepared to leave for his morning swim, all he could think about was the softness of Lou's skin under his lips, of how much he'd wanted to kiss her properly. But he'd felt her resist his second hug and had decided to bide his time.

He was looking forward to being in the ocean again, but when he reached the beach, the sight of the large waves changed his mind, forcing him to walk along the shoreline instead. He was later than usual again this morning, and there was no sign of the wild swimmers, only a woman and her dog walking along the edge of the ocean like himself.

As they drew closer, he saw that it was the old woman he'd noticed there before, her white hair blowing wild this morning and her long skirt trailing in the shallow water, while her dog – a spaniel – frolicked in the waves.

'Good morning,' he said, and was about to walk past, when something in her expression made him stop.

'I know who you are,' she said, pointing a bony finger at him. 'Your daughter is the masseuse at the wellness centre. I've seen you together with her and her two children. They'd be your grandchildren.'

'Harper and Noah.' Blair nodded, amused that she recognised him. Pelican Crossing really was such a small town.

'You frequent the bookshop too,' she continued, 'and I know the attraction. But you have your work cut out if you think you can get anywhere with Lou Chalmers. She was badly hurt once and won't want to risk it again. But good luck to you.' She nodded wisely before calling, 'Lady!' to her dog and continuing on her way.

Blair stared after her. Who was she and what did she know? He continued on his walk. Was the old woman right? Had Darren Ross – and Fleur – hurt Lou so badly that she would never risk falling in love again… with him? Blair's heart sank. But this was just the idle talk of an old woman, who probably wasn't even in her right mind. He should ignore it.

But the old woman's words stuck in Blair's head. What if she knew Lou better than he did? She looked ancient. She must have lived here when Lou was a teenager, when her sister left town. He needed something to take his mind off her. Deciding breakfast was the answer, he made his way to *The Blue Dolphin Café*.

There was a man sitting at one of the outside tables with his dog, a chocolate labrador. He looked up as Blair was about to walk past. 'Hello,' he said, rising to his feet and holding out his hand. 'We've not met, but I know who you are. Troy Piper has told me about you. I'm a neighbour of his, Joe Harris. This is Coco. Care to join us?' The dog looked up at the sound of its name, before dropping its head onto its paws again.

Blair was surprised to hear a second person say they knew who he was, but this time he recognised the man from a photo he'd seen in the local paper. 'I know who you are too,' he said to the local mayor. 'I'm delighted to meet you and would be happy to join you.'

When he had ordered coffee and the Big Breakfast and answered Joe's questions about how he was finding Pelican Crossing and how he liked living in *The Haven*, Blair said, 'I had an odd experience on the beach earlier. I met this old woman who said she knew who I was… a bit like you did,' he chuckled, 'but she then offered me some advice.'

Joe chuckled too. 'Oh, that's old Agnes. She lives by the river and takes care of sick pelicans. She's harmless, often walks on the beach with Lady, her dog, and makes odd pronouncements. I should warn you, she usually knows what she's talking about.'

'Oh,' Blair said, his hopes of having a closer relationship with Lou dashed.

'I won't ask you what she said, but I wouldn't let it worry you. I hear you've met another of my neighbours… Lou Chalmers,' he added, when Blair clearly appeared puzzled.

'Troy introduced us, though we'd already met at the bookshop. I'm a sucker for bookshops, and I was intrigued by her *Book Café*. It's a brilliant idea.'

'Yeah, I'd heard about that. You're into family history too, I hear.'

Blair stared at his companion. *How did he know that?* He could see what made Joe Harris such a popular mayor. He seemed to have his finger on everything that happened in the town, even Blair's own interests.

'It was something Troy said.' Joe looked embarrassed. 'People tend to tell me things, and I have a good memory.'

'Hmm.'

The waitress appeared with Blair's meal and another coffee for Joe, and no more was said while Blair enjoyed his breakfast. Then Blair asked, 'You've lived here all your life?'

'I have indeed. Been mayor for the past few years too… for my sins.' He laughed.

'And a good one from what I've read.'

'Oh, you shouldn't believe all you read in *The Echo*, though for the most part it's fairly accurate in its reporting.' Joe laughed again.

Taking what he felt was a wild shot, Blair risked asking, 'You'd have known Lou for a long time then?'

'We all grew up together, though of course, I was a good bit younger than Lou, Troy and Phil. We all chose to stay around and all three have done well for themselves. A group of guys in my group stayed around too. Now Poppy owns *Crossings*, Cam heads up *Pelican Marine*, and Jamie runs the fishing charters you may have seen advertised.'

'I've not only seen them advertised, I've been on one. It was a great trip.' He didn't know why he was surprised to learn that Joe and Jamie Whittaker were friends. He was fast learning that in Pelican Crossing, everyone knew each other, and if they hadn't grown up together, they soon found themselves caught up in the friendly community. He had only been living here for a couple of months, look how many people he'd met already, and here he was talking with the mayor as if they were old friends.

As if reading his mind, Joe said, 'You don't remain a stranger for long in Pelican Crossing. You've found your way to *The Grand*, I hope?'

'I have indeed, a lovely old hotel.'

'It's a favourite spot with all the old timers – though it's becoming popular with the younger set too. You'll always find someone to drink with there.'

'What's its story? It looks pretty old.'

'It is, been there as long as I can remember. It was originally called *The Grand Hotel*, shortened to *The Grand* by the locals. It's changed hands a few times over the years, and there have been attempts to modernise it, change the name. None succeeded.'

'Mmm. And what about the row of cottages where you and Troy live? They must be pretty old too. I've been meaning to research them. Old things and places fascinate me. I guess it's my love of family history and because I taught history for so many years.'

'How long have you got?' Joe chuckled again. 'No, seriously, if you're really interested, I do have some information on the history of the town. It's always fascinated me too. Why don't you come to dinner with me and Gill, and I can show you some of the archives I discovered in the town hall when I became mayor.'

'Really? I'd love that.'

'Let me have your number and I'll be in touch. Oh, and...' Joe said, when they'd exchanged numbers, 'don't let anything old Agnes told you about Lou put you off.' He grinned before leaving.

Thirty-four

Lou was wishing she'd refused Katrina's invitation to dinner. The prospect of meeting Blair's family hung over her like a cloud all day while she smiled and served customers. She'd been right about the weather. The storm had passed, leaving the sky clear and blue, perfect for the holidaymakers who were flooding into the town. Some of the schools interstate had finished early, and parents had been quick to book accommodation for a pre-Christmas getaway.

Since it was Saturday, both Zoe and Georgia were there to help and, now that Georgia had completed Year Twelve, she'd be helping out till well into the new year, until after Lou's January sale. Lou was glad, especially since next week they were hosting the local schoolchildren again for Zoe's Christmas story time. If it was anything like Halloween, that, plus the increased customer presence, would create chaos. But it would be the sort of chaos Lou loved.

While she worked, Lou kept an eye on the shop door. Blair had promised to pop in today, as he did every day, whether she had time to spend with him or not. It always gave her a warm glow to see his cheerful face, and she hadn't forgotten his admission that he had feelings for her. She only hoped Katrina hadn't guessed and had believed him when he claimed they were only friends.

It would be strange to meet her masseuse socially, another reason to go to the physio instead, even though she knew Dan Parker socially too. He had recently moved into a neighbouring cottage with Lou's friend, Livvy, and they'd met at several of the gatherings the cottage owners held on the beach. There was one due to occur soon. It would be an early Christmas celebration for the group who were close friends as well as neighbours.

As she'd expected, Lou had no time to spend with Blair, and they only exchanged a few words as he purchased yet another book to add to his collection, joking as he did so that he'd soon have to buy another bookcase.

Finally, the crowd thinned, and Zoe was able to lock the door behind the last customer, while Lou checked the day's sales. Then, with nothing to keep her in the shop, Lou drove home, feeling sick at the thought of the evening ahead.

As soon as she got home, Lou fed Tilly who, sensing Lou's nervousness, ignored her food to pace around the kitchen meowing loudly before hiding under the table. Unable to coax her out, Lou gave up and went to the bedroom to freshen up and change into something suitable for dinner with Blair's family.

A short time later, she emerged wearing a loose beige dress to find Tilly eating her food. *Cats!* She just had time to apply a touch of makeup and a spritz of perfume, and to brush her hair before it was time for Blair to arrive.

'You look very nice. Nervous?' he asked, when she opened the door, and he'd given her his usual hug.

'Thanks, and just a bit,' she lied. She was terrified. *Why had she agreed to this?* She could perhaps cope with meeting Katrina socially, but her husband… and Blair's grandchildren? What would they think of her? 'Should I take something? I have wine, and I brought home a couple of books I thought your grandchildren might like.' Lou was accustomed to dealing with children at work but hadn't had much to do with them outside the bookshop.

'I have wine, but the kids are great readers and love to get books.'

'Okay.' Lou picked up the two new releases by popular children's authors she'd chosen, hoping they'd make an appropriate gift.

'Ready? They won't bite, and you know Katrina.'

'Yes, but I only know her as my masseuse. She's never seen me as…' Lou swallowed, '… her dad's friend.'

'You'll be fine,' Blair assured her as he ushered her out of the cottage and into his car.

Lou's stomach churned all the way to the new development where Blair's family lived, despite his attempts to put her at ease by telling her about some of the exploits his grandchildren got up to. She thought he might be making it worse.

To Lou's relief, Katrina was smiling when she met them at the door. 'I'm so glad to meet you properly,' she greeted Lou, giving her a peck on the cheek. 'These are Harper and Noah,' she added, as a boy and girl appeared behind her, yelling, 'Grandad!' and vying with each other to be first to hug Blair.

'Steady on, guys,' Blair said. 'I've brought a friend to meet you.'

They both turned towards Lou, as if seeing her for the first time. 'It's the lady from the bookshop,' they called in unison, before turning back to Blair. 'Did you bring us something, Grandad?' Noah asked.

'Noah! Grandad can't always be bringing you things,' Katrina said. 'Sorry, Lou, they're always like this. It's Dad's fault. He spoils them rotten.'

Blair shrugged. 'I think *Lou* has something for you tonight,' he said.

The two children turned back to Lou, suddenly shy.

Lou handed them the books. 'I don't know your tastes, but these have newly arrived in the shop. No one else has seen them yet.'

'Wow!' Harper said, looking at her copy. 'I love this author. Wait till I tell Ellie. Thank you,' she said, looking up at Lou with a smile.

'Noah!' Katrina said to her son who was busy checking out his book.

'Oh,' he said, looking up too, 'thanks.'

'Thanks, Lou. You didn't need to do that. But it'll keep them quiet for a bit so we can have a glass of wine before dinner. You're probably ready for one. Come and meet Brett. He's getting the barbecue ready. I hope you like steak?'

'Yes, thanks.' Lou had already realised that Katrina was a very different person at home from what she was in the clinic. With two children to look after, she had a tendency to run her sentences together without waiting for an answer, while at work she spoke more sparingly, making every word count.

Outside, a tall, dark-haired man was standing over the barbecue. He came towards Lou, smiling, hand outstretched. 'Hi, Lou. It's good to meet you. I'm always happy to meet a friend of Blair's. I'm Brett.'

'Hello, Brett.' Lou shook his hand. 'It's good to meet you too.'

'Sit with me,' Katrina said, pulling out a couple of chairs, while Blair joined Brett at the barbecue.

'Thanks for coming,' Katrina said. 'I know this is probably awkward for you. It is for me too. I'm really glad Dad is making friends in Pelican Crossing. I've been worried he might decide to go back to Tassie. I admit, it felt a bit odd to learn he had a woman friend. Not that I'm reading anything into it,' she said quickly, as Lou opened her mouth to speak. 'Though both Chels and I would be happy if Dad did find someone… Chels more than me, I think. Mum and I were always close. It would be difficult to think of someone taking her place.'

Lou was shocked. 'Katrina, I have no intention of taking your mother's place. I've heard your dad talk about her. He still loves her and is grieving her loss.'

'I know, I know. But, as Chels says, it will probably happen one day, and better the devil you know…' She took a sip of wine.

Lou almost choked. *Was she the devil Katrina knew?* She'd been called many things over the years, but this was a first.

'Hey, you two. Steaks are ready,' Brett called.

Katrina rounded up the children and brought out some salads, and they all sat down to eat. It was a lively meal, unlike what Lou was accustomed to. But she enjoyed the children's chatter, their excitement about the approach of Christmas and their interest in what books were to be read at the Christmas story time in the bookshop.

'You'll have to wait and see,' was her answer to that, to be met with wails of disappointment.

As soon as they had finished eating, Harper and Noah begged to be excused so they could go back to reading the books Lou had brought them.

'You've won a couple of hearts there,' Katrina said, smiling fondly as they dashed off. 'They won't forget you in a hurry.'

'I'm glad they liked my choices.' Lou was relieved. It was always tricky to choose books for children she didn't know.

With the children gone, the conversation turned to local events, the next of which was the carol singing in Pelican Plaza on Christmas Eve. It was an event Lou always attended and enjoyed, celebrating as it did the spirit of Christmas. Afterwards, she always returned home to enjoy a glass of sparkling wine and a piece of the Christmas cake brought home from the café, with Tilly for company, before heading to bed, knowing she could sleep till late next day.

'What's the story behind Pelican Plaza?' Blair asked, curious as always.

'Lou?' Katrina asked. 'You've been here longer than we have.'

Lou smiled. 'Well,' she said, 'it all started a long time ago when staff at the local fish shop fed scraps to the pelicans every day. Some people say that was where the town got its name. Anyway, the gathering of pelicans became so popular that eventually the local council arranged the building of a proper feeding platform. It became known as Pelican Plaza and in tourist season, crowds of people gather there at two o'clock every day to watch the birds being fed. In addition to feeding the pelicans, the volunteers who conduct the sessions also educate the spectators about the birds and check their health. If you haven't been there to see it yet, Blair, you should go. It's quite a spectacle.'

'The kids love it, Dad. You could take them in the school holidays,' Katrina said.

Blair met Lou's eyes. She could see what he meant about his daughter. Katrina did have the habit of organising him. But most of the time, he didn't seem to mind.

'The carols sound fun too,' he said. 'Will you be going, Lou?'

She nodded. 'I go every year. It's a lovely event.'

'Maybe we could go together.'

There was a sudden silence, then, 'Maybe,' Lou said. A lot could happen between now and then, and she didn't want to do anything to jeopardise Blair's relationship with his family. Despite her comment about the devil she knew, Lou was aware Blair's invitation to the carols had stunned Katrina. It had stunned Lou too. The carol service was a family event, and she wasn't part of Blair's family.

Lou and Blair left soon afterwards. On the drive back to Lou's cottage, Blair took a detour along the beachfront. It was beautiful at this time of night, the moon and stars reflected in the ocean, empty apart from a ship anchored far out to sea.

'I can see why you love it here,' Blair said when he parked outside her cottage. 'The more I get to know Pelican Crossing and its people, the more I like it.' He got out and walked Lou to her door. 'Thanks for coming along tonight. I know it was a big ask. It went well, and Harper and Noah loved you.'

'They're delightful children. Thanks for inviting me. I enjoyed it too.'

'I hope Katrina wasn't too hard on you, when Brett and I were at the barbecue.'

'No, not at all.' Lou didn't intend to tell Blair what his daughter had said. She wasn't sure herself what Katrina had meant.

'I'm sure she likes you. But it doesn't matter, because I do.' Blair pulled Lou into a warm hug, his lips brushing her forehead again, sending a shiver down her spine and making her wonder what it would feel like to have those lips on hers.

Thirty-five

To Iris's delight, the next few days were perfect, the brilliant sunshine exactly what all the ads promised. Violet was in her element as they spent each morning at the beach, swimming and playing in the sand before heading back to their motel to change for lunch which was either a meal at *The Blue Dolphin*, or fish and chips by the beach.

Despite making several visits to *Books and Coffee*, Iris hadn't been able to approach the woman she knew to be her aunt. Lou Chalmers was different to what she'd expected, not at all like Fleur. Iris's mother had been daintily built, pretty, always concerned about her appearance, and very charming… as long as she got her own way.

The bookshop owner was a tall woman, elegant rather than pretty, and always dressed in pants and a tunic which hid her shape. There was something formidable about her that made Iris wary of approaching her. How she wished her mother had been able to tell her more, to tell her what she needed to apologise for. It must have been something dreadful to have kept the sisters apart for all those years – Iris had seen the postage dates on the letters.

Despite that, Iris and Violet were enjoying their time in Pelican crossing. They had been to see the pelican feeding at Pelican Plaza, watched a beach volleyball game, admired the prowess of a group of kitesurfers, and Violet had taken lessons in stand-up paddle boarding which she loved.

Being a librarian, Iris gravitated to the town library and, while Violet found a corner in which to curl up and read, Iris met the

Heritage librarian who'd introduced her to the Heritage room with its collection of archives. As soon as she realised the collection included copies of old school magazines, she was hooked and trawled through them looking for mention of Fleur.

After a few false starts she found several photos of Fleur in different costumes she'd worn in school productions and one of her in a group all dressed for their school formal. She stroked the photo with her finger. Her mother had been so pretty at eighteen.

Next, she searched the archives of the local paper, which appeared to have been called *The Crossing Courier* before being changed a few years earlier to *The Echo*. Iris was sure there was a story behind the change of name but wasn't interested in pursuing it. She was more interested in reading about Pelican Crossing when her mother was growing up here.

'I'm hungry, and we were going to go to the bookshop again today.' Violet sidled up to Iris, interrupting her concentration. She had just discovered an article about a performance of Romeo and Juliet, which Fleur had starred in, playing Juliet to a handsome young Romeo.

'Look!' Iris said, showing Violet the article. 'That's Grandma, when she was in high school.'

Violet peered at the photo for a few moments, before saying, 'She's pretty. Why is she all dressed up?'

'She's acting in a play, and she was always pretty… until she became sick.' Iris felt a lump form in her throat. She missed her mother so much. Maybe the time had come to speak to her aunt. 'Let's have lunch and go to the bookshop,' she said.

'Can we have lunch in the café part of it today?'

'Okay.' Until now, Iris had avoided eating or having coffee there. She didn't know why. But, today, it seemed right.

Iris and Violet were enjoying miniature quiches with salad accompanied by coffee for Iris and lemonade for Violet, when the man at the next table folded the newspaper he'd been reading, rose and made his way into the bookshop. Iris thought he looked vaguely familiar, before realising where she'd seen him before. It had been at the library. He'd been poring over the Heritage collection one day, sitting at another computer.

'Do you know him?' Violet asked, seeing her looking at him.

'No, Vi. I recognised him, but only because I've seen him in the library.'

When Iris couldn't delay any longer, she paid for their meal and she and Voilet walked through into the bookshop. As on all their previous visits, the shop was crowded with people, all seemingly intent on giving books as gifts for Christmas. Carols were playing quietly in the background.

Suddenly the door opened, and a line of schoolchildren filed in, pushing and shoving each other and chatting excitedly. They headed to what Iris now knew was the children's area and sat down on the floor. A young woman Iris had seen in the bookshop before took a seat on a chair in front of them, opened a book and began to read.

'Can I?' Violet pleaded with Iris. 'I can slip in at the back,' she added when Iris appeared doubtful.

'Well… okay,' Iris said, realising this might give her the opportunity to approach Lou on her own.

Violet ran off and, checking that there was only one customer waiting to be served, Iris took a deep breath and made her way towards the counter.

'Can I help you?'

Iris stared at the woman who was her aunt, her stomach churning. She took another deep breath. 'Are you Lou Chalmers?' she asked.

Lou nodded.

Iris hesitated for a moment before saying, 'I'm Iris Ross, Fleur's daughter. I think I'm your niece.'

Thirty-six

Lou stared at the woman, unable to believe her ears. For a moment, everything went black.

She'd just farewelled what had been her most difficult customer of the day so far. Her feet and back were killing her, and the final group of schoolchildren had just arrived for their story time. Zoe was doing a great job with them, and it was resulting in a lot of extra sales, but they should have considered how it would affect Lou and Georgia at this busy time of year. She'd be glad when the day was over and she could go home to Tilly, have a hot shower and a glass of wine.

She'd been wondering if she could manage to ease her feet out of her shoes for a little while, when she noticed the woman hovering to the side of the counter. She'd seen her in the bookshop before, accompanied by a young girl, but she had never bought anything... and she looked vaguely familiar.

'Can I help you?' she'd asked, hoping the woman wasn't going to be another customer who was difficult to please. Perhaps she'd left her daughter somewhere today so as to be able to buy something for her.

The woman looked at Lou, something in her expression sending a shiver down Lou's spine. 'Are you Lou Chalmers?' she'd asked.

Then, when Lou nodded, she'd said...

'Are you okay?' The voice seemed to come from a long way away. Lou forced herself to focus on the present. It was as if she was coming out of a long tunnel. Had she heard correctly? Had the woman said she was Fleur's daughter? Where was Fleur? Had she sent her? 'I think so,' she said, not at all sure she was.

Fortunately, Georgia appeared at her side to cope with the next few customers, and when Lou looked around, the woman, Iris, was still there, looking as panicked as Lou felt.

'You… you're Iris?'

The woman nodded.

Lou felt as if there was an explosion in her head. She wanted to… She didn't know what she wanted, but she knew she had to talk to her, to find out why she was here. 'I can't talk here. We close at five. Where…?'

'This is where we're staying.' Iris handed her a card with the name of a local motel. 'You can find us there.'

Us? Lou's heart raced. Was Fleur here… in Pelican Crossing?

'My daughter and I. She's…' At that moment the class of schoolchildren began to leave the children's corner, and one small girl ran towards Iris. 'This is Violet, Vi,' she said.

Lou was too overcome to speak. She couldn't believe that Fleur's daughter and granddaughter were standing right there in her bookshop. Now that she looked closely, both bore a slight resemblance to her sister. It was why she'd thought the woman looked familiar.

As if realising Lou's discomfort, Iris said, 'We'll be off now. I hope to see you later. My mum gave me a message for you.'

At those words, Lou's heart leapt. Fleur had received her letter. Something had prevented her from coming herself, but her daughter and granddaughter were here and had a message for her. Lou wondered why Fleur couldn't come herself, why she hadn't replied to Lou's letter. She'd included her email address and phone number. But perhaps after all those years, she was feeling as nervous as Lou was about their reunion.

Lou tucked the card into her pocket, though there was no need. The motel was one she knew, and now its name was imprinted on her brain.

She wasn't sure how she got through the rest of the afternoon, serving customers automatically. Several times, she caught Zoe glancing at her as if she was going to ask her what was wrong. She even forgot about her aching back and feet, her mind filled with the knowledge that Fleur's daughter and granddaughter were here, in Pelican Crossing and, as soon as she closed the bookshop, she could see them and talk to them, hear the message Fleur had sent to her.

*

Of course, it wasn't as simple as it seemed. Although, once she'd locked the shop, Lou wanted to go straight to see Iris and Violet, she knew she had to go home first and feed Tilly who had been on her own all day and would be hungry and in need of a cuddle. Also, she knew she'd feel much better about meeting Iris and Violet again if she took time to shower and change first.

So, despite longing to discover what her sister wanted to say to her, Lou made her way home to be greeted by Tilly winding herself around her ankles as if she knew something was bothering Lou. 'You'll never guess who I met today,' she said to her pet, picking up the cat and rubbing her nose into Tilly's fur. 'I have a niece and great-niece – or is it grandniece? And I'm going to meet them.' Indifferent to Lou's excitement, Tilly gave a yowl and slid out of her grasp to head to her food bowl, standing over it till Lou filled it with her special Fancy Feast Classic Pâté with Chicken.

Trembling with excitement, Lou had just showered and changed into the beige outfit she'd worn to dinner at Katrina's when her phone rang, and she saw Blair's number. In the tumult of her emotions, she'd forgotten he'd said he'd call.

'Blair.'

'Lou? Has something happened? You sound… different.'

'Oh, Blair. I still can't believe it. Fleur's daughter and granddaughter – Iris and Violet – came into the bookshop this afternoon. She had a message for me from Fleur. I'm going to meet her.'

'How wonderful. I'm happy for you. Did she say why your sister didn't come herself?'

'No, but I'm sure she has a good reason.' Lou had been trying to figure this out but hadn't come to any conclusion.

'Do you want me to come with you? I could wait in the car, be there, in case…'

'No, I'll be fine. It's good of you to offer.' He really was such a kind man.

'Well, why don't you come round to my place afterwards… if you feel like it, that is. We can eat here, and I have wine.'

Lou felt a warm glow wash over her, the same one she often felt with Blair and which she didn't want to analyse. 'Thanks, I might do that. I'll call if I can't make it.'

'Okay. Take care, and I hope all goes well.'

'Thanks.' It was good of Blair to be concerned, but what could possibly go wrong?

Lou drove into the motel surrounds and parked outside, checking the room number before knocking on the door.

'You came!' Iris greeted her when she opened the door. 'Come in.'

Violet was sitting on one of the twin beds with a book. She stared at Lou. 'Are you really my aunt?'

'Vi!' Iris said. 'Sorry, this is all so new to her, to me too. Why don't you take a seat? Wine?' She gestured to one of the chairs by a small table on which sat a bottle of wine and two glasses.

'Thanks, that would be lovely.' And it might help calm the butterflies doing cartwheels in her stomach. 'It's very new to me too. I never thought...' Lou accepted a glass of wine and took a sip. 'You have a message for me?' she asked, eager to hear what Fleur wanted to say to her.

'Mum wanted to apologise to you. It was her last wish that I tell you she was sorry. She didn't say what for.'

Lou felt the room spin. *Her last wish? Fleur was dead? Her sister was dead? There could be no reunion, no opportunity for forgiveness? She'd never see her little sister again?* She became aware of the tears trickling down her cheeks, her breath coming in gasps. She reached out a hand to find Iris's in hers.

'I'm sorry. Of course you didn't know.'

It was some time before Lou could speak. 'I thought... I wrote to Fleur... When you said you had a message for me, I thought she'd sent you instead of coming herself. I never imagined. Oh, poor Fleur!' Lou burst into tears and suddenly, she and Iris were hugging each other, both in tears.

There was so much Lou wanted to know, to ask Iris, but not now. Now, all she wanted to do was to get away, to try to absorb the fact that her little sister was dead, that there would be no happy reunion, no chance to make amends. It was as if part of her had died with Fleur, her entire childhood with all its memories.

'I'm sorry. I shouldn't have broken it to you like that,' Iris said, when they had separated and were each taking another drink of wine.

'No, it's all right.' But it wasn't. Despite being estranged from her sister, Lou had always known Fleur was there, somewhere, and hoped that one day... *How could she not have sensed her sister was dead? What had happened to the letter she'd sent, the letter which had been so difficult to write? Had Fleur already been dead when Lou dropped it into the mailbox?*

'I'm sorry. I can't...' Lou took a card from her bag, one of the *Bookshop and Coffee* cards, and picking up a pen, quickly wrote her home address and phone number. 'Tomorrow. Come to dinner. Both of you. Seven o'clock. We can talk then.'

She rose and, stumbling, made her way out of the motel room gulping in the fresh air on the way to her car, where she sat in shock, her eyes squeezed shut as if she could shut out the news. Then she turned on the ignition and drove to the villa in *The Haven*, to the comfort she knew she'd find there.

Thirty-seven

As soon as Blair opened the door, Lou fell into his arms, sobbing uncontrollably. He knew something was wrong, terribly wrong. He led her inside, still holding her in his arms, settled down with her on the sofa and waited.

It was some time before Lou spoke and at first, her words were incoherent. Blair listened, making no comment, too afraid to move, fearful of making things worse.

Finally, Lou's words started to make sense. 'She's dead, Blair. Fleur's dead,' she said, before breaking down again.

Gently, Blair released Lou. 'I'll be right back,' he said before going to the kitchen to pour a glass of whisky, then returning to join Lou on the sofa. 'Drink this. You've had a shock. It'll help.'

Trembling, Lou took the glass and put it to her lips, grimacing as the fiery liquid slipped down her throat. She clasped the empty glass in both hands. 'Thanks. I can't believe it. If only I'd tried to contact her earlier, if…'

'Shh. You did what you could, when you could. Perhaps you weren't meant to meet again in this life. Everything happens for a reason. What did Iris say?' He took the glass from her trembling hands and put an arm round her shoulders again.

'She said…' Lou paused and wiped her eyes, '… she said it had been her mother's last wish that she see me and pass on her apology. Oh, Blair, to think that all this time…' Lou began to weep again.

'Then perhaps it wasn't till then that she found it in herself to regret the hurt she caused you. People often try to make amends in their final moments. It's a way of making confession for their sins. You have to try to accept it for what it is, not to blame yourself for something over which you had no control.' Prue's last moments flashed behind Blair's eyes, before he blinked and refocussed on Lou.

'You're right,' she sniffed, 'but I wish I could have seen her one last time, that she'd known I'd forgiven her.'

'I'm sure she does.'

'I wish I could believe that.' But Lou's tears were drying.

'Could you face something to eat? I have a chicken pie in the oven, and I made a salad. You can tell me all about it while we eat. I also have a bottle of some pretty good cab sav.'

'Thanks. I'm not sure if I can eat anything, but maybe a few mouthfuls.'

'Good. Now, why don't you wash that lovely face of yours while I dish up?'

When Lou returned, her eyes were still red, but she appeared to be more composed. 'I'm sorry, what must you think of me?' she said.

'You had a shock. Fleur was your sister. It's only natural for you to be upset.

'Thanks. That pie smells good.'

'It does. Sit down and I'll dish up.'

'Thanks,' Lou said again and took a seat.

Blair poured them both a glass of wine and served up the salad and chicken pie, giving Lou only a small portion of both. He watched as Lou took a sip of wine and picked at the food, her dejection obvious. Finally, she pushed the plate away. 'It's lovely, Blair, but I'm sorry…'

'It's okay.' He felt bad, wolfing down his own meal, but he was hungry. 'Do you want to tell me about Iris and Violet?'

Lou gave a weak smile. 'Iris reminds me of her mother. I'd seen her in the shop before and thought she looked familiar. She doesn't have Fleur's features, but there's something about her. She was nervous in the shop, a little better at the motel. I had to leave as soon as she told me about Fleur. I couldn't bear to…' A tear trickled down her cheek again. 'Sorry, I don't seem to be able to stop crying.'

'It's okay.' Blair got up, went to a cupboard, and returned with a box of tissues.

'Thanks,' Lou said, taking a tissue and wiping her eyes.

'And Violet?' Blair asked.

'I barely noticed her. Iris was on her own when she first spoke to me. I think Violet – she calls her Vi – was at Zoe's story time. Then, in the motel, she was reading. She…' Lou seemed to remember, '… she asked me if I was her Aunt Lou. I don't think I replied. Oh, what must she think of me?'

'It must be strange for her too.'

'I suppose so.'

'Did you arrange to see them again?'

'Yes. I asked them to come to dinner tomorrow at the cottage. Hopefully, I'll be making more sense by then.' She gave a wry smile. 'They came all this way to pass on Fleur's apology. Imagine?'

'You'd have done the same in their place.'

'Mmm. Thanks for being here for me, Blair, and for listening.'

'No problem. I'm always here for you, Lou. I hope you know that.'

'I don't know why you bother with me,' she shook her head, 'why you've done so much to help me.'

'It's because I care about you, about what happens to you. And I hate seeing you as upset as you were when you arrived this evening.'

'Thanks, Blair. You're a good friend. I'm lucky to have you.'

Blair didn't respond, knowing that while he was happy to be Lou's friend, he'd like to be more, much more.

'Will you be okay to drive home?' Blair asked, when they were standing in his doorway. Lou still appeared distraught.

'Yes, I got here, didn't I? And that last cup of coffee helped.'

Blair was glad he'd insisted on the coffee. He pulled Lou into his arms for one last hug, intending to brush her forehead with his lips as he'd done before. But, at the last moment, she raised her head, her eyes met his, then his lips were on hers in a kiss that seemed to last for ever.

*

Lou drove home in a daze. She didn't know what had made her raise her head just at the moment when she knew Blair was about to brush her forehead with his lips, something she'd become accustomed to.

Had she known his lips would meet hers? If she had, would she have done anything differently?

Blair Stevens had kissed her, and she'd enjoyed it. Lou hugged the knowledge to herself all the way home, and there was a smile on her face when she walked in to be greeted by an irate Tilly. After fondling the cat's ears, then filling up her food and water bowls while telling her what a good girl she was, Lou made herself a mug of hot chocolate and curled up in her favourite armchair, the moonlight shining in through the window, her thoughts swirling around in her head.

What a day it had been! First, the appearance in the bookshop of Iris, Fleur's daughter and her niece, then the news of Fleur's death which had knocked her for six, followed by Blair's concern and comforting presence. Then that kiss! Lou hadn't been kissed in over forty years, not since Darren… She'd never thought she'd ever be kissed again. Yet it had seemed so natural to feel Blair's lips on hers. She put a finger on her lips, where Blair's had been only a short time earlier. Then she remembered Fleur. How could she be feeling happy about a kiss, when her sister was dead?

Tilly padded in and leapt on to Lou's lap, her hand automatically going down to pet her. 'They're coming to dinner tomorrow, Tilly… Iris and Violet, my family.' It felt odd to say the word. For so long, she'd had no family. It had only been her and Tilly. Now she had a niece and grandniece, and they'd be here tomorrow.

Thirty-eight

To her surprise, Lou slept soundly, wakening at her usual time. She was feeling much better this morning, though couldn't shake the thought that Fleur had died, and she hadn't known. It must have happened recently, as Blair had found nothing about it in his search of births, marriages and deaths. She should have asked Iris more about her mother. Had she been sick? When had she died? But she'd been too overcome with the shock and had just wanted to get out of the motel room and into the fresh air where she'd taken gulps of it before sitting in her car for ages.

Now she'd had a good sleep and time to think, she realised she'd been very rude to leave Iris the way she had and was glad she'd had the presence of mind to invite her and her daughter to dinner tonight. She'd apologise for her unseemly departure and make an effort to get to know them. With Christmas approaching, they'd no doubt be going home for the days leading up to it, and she wanted to make the most of what little time they might have together. It was a pity it was her busiest time of year in the bookshop, but there were always the evenings – evenings which she might otherwise have spent with Blair.

At the thought of Blair… and that kiss… Lou shivered. It had been so unexpected to feel his lips on hers, so natural, so… She shivered again, shaken by how much she wanted to repeat it. She'd thought she was past all that – not exactly sure what she meant – but happy to have made a life for herself without the trammels of a man or emotion to disturb her tranquil existence. Was this what her friends meant when they tried to tell her that there was more to life, what they'd found in the relationships they now enjoyed. She thought about Rachel, now happy with Luke, Poppy and Cam, Livvy and her Dan. Could she bear to give up her solitary existence, let a man into it?

Tilly, tired of being ignored, yowled loudly.

'You're right, Tilly. It was one kiss, nothing to get all tied up in knots over. Blair might already be regretting it.'

The twinkling lights of the Christmas tree greeted Lou when she walked into the shop, reminding her of her priorities. She loved the bookshop at this time in the morning, before her staff and the customers arrived, when it was just her, the sounds of the espresso machine and the aroma of coffee filtering through from the café. She turned on the playlist of Christmas carols Zoe had put together and allowed the joyful strains of *We wish you a Merry Christmas*, *We Three Kings* and *Little Drummer Boy* to set the right mood and help her focus on the day ahead.

To Lou's relief, Blair appeared as usual at ten o'clock, giving her a smile and a wave as he passed through on his way to the café. So, nothing had changed. She was glad to see his smiling face, and the resulting tingle she felt only heightened her pleasure. The queue of customers meant there was no time to have coffee with him, but it was enough to know he was there.

The day passed quickly, closing time arriving before she knew it, and Lou was on her way home, anticipation and apprehension warring with each other as she thought about the evening ahead. Luckily, she'd picked up a quiche and plenty of salad makings in her last shop, so there was no need to stop at the supermarket. And she still had a carton of lemon sorbet in the freezer.

Once home, Lou fed Tilly, then dashed around the cottage, picking up all the odd bits and pieces that were lying around, before setting the table in the dining area. Then she took a long shower, the shock of cold water invigorating after her busy day in the bookshop, and changed into a pair of navy pants with a multicoloured top in which she felt comfortable. A touch of makeup, and she was ready.

Back in the kitchen, Lou popped the quiche into the oven and put together a salad. She considered pouring herself a glass of wine to still the butterflies in her stomach but decided to wait till Iris arrived.

Tilly, sensing something was afoot with all the activity, had already disappeared out the cat door.

Glancing around to make sure everything looked in order, Lou jumped when there was a knock at the door.

With her heart racing, she opened the door to see Iris and Violet standing there. Iris handed her a bottle of wine, and Violet gave her a bunch of flowers.

'Oh, thank you so much,' Lou said.

'We didn't know what…' Iris stammered, making Lou realise her niece was as nervous as she was. This was new to both of them.

'Come in,' she said. 'It's lovely to see you again. I'm sorry I left so abruptly last night. I…'

'I understand.' Iris said. It must have been a shock to learn about Mum. I'm sorry too. I didn't know how to tell you. I had no idea you existed until…' Her eyes moistened.

Iris and Violet followed Lou into the kitchen, standing awkwardly while Lou put the wine and flowers on the benchtop. 'Would you like something to drink? Wine, Iris? And I have juice if you'd like that, Violet… or would you prefer me to call you Vi?'

'Yes, please, and juice would be great,' Violet said shyly.

'Wine sounds good,' Iris said.

'Please take a seat,' Lou said, taking out three glasses and pouring wine into two and juice into the other.

When they were seated around the kitchen table, Lou said, 'I had no idea about you either until recently, when I discovered Fleur and Darren had gone to Melbourne, then a friend discovered she'd had a daughter – you, Iris. I wrote to her, but…'

'We must have left before it arrived. I think Mum would have been pleased to hear from you. It was difficult for her after Dad died, after we moved in, but she loved Vi so much and she was a big help to me.'

'She was lucky to have you.'

'You never married?'

'No.' Lou didn't want to think of her reasons for remaining single, not while she was sitting beside Fleur and Darren's daughter, the daughter who might have been hers if things had been different. 'Tell me about Fleur,' she said. 'Were she and your dad happy? When did she die? Was she ill?'

Iris smiled, a smile that reminded Lou so much of her sister. 'Mum and Dad were one of the happiest couples I've known. She was devastated when he died, and I don't think she could have gone on if it hadn't been… Vi was only a baby, and I was struggling to make ends meet as a single mother. When we moved in with her, it was a good solution for both of us.'

Lou felt a wave of relief at the news Fleur and Darren had continued to be in love. She didn't think she could have borne to hear that their marriage had been unhappy, that all her hurt had been for nothing. 'I'm glad,' she said. 'And when did she…?'

'Mum died three weeks ago. She hadn't been sick for long, only lived for a few weeks after her diagnosis. It was a shock.' She wiped her eyes. 'I'd never heard of Pelican Crossing, had no idea Mum grew up here. I thought she and Dad had always lived in Melbourne. They never talked about the past, about before they met. I found your address on a bundle of unopened letters, along with some newspaper clippings. One was about the opening of your bookshop.'

'Oh!' So, Fleur had kept those letters all those years. Had she been hoping to reunite with Lou, or had she kept them as a reminder of Lou's bitterness towards her and Darren? And the newspaper clippings? Lou's breath caught.

'We waited till Vi was on school holidays before leaving, and I had to arrange leave from work.'

'What sort of work do you do?' Lou asked, anything to take her mind away from those letters she'd returned. Now it was too late, she wondered what Fleur had written.

'I work in our local library. Christmas is a quiet time for us, so it was easy for me to get time off. And I was curious to discover I had an aunt who owned a bookshop. It's a lovely shop. You must be so proud of it.'

'I am,' Lou smiled. 'I started off as a librarian like you. I always wanted to own a bookshop, so I saved like mad, and *Books and Coffee* is the result.'

'Wow! That's always been my dream too, but I can't imagine it ever becoming a reality.'

The oven beeped and, as if she'd been waiting for the sound, Tilly appeared through the cat door, letting out a loud meow when she realised Lou had guests.

'Oh, you have a cat!' Violet, who had been sitting quietly, sipping her juice, became animated. 'I love cats. What's his name? Can I pet him?'

Lou chuckled, as Tilly glared at the two visitors. 'Tilly's a lady cat, and she doesn't often take to strangers but if you go gently, she might allow you to pet her. She likes to have her ears scratched.'

While Lou took the quiche out of the oven, Violet slipped from her chair and, her hand held out and calling, 'Here, puss,' in a soft voice, moved slowly towards the cat. For a moment, Tilly looked as if she was about to flee, but to Lou's surprise, she raised her tail and began to purr, allowing Violet to get close enough to touch her.

'Vi's always wanted a cat,' Iris said sadly, 'but with Mum allergic, it wasn't possible. Maybe now…'

Lou stared at Iris. To the best of her knowledge, Fleur hadn't been allergic to cats, not when she was growing up. Was it something she'd developed as she grew older, or an excuse she'd used because she didn't want to have a cat in the house? Lou suspected the latter, a sign that the years hadn't changed her sister much. She'd always been good at getting what she wanted, by fair means or foul.

'I hope you both like quiche,' Lou said, cutting the quiche into slices and picking it up with one hand, the bowl of salad with the other.

'We certainly do,' Iris said. 'I'll bring the wine, shall I?' She picked up the bottle and empty glasses. 'Vi, leave the cat now, and wash your hands before you come to the table.'

Violet sighed and did as she was asked, picking up her glass of juice on the way.

'You have a nice place here,' Iris said, her eyes roaming around the large open area with the windows at one end. 'Do you look out onto the beach?'

'It's just across the road, quieter than the main beach where all the tourists congregate, and the surfers.'

'We watched some kitesurfers there too, and a beach volleyball game,' Violet said, coming out of her shell.

'You should come here in daylight,' Lou said. 'It's a pity I can't leave the bookshop at this time of year, but it's usually still light when I get home. Maybe… How long do you intend to stay in Pelican Crossing?'

Iris turned red. 'We plan to stay till after Christmas. There's nothing to go back home for, and with Mum being sick, we hadn't made any plans so… when I saw where you lived, it seemed like the perfect opportunity for a bit of a holiday.'

'Oh!' Lou felt a small vestige of hope unfurl in her stomach. 'So, you'll be here for Christmas?'

'Oh, we don't want to interfere with your plans. It just seemed like a good idea…'

'No, I'm sure we can arrange something.'

'I can't imagine why Mum never told me about you, about Pelican Crossing,' Iris said, when they had finished eating, and after politely asking to be excused, Violet had gone to look for Tilly again.

'I'm sure she and Darren had their reasons,' Lou said.

'How did you discover where we lived? You said you wrote to Mum?'

'A friend who lives in an over-fifties resort met your dad's brother, and…'

'Dad had a brother?' Iris interrupted, her voice rising. 'I can't believe this. How could they have kept you and him secret from me? If Mum hadn't said when she was dying, I'd never have known. I always thought they were both only children, and their parents were dead. Don't tell me I have grandparents too?'

'No, sadly, both my parents and Darren's died several years ago, and Stan is your dad's half-brother. He only returned here after his parents passed away. He's a lot older than Darren and all he knew was that Darren and Fleur had gone to Melbourne. It was my friend, Blair, who found your address from the electoral roll.'

'Does that mean Darren lived here too?'

Lou nodded

'Wow! I feel I'm living in one of those books about long-lost families.'

Lou felt that way too. She wanted to pinch herself to make sure that Fleur's daughter and granddaughter were really here, sitting in her cottage, and they had eaten dinner together.

'So, Dad's brother. Can I meet him too?'

'Stan?' Why hadn't Lou thought of that? She had been so wrapped up in her own feelings, in the emotion of meeting Iris and Violet, in learning about Fleur's death, that she had forgotten they were Stan's relatives too, and that of course, Iris would want to meet him. After learning Fleur had gone to Melbourne, she hadn't given Stan another thought. Did he know Iris was here in Pelican Crossing? Had Blair told him?

'Of course.'

'Can you introduce me to him?'

'I suppose… but I barely know him. He's Blair's friend.'

'Blair's your friend?'

'Yes.' Lou was trying to figure out how best to arrange this, when Iris asked, 'Can I meet *him?*'

Suddenly, Lou had the answer. It would provide her with an opportunity to see Blair again too. 'Why don't I contact Blair and arrange for us to meet – Violet too. Maybe over an early dinner at the yacht club. Have you been there yet?'

'Not yet. We've seen it, and it's on my list of places to visit. When do you think you can arrange it?'

'I'll call Blair tonight, see what he says, then I'll get back to you. Regardless, why don't you and Violet come back here tomorrow? I won't be home till five thirty, but if you come earlier, you and Vi can take a walk on the beach and see the sunset.'

'That sounds wonderful. Thanks. It's been so good to meet you again, to get to know you, and thanks so much for dinner.'

'No problem. It's been good getting to know you too. It seems we may have more in common than your mum.'

'We do.' Iris laughed. 'I wish I'd known about you before now,' she said, a note of regret in her voice.

'Me too. But we've met now, and we can make the most of the time you have here in Pelican Crossing.'

'I'd like that too.'

At that point, Violet appeared, carrying a seemingly compliant cat.

'Oh, Tilly!' Lou said. 'She must like you, Vi.'

'I like her too,' Violet said, as Tilly managed to slip from her grasp.

'It's time to go, Vi,' Iris said. 'Thanks again, Aunt Lou.'

'I'll look forward to seeing you again tomorrow,' Lou said, tickled pink at being called Aunt Lou.

When Iris and Violet had left, Lou was left with the sort of warm fuzzy feeling she hadn't experienced for years, and the thought that she might not spend this Christmas alone. She picked up her phone to call Blair.

Thirty-nine

Blair had spent the evening wondering how Lou was faring with Iris and her daughter. When his phone rang at ten minutes past nine, and he saw Lou's number, he grabbed it eagerly. 'Lou, I was just thinking about you. How did it go?'

'Pretty well, I think. I like Iris, and Violet started to open up when she met Tilly, who took to her right away.' She sighed. 'I wish I'd known about her sooner, but it is what it is.'

'Will they be staying long?'

'Yes! Till after Christmas.' Blair could hear the elation in Lou's voice. 'They'll be here for Christmas.'

'That's great. I'm so happy for you.'

'One thing we hadn't thought of… Stan.'

'Stan?' Blair frowned.

'When Iris asked how I found her, I told her about Stan. She wants to meet him. It hadn't occurred to me that…'

'Of course! He's her uncle. I didn't think of that either. I'm sure he'd be delighted to meet with her and her daughter.'

'The problem is that he's *your* friend, not mine. So, I wondered…'

'I'd be happy to introduce them, once I've met Iris.'

'I hoped you'd say that. Could we have dinner at the yacht club, an early one to suit Violet? Any evening works for me. I intend to spend as much time with them as possible while they're here, and Iris is eager to see as much as she can of Pelican Crossing. Imagine? She had no idea that Fleur and Darren grew up here.'

'Why don't we do it tomorrow? I'll book a table. The club's probably busy on a Friday. How does six-thirty sound? Meantime, I can talk to Stan, give him the heads up and tee up something with him.'

'Wonderful. Thanks, Blair. I don't know how I can thank you.'

Blair could think of several ways, but that was for another time. Right now, Lou's focus was on her newly discovered family. But once things settled down for her, Blair hoped there would be an opportunity to repeat that kiss.

*

Blair had already made arrangements to join Stan and his two friends for another game of pickleball next morning, so, after his swim and breakfast, he headed over to meet them.

This time, he enjoyed the game more and managed to put up a better showing. As before, the group insisted he join them for lunch at the yacht club which suited Blair perfectly. He hoped there would be an opportunity to bring up Iris over their meal, but Fred and Ewan were full of chatter about a concert they'd attended in Brisbane the previous week. There was no way Blair could have a quiet word with Stan. It wasn't till they were all leaving, that he managed to take him aside. 'I need a word, Stan. Can you drop in for coffee when we get back?' he asked.

'No problem. There's something I've been meaning to ask you about too. See you shortly.'

Back home, Blair had set the coffee machine going and was finishing tidying away some papers he'd left on the table when he heard Stan at the door. 'Come on in,' he called from the kitchen.

'Coffee's ready,' he said, when Stan joined him. 'Take a seat.'

'Thanks, mate. I wanted to ask you about what you talked to me about… about Darren going to Melbourne. Did anything come of it?'

'Funny you should ask,' Blair said, handing Stan a mug of coffee and joining him at the table. 'It's what I want to talk to *you* about.'

Stan raised one eyebrow and took a drink of coffee. 'Good stuff this. You must tell me where you get it. So…?'

'As I think I told you, I was helping a friend trace her sister, the woman your brother went to Melbourne with. The long and short of it is that I found her, or her address. Then, damned if her daughter didn't turn up here, in Pelican Crossing with *her* daughter. Seems your brother and his wife have passed away, and the woman, Fleur, told her daughter about her sister when she was on her deathbed. You couldn't make it up.' He took a sip of coffee.

'So, Darren had a daughter and she's in Pelican Crossing, right now? Wow!'

'And she wants to meet you.'

'My niece? Fancy! Never thought I had any relatives. And she has a daughter too? Have you met them?'

'Not yet. I'm meeting them tonight. And Lou wants me to introduce them to you. If you're okay with it, maybe I can ask them here on the weekend?'

'Hell, yes! Darren's daughter and granddaughter. After all this time. Who'd have thought it?' Stan shook his head in bewilderment.

'Great! I'll let them know tonight. When suits you?'

'Anytime. I don't have any plans. Darren's daughter,' he said again incredulously.

'Okay, I'll get back to you.'

'Thanks, mate. I can't wait.'

That settled, Blair felt more relaxed. He'd been worried Stan might have no interest in his half-brother's family, and he didn't want to disappoint Lou. The two men chatted for a bit, Stan reminiscing about his time in Vietnam which had taken him away from Pelican Crossing and his delight at being back again. As soon as he'd left, Blair sent a text to Lou to let her know Stan's reaction and confirm dinner that evening. He was glad he was going to be able to see her then. He'd missed his coffee in the café that morning, and even though he knew she'd be unlikely to join him, it always gave him a warm feeling to see her in the bookshop as he walked through.

*

Blair had been right. The yacht club was packed when Lou arrived, mostly families with young children. She glanced around, relieved when she saw Blair was already there, seated at a table in the far corner, close to the window. 'There he is,' she said to Iris and Violet, who had come over to the cottage earlier and taken a walk on the beach as she'd suggested. When she'd arrived home, Iris had been sitting on the front veranda, and Violet had been playing with Tilly, who was happy with her new friend.

They made their way across the club to join Blair, and Lou introduced them.

'I'm so pleased to meet you both,' Blair said, standing to greet them with a smile. 'I know how delighted Lou is that you're here.'

'Thanks,' Iris whispered while Violet tried to hide behind her mother.

'Let's all sit down,' Lou said, pulling out a chair. She sat next to Blair to allow Iris and Violet to sit together.

'This is nice,' Iris said glancing around. 'A popular spot.'

'Especially on a Friday night,' Blair agreed. 'I think half of Pelican Crossing is here tonight.'

'You may be right,' Lou said, catching sight of Rachel and Luke with her children and grandchildren and waving to her. She'd have a lot of explaining to do to her friend later.

'What would you like to eat?' Lou asked Violet who was now trying to hide behind a large menu. 'I'm going to order fish and chips.'

Violet smiled and pointed to the pizza on the children's menu.

When they had all ordered and been served wine for the grownups and juice for Violet, Blair said, 'Have we met before, Iris? I feel I've seen you somewhere.'

Iris blushed. 'In the library. I was looking up old school magazines and copies of the local paper for any mention of Mum. I didn't know about Dad then, that he'd grown up here too. You were on one of the other computers in the Heritage Room.'

'Of course!' Blair snapped his fingers. 'That's where it was. I spend a lot of my time there.'

'As I told you, it's thanks to Blair I found out about your mum,' Lou said. 'But you managed to find me too.' She smiled. 'Now, I believe Blair has something to tell you.' She turned to face Blair.

'I spoke to your dad's brother, Stan, today,' Blair said. 'He'd be delighted to meet you. He was thrilled to learn about you, and that you're here in Pelican Crossing. Anytime on the weekend suits him. He and I are neighbours, so we could meet at my villa… or somewhere public if you'd prefer.'

Iris looked across the table at Lou, as if seeking for guidance.

'It's up to you, Iris. Would you feel more comfortable meeting in a café?'

Iris nodded. 'It's a lot. First you, then this. I didn't even know dad had a brother.'

'How about the café at *Books and Coffee*?' Blair suggested. 'Then Lou will be close by if we need her.' He grinned at Lou, who smiled back. He was so thoughtful. A warm glow washed over her once again. She'd never known anyone quite like him. The sudden memory of his lips on hers made her blush.

'That would be good,' Iris said, clearly relieved. 'What's Stan like? Iris said he's a lot older than Dad.'

'Stan's in his eighties. He was a Vietnam Vet, left Pelican Crossing when he signed up and from what I can gather, wasn't back much till a few years ago. But he'll be able to tell you everything himself. He's a good guy. You'll like him.'

'It would be good for Vi to have… She never knew her dad… or her grandad.'

Lou tried not to wince. She may have forgiven her sister, but the memory of Darren still had the power to hurt her.

During dinner, Blair kept Iris and Violet amused by stories of his grandchildren and of his life growing up in Melbourne. They were interested to hear he shared their love of many special spots in the southern city.

'Blair's a lovely man,' Iris said, when they all got out of Lou's car back at the cottage. 'Are you and he…?'

'No, nothing like that. We're just friends,' Lou said, glad it was dark, because she was blushing furiously, remembering the kiss again. They hadn't been alone together since. Would he kiss her again, or had it been a spur of the moment thing because she was so upset?

'That's a pity.'

'Looking forward to tomorrow?' Lou asked, eager to change the subject.

'I think so. I still can't believe I have a new aunt *and* an uncle I didn't know existed. It's a lot for Vi to take in too. For all her life, there's only been Mum and me, now…'

'Now you have a family, and I have one too.' Lou hugged Iris and Violet as she said goodbye.

Lou's phone started ringing when she walked inside. She smiled to see Blair's number.

'I thought you might be home by now,' he said. 'Can I drop round for a nightcap? I promise I won't stay late.'

Lou's heart started pounding. A nightcap? Did that mean…?

'Lou? You there?'

'Yes… Yes,' she said. 'That would be lovely.'

A few minutes earlier, Lou had been looking forward to an early night. Now, she couldn't wait to see Blair. Would he kiss her? Would she kiss him? Did having a nightcap mean something more these days?

Lou rushed to the bathroom, threw water over her too-warm face and stared at herself in the mirror.

She needed a drink more than ever. She hoped the *nightcap* would be a strong one.

Forty

It had been a stroke of genius to call Lou last night, Blair thought, as he drove to *Books and Coffee* next morning. Stan had said he had a couple of things to do in town and would meet them there. Iris and Violet, who he must remember to call Vi, were making their own way to the café too.

When he'd arrived at Lou's cottage only a few minutes after he'd called, she'd greeted him at the door so warmly, he'd pulled her into his arms for a kiss which had gone on for some time. 'Sorry,' he'd said when they finally drew apart and became aware of Tilly glowering at them and hissing her annoyance at being ignored.

'Don't be... unless you were speaking to Tilly,' Lou said with a smile. 'You mentioned a nightcap?' She'd taken his hand and led him into the kitchen. 'I have wine, brandy, whisky and...' she picked up a bottle of Kahlua, '... this liqueur which the boys in the café gave me last Christmas and I haven't had occasion to open. It could go well with coffee.' Her cheeky smile had sent Blair's heart racing.

They'd each had a small glass of the liqueur with coffee and rehashed the evening, with Blair saying what a lovely pair Iris and Violet were and asking Lou how she was feeling about her sister's death now. He'd taken her into his arms again when her eyes moistened, and they'd remained like that for the rest of the evening. By the time he left, Blair had the feeling that their relationship had moved forward.

Today, he was feeling buoyant at the prospect of doing something else to help out by introducing Lou's niece to Stan. There was a swing in his step as he walked into the bookshop to experience the familiar warm glow at the sight of Lou standing behind the counter, a line of customers waiting to be served. The bookshop looked amazing with the brightly lit tree and garlands of tinsel scattered around the shelves. The soft music of Christmas carols added to the festive atmosphere… and there was still over a week to go till Christmas.

Blair grinned as Lou's eyes met his and he gave her a small wave before making his way to the café. There was no sign of the others, so he chose a table where he considered they wouldn't be disturbed and would be able to talk in private and ordered his usual long black. He added a plate of the caramel salted brownies he'd become addicted to, thinking the others might enjoy them too. Then he settled down to wait.

He didn't have to wait long. Stan was first to appear, seemingly on friendly terms with the two young men who ran the café. He ordered, then joined Blair. Only a few minutes later, Iris and Violet walked in and looked around cautiously. Iris smiled when she saw Blair. 'Sorry we're late,' she said. 'We decided to walk, and it took longer than I expected.'

'Not at all. We just got here. What can I get you?'

'Coffee for me – a flat white – and… Vi, what would you like?'

'Can I have a Coke?'

Iris frowned then nodded when Blair said, 'Maybe this once?'

When their drinks had arrived, and Blair had introduced Iris and Violet to Stan, Stan said, 'This is as much a shock to me as it must be to you. I had no idea…' He stroked his thinning white hair, his eyes moistening. 'Darren was only a nipper when I left for Vietnam, around your age, Vi,' he said to the little girl. 'I didn't really have a lot to do with him. And after Vietnam, I re-enlisted, spent the rest of my life in the forces, going from one conflict to another. When I got leave, home was Sydney. I got news from the oldies from time to time. It's how I knew Darren had gone to Melbourne. But I'm afraid I can't tell you any more about him.'

'Oh!' Iris appeared deflated. 'I'd hoped… being his brother…' She picked up her coffee.

'I'm sorry,' Stan said again. 'But I'm real glad to meet you, that you've come to Pelican Crossing. It's a good town. It was a good place to grow up.' He seemed to think for a few moments, then added, 'There might be some photos… of Darren. When I cleared out my folks' house, I packed some stuff into boxes to check out later. They're still sitting in the garage. If you like, I can take a look.'

'Oh, would you? And now I know Dad grew up here too, I plan to go back to the library. I should ask Aunt Lou if she has any old photos of Mum too. I never wondered why there were none of the two of them as children,' she said, almost to herself.

'Now we've met, I'd like it if we could keep in touch,' Stan said. 'How long do you intend to stay in Pelican Crossing?'

'We're here till after Christmas,' Iris replied.

'Wonderful. Maybe we can do a few things together? There are the Christmas carols on Christmas Eve, and *The Haven* is putting on a special Christmas splash.'

'Thanks. I'll have to see what Aunt Lou's plans are, but we'd love to spend some time with you too, wouldn't we, Vi?'

Violet, who'd been silent throughout the conversation, nodded, then asked, 'What should we call you?'

'How about Uncle Stan? I haven't been an uncle before.'

'Okay, Uncle Stan,' Violet said, as if trying the title out.

'Thanks,' Iris said. 'This visit is turning out to be full of surprises.'

*

Blair was eager to let Lou know how the meeting with Stan had gone, but the bookshop was busy when he walked through on his way out. Before Iris's arrival, he'd have suggested Lou meet him for dinner, but he knew she'd find out about the meeting with Stan from Iris.

Aware that Lou was spending her evenings with Iris and Violet, Blair had accepted an invitation from Joe to dine with him and Gill in their cottage at the end of the row where Lou lived. He was interested in seeing another of the cottages which intrigued him so much, and Joe had promised to show him some documents relating to their history. Also, if he was lucky, Lou might be home on her own by the time he left Joe's. He could always walk past to check.

From the outside, Joe's cottage looked similar to Lou's and Troy's, but when Blair walked in, he was surprised to see how different it was. Joe and his partner had renovated the inside of the cottage in a way which maintained its original character, creating an eco-friendly approach by recycling, repurposing and repairing materials wherever possible—just as the old fishermen had done.

'Not what you expected?' Joe laughed. 'We had a few battles about it. Gill favoured a more austere approach similar to her old apartment but she eventually saw sense, didn't you, sweetheart?'

Gill smiled. 'Joe persuaded me it made more sense to try to keep to the original design as much as possible, though I did draw the line at the kitchen and bathroom.'

'It looks good,' Blair said, 'and you mentioned some archives.'

'I looked out some documents to show you, but let's have a beer while Gill works her magic in the kitchen.'

Blair followed Joe through to a modern kitchen, where the chocolate labrador he'd met at *The Blue Dolphin* greeted him, her wet nose pushing into his hand. 'Hello there,' he said, ruffling the dog's ears and being rewarded by a low-pitched sound of pleasure.

It was an enjoyable evening. Over dinner, Blair learned about Pelican Crossing politics from Joe, while Gill expressed interest in Blair's time in Tasmania and his impressions of the town. When she learned Katrina was his daughter, she told him that, while she hadn't used her services, she couldn't praise the wellness centre highly enough. 'One of my friends works there too,' she said. 'Livvy's an amazing counsellor.'

'And another of our neighbours,' Joe said with a grin. 'I understand you already know Troy and Lou.'

Blair saw Gill react when Lou's name was mentioned.

'Weren't you helping Lou trace her sister? Did you manage to get a result?'

'It's up to Lou to share that with you. You'd best ask her.' Blair shifted uncomfortably in his seat, picked up his wine glass and drained it. He didn't know how much Lou wanted to share about Fleur and Iris, of how well she and Gill knew each other. Though he was fast discovering what a small community Pelican Crossing was, he didn't want to do or say anything which would upset Lou.

Dinner over, Joe took Blair into his study, where they pored over copies of old maps and plans showing the history of this part of Pelican

Crossing. 'These shacks were built in the eighteen hundreds to house local fishermen and their families,' Joe explained. 'Initially, they were simple shelters built from salvaged materials, evolving over time into more substantial structures while retaining their distinct character, as we've tried to do with this one.'

'Wow!' Blair couldn't hide his admiration. What he'd give to live in one of these, instead of the impersonal villa in *The Haven* which had no history.

When he finally left Joe and Gill, it was with a promise to catch up again. Joe had mentioned a neighbourhood get-together planned for closer to Christmas, which he thought Blair would enjoy even if he didn't live there. Blair didn't make any promises about that, preferring to wait to see if Lou mentioned it to him.

It was as he was leaving, that Joe surprised Blair by saying, 'Of course, the cyclone may put paid to all our plans.'

'The cyclone? I thought it was farther north?'

'It was, but the latest prediction is that it has changed direction and may come closer to us. Best to keep an eye on it.'

'Thanks.' Blair hoped Joe was wrong. Hadn't Lou told him they never got cyclones this far south?

As he'd planned, before getting into his car, he walked down past Lou's cottage, disappointed to see it was all in darkness. Realising that he'd been standing there for way too long, staring at Lou's front door, recalling their kisses, the way Lou responded so warmly, and not wanting to appear as a stalker should anyone pass by, Blair chuckled to himself and headed back to his car with a smile on his face, looking forward to kissing those gorgeous lips again.

Forty-one

Lou was anxious to find out how Iris's meeting with Stan had gone. She'd seen first Blair, then Iris and Violet, pass through the bookshop on their way out, but had been tied up with customers. All she could do was meet their eyes apologetically and keep a smile on her face. She was glad she'd arranged to see Iris and Violet again that evening. She'd find out then.

Back home, Lou had just put Tilly's food bowl down when her phone rang. She wasn't surprised to see it was Rachel. She'd been expecting her friend to get in touch since she'd seen her at the yacht club with Blair, Iris and Violet. She took a seat at the kitchen table and answered the call.

'Hi Rach, how are you?'

'I'm good, but how are you? And who was that with you and Blair at the yacht club last night? I couldn't believe my eyes. Does he have another daughter, besides Katrina?'

Lou sighed, but Rachel would have to know sometime, and she had known she was trying to find Fleur. But she'd hoped to keep Iris and Violet as her secret for a little bit longer. 'He does, but that wasn't her we were with. It was Fleur's daughter and granddaughter.'

There was a stunned silence on the other end of the phone, then Rachel said, 'Oh, you found her. I'm so pleased for you. But why wasn't she there too? Is she sick, too infirm to travel?'

'Rach…' Lou's voice broke, '… Fleur's dead.' It was only the second time she'd said it out loud and it sounded harsh, even to her own ears.

'Oh, Lou! I'm so sorry. Is there anything I can do? I know what it feels like to lose a sister.'

Lou shook her head, then realising Rachel couldn't see her, said, 'No, but thanks. It was a shock.'

'Oh, Lou!' Rachel said again. Rachel could understand her suffering, having lost her own sister… but *they* hadn't been estranged.

'I just wish I'd been in time, that I'd found her before…'

'Of course you do.' She was silent for a moment. 'Her daughter and granddaughter? How did that happen?'

'It seems Fleur told Iris about me on her deathbed, asked her to come to apologise to me for her.'

'Wow! Heavy!'

'Yeah!'

'So, what's she like, your niece?'

'I'm still getting used to the fact I have a niece, but she's lovely, and her daughter is a dear. By coincidence, Iris is a librarian like I used to be. She reminds me of Fleur but doesn't look like either her or Darren. She's met Stan too now, Darren's half-brother.'

'How did that go? Liz says he's a good guy.'

'I don't really know him. He's a friend of Blair's.' Lou bit her tongue, wishing she hadn't mentioned Blair and given Rachel something else to comment on. But, to her relief, her friend didn't pick up on it. 'I'm seeing Iris again tonight, so I'll find out then. The good news, Rach, is that she'll be here for Christmas, she and Violet.'

'How lovely for you. Well, I should let you go now. Do you want me to keep quiet about this?'

'There's probably no need. Their presence in Pelican Crossing isn't a secret. Half the town most likely knows already.'

Rachel chuckled. 'You're probably right. Be sure to let me know if there's anything I can do.'

'Thanks, Rach, I will.' Lou finished the call with a smile. Rachel was a good friend, and she'd known Fleur. She was the one person among Lou's friends and acquaintances, who'd understand what Fleur's death and Iris's arrival in town meant to her.

By the time Iris and Violet arrived, Lou had showered and changed into a comfortable pair of jeans and a linen shirt. She was segmenting a roast chicken she'd picked up on the way home when she heard them at the door.

Hurrying to open it, Lou greeted them with hugs, trying to stifle her curiosity about their meeting with Stan. She needn't have bothered because Iris immediately said, 'Thanks so much for introducing me to your friend and having him arrange for us to meet my uncle. Stan's a lovely man. It feels so strange. A few weeks ago, it was just Mum, me and Vi. Now Mum's gone, and I have an aunt and uncle.'

'So it went well?'

'Very well. We plan to meet again, and he's going to look out some photos of Dad when he was growing up. I don't suppose…' She gave Lou a pleading look.

Lou winced. She should have thought that Iris would want to know what Fleur had been like as a child. 'I have some photos of your mum somewhere. I can look them out too.' There was no need to tell Iris that for years she hadn't been able to look at them, to see her sister's face.

'Thanks.'

'Not a problem,' Lou said, realising that she too was curious to see those photos again.

'You can't keep feeding us,' Iris said, when they were enjoying the chicken and salad Lou had served. 'Let me treat you next time.'

'It's no trouble, and you are family.' Lou couldn't believe how good it made her feel to be able to say that.

'Still. Let me take you to dinner tomorrow evening. I've heard *Crossings* is the best place in town to eat.'

'It is, but…'

'No, I insist.'

'Okay.' Lou smiled. In some ways, Iris was just like Fleur, determined to get her own way, but in her case, it was because of her concern for others, not herself.

'I like your friend,' Iris said as she and Violet were leaving. 'Would you like to bring him along to dinner tomorrow?'

'Oh, no. We're not… It wouldn't be…' Lou felt flustered. 'Thanks, but no.'

She thought Iris gave her a strange look. 'Okay,' she said.

It was still early when Iris and Violet left, and Lou considered pulling down the boxes from the attic which she knew contained the old photo albums. She'd stashed them up there after her parents died, meaning to go through them one day. Now Iris wanted to see photos of Fleur, it seemed that day had come, and Lou was more curious than ever to see them again. But not tonight. Lou sighed, gave Tilly a cuddle, and headed to bed where, as she drifted off to sleep, images of a smiling Blair floated behind her eyes, and she wondered when they would manage to be alone together again.

Forty-two

Lou beamed when Blair walked into the bookshop next morning at his usual time. Being Sunday, it was quieter than usual and there were only a few people browsing the shelves.

'Time for coffee?' he asked, smiling when Lou nodded.

In the café, Ron grinned to see them sitting together. 'Not too busy this morning, Lou?' he asked.

'Taking a well-earned break. It's good to have the chance to relax.'

'Enjoy it while you can.'

'You work too hard,' Blair said, when they'd been served. 'I feel tired watching you with all those customers.'

'It's what keeps me going.' Even as she spoke, Lou realised it was no longer true. For years, the bookshop and Tilly were her life. But now there was Iris and Violet… and Blair. She looked at the man sitting opposite, amazed at how quickly he'd changed from being a stranger to becoming part of her life.

'Penny for them?'

'I was just thinking how my life has changed so much in the past few weeks… meeting you… then Iris and Violet.'

'I can understand how finding your sister's family has had an impact on you. I'm happy to hear you mention me too.'

'Of course. Without you, I might never have found them.'

'They did find you.'

'You're right.' But Lou knew she owed a lot to Blair. He had been the catalyst which had changed her life, he and the photo on Troy's fridge. Before then, she'd been looking at the years ahead in despair, wondering what she was going to do when she could no longer manage the bookshop. Blair was so proactive, swimming every morning, researching his family history and writing a book. He had shown her there was a life after retirement.

Had she become too self-absorbed, too set in her ways? Had it taken meeting Blair, the news of Fleur's death and the arrival in town of Iris and Violet to pull her out of it?

'Thanks,' she said, 'for being my friend, for helping me see I could have something to look forward to.'

'I'm not sure what…'

'You've shown me retirement might not be so bad, and meeting Iris has given me an idea.'

Blair appeared puzzled.

'It was something that came to me last night, when I was having trouble sleeping. It may be crazy, but can I run it past you?'

'Please do.'

'It goes back to when I was working as a librarian. I always loved books and wanted to own my own bookshop, so I saved madly. It took me years to establish *Books and Coffee*, but recently, I've wondered what I'll do when I can no longer manage. I'm not getting any younger and my back and feet are beginning to give out.' She grimaced.

'I'm with you so far. I often have problems with my back too. It's a sign of getting older, but we're both still fit.'

'I agree, but I won't always be able to spend all day every day on my feet as I do now. This busy Christmas period has shown me that. It was when Iris said that owning a bookshop had always been her dream too, that the seed of an idea took root. I suppose, subconsciously, I've been thinking about it ever since, but I haven't put it into words till now.'

'You mean…?'

'It's the perfect solution. Iris and Violet move to Pelican Crossing and when I'm ready to retire, she can take over from me. In the meantime, she can either get a job in the local library or learn the ropes in the bookshop. What do you think?'

'I think it's a brilliant idea. Have you mentioned it to Iris?'

'Not yet.' Lou's smile disappeared. 'What if she doesn't like it, doesn't want to move here? It's very different from Melbourne. She says she loves Pelican Crossing, but being here on holiday is very different from living here. And there's Violet – she's only ten, she has her school, her friends. Iris may not want to uproot her.'

'There's only one way to find out.'

Lou nodded. 'I thought I'd ask her tonight. We're having dinner at *Crossings*, her treat. She's such a lovely girl. I still have to pinch myself when I remember she's now part of my life.'

'Good luck.' Blair covered Lou's hand with his, sending shivers down her spine.

'Thanks,' she said, placing her other hand on top of his. He really was such a lovely man.

*

Lou had psyched herself up to make her suggestion to Iris, unsure how she would react. But everything she'd planned to say flew out of her head when she saw the distraught expression on Iris's face.

'What's the matter? Has something happened?' she asked, trying to imagine what had changed her from the cheerful woman who'd left the cottage last night.

'We're going to have to go back to Melbourne.'

'What?' Lou's heart sank. All she could think of was that she'd be alone for Christmas again.

'We have to move out of the motel. Evidently the storm we had damaged the roof which will leak next time it rains, and the owners need us to vacate. They've been very nice about it, refunding all we paid, and ringing around to try to find us alternative accommodation, but everywhere else is booked, so…' Iris lifted her hands in the air. 'I'm so sorry. I was looking forward to spending Christmas with you.'

Without thinking, Lou said, 'You can move in with me. I have spare rooms I never use. There's no need for you to leave… unless you'd rather…'

'Of course not. We've love to, wouldn't we, Vi?'

Violet nodded enthusiastically.

'That's settled then,' Lou said, before she could regret her offer. What was she thinking, inviting Iris and Violet to stay with her, in her cottage, her private space? It would be a disruption to her routine, to Tilly. But Iris was Fleur's daughter, and Violet was her granddaughter. They were family.

Forty-three

Blair paused and gazed into space, the memory of the call from Lou the previous evening interrupting his flow of thought. Since he'd completed his search for Lou's sister, he'd been making progress with the novel he'd been dreaming about for years. Prue would be pleased, though she'd never really believed he'd do it. But Lou's call, plus the news on the radio this morning, had destroyed his concentration. How could he focus on the plight of the early convicts and colonists when Lou's life was about to be turned around, and a cyclone was approaching the coast?

Blair was on his way out of *The Haven*, driving carefully and keeping to the 10k limit, when he saw Stan walking towards him. He stopped and lowered the window.

'Thanks again for helping me meet Iris and Violet,' Stan said. 'I'm still reeling from the fact Darren had a daughter, and none of us knew. Mum would have loved to have had a granddaughter to fuss over.' He sighed. 'I guess he was too embarrassed to come back after what he did. I hope they were happy, he and Lou's sister.'

'Lou said they were, or so Iris told her. It makes you wonder, though.' He thought of his own happy marriage, the way his family had always got together for birthdays and Christmases until his parents and Prue's passed away. They had been occasions for rejoicing, for their girls to be spoiled rotten by their grandparents. It wasn't only the grandparents who'd missed out. Iris had too.

Stan must have been thinking the same, because he said, 'I intend to do my best to make it up to them while they're here. Thought I'd drop round to that motel they're staying in today, maybe take them out to lunch.'

'Good idea, but they're moving. Some problem with the roof. They're going to be staying with Lou. You know where that is? She lives in one of those cottages on the other side of the harbour.'

'I know them. Thanks for the heads up. Guess the motel has storm damage like a lot of other places. We were lucky here.' He lifted his gaze to the surroundings of *The Haven*, where the only damage had been a couple of fronds dropping from the palm trees at the entrance.

'Too right. You heard the news… about the cyclone?'

'Yeah, but these meteorologists don't know everything. We don't get cyclones this far south. Just look at that sky.' He gestured to the clear blue of the sky with not a cloud to be seen.

'Hope you're right. Have a good time with Iris and Violet.'

'Thanks, will do.'

Blair drove on, feeling more reassured. Stan grew up here. Surely he knew as much as the guy on the radio, if not more.

When Blair walked into the bookshop, he was surprised to see it wasn't as busy as it had been the previous week. There was no line of customers at the counter, and Zoe appeared to be taking advantage of the lull to reorganise the display of Christmas books. When he approached Lou and suggested coffee, she was quick to agree.

'Where are all your customers today?' he asked, when they were settled in the café with coffee and the inevitable salted caramel brownies which he was sure were contributing to an increase in his weight. He'd need to buy a larger size in pants if he continued to indulge in them.

'I guess they've been listening to the news of the cyclone,' Lou said, her forehead creasing. 'I checked the Bureau of Meteorology site this morning and it does look as if we're in the target zone. Let's hope it changes direction and goes out to sea. But if it hasn't by tonight, we'd be wise to take precautions.'

'I spoke with Stan this morning. He didn't think it would hit here.'

'I hope he's right. He's probably counting on the fact we don't have them this far south, but the climate seems to have changed so much, we can't be sure.'

Despite having been reassured by Stan, Blair felt stirrings of concern, more insistent than when he heard mention of the cyclone on the radio… and he remembered Joe saying something about it too.

'What should we do?'

'Wait and see. Keep watching and listening to the news. Check your phone for warnings. I was in Cairns years ago when one was predicted, and I remember how scared I was, the tense atmosphere. I was lucky. I managed to get a flight home before it hit.'

'Right.' He could do that. 'On another topic. Stan plans to catch up with Iris and Violet today. I told him they were moving to your cottage. Hope that was okay.'

'Of course. They should be there by now. I gave Iris a key. Tilly will be delighted to have company during the day, and she's bonded with Violet. She'll miss them when they leave.'

'You will too. You still intend to ask Iris about moving here?'

'I do, but I want to pick my time, maybe wait till this cyclone scare is over.'

'Mmm.' Blair thought Iris would jump at the idea. It was a perfect solution for her and her daughter. But what did he know? They had a life back in Melbourne, which they might not want to leave, and as Lou had already pointed out, young Violet was only ten, and had her school and her friends there. He remembered how reluctant he'd been to leave Tasmania. But it had worked out well, better than he could have hoped, he thought, glancing across at Lou.

*

Lou was glad she'd managed to take time to have coffee with Blair this morning. While she'd been delighted the bookshop had been so busy, she'd missed their morning chats over coffee more than she'd expected. As they chatted about the prospect of the cyclone and Iris and Violet moving into her cottage, she thought how much her life had changed in just a few months. It seemed only yesterday that she'd been dreading the approach of yet another Christmas she'd spend alone, while now she'd have her family with her, a family she hadn't known existed. And there was Blair…

'Why don't you join us for dinner?' she asked, when they had finished their coffee and the brownies he seemed to love. She did too but tried to limit her intake of them. 'I'm not sure what it'll be, but…'

'I'd love to, and don't worry about cooking anything. I can bring fish and chips again. Do you think Iris and Violet would like that?'

Lou grinned. 'Who doesn't like fish and chips?'

Lou returned to the bookshop with a smile on her face, and the hope that her life was about to change for ever… if Iris agreed to her proposal. But she knew she'd have to be careful, to choose her moment wisely, give her time to become used to being here in Pelican Crossing, maybe even ask for her help in the bookshop. With these thoughts swirling through her head, the rest of the day passed quickly and she was putting the closed sign on the door before she knew it.

It was a strange experience to return home to find Iris and Violet already settled in, and Tilly happily ensconced on Violet's lap. The cat leapt down when she saw Lou and padded towards her, but it was clear Lou was no longer her favourite person. 'I'm glad you got here okay,' she said. 'Blair is coming round later and bringing fish and chips.' She looked out the window to where there was still a vestige of sunlight. 'How about a walk along the beach before he arrives? It's still light enough.'

'Yay!' Violet said.

'We fed Tilly. I guessed where you'd keep the cat food. I want us to do what we can to help, not be a burden,' Iris said.

'You're family. You could never be a burden. Just let me freshen up and put on a pair of sandals.'

A few minutes later, they crossed the road and made their way down to the beach. The tide was out, and it was a perfect evening with only a light breeze ruffling their hair and the ocean.

'Stan came round to see us,' Iris said. 'He brought photos of Dad. He was handsome as a young man.'

'Mmm.' Lou didn't want to think of the handsome young man who'd stolen her heart, but to her surprise, thinking of him didn't hurt the way it used to. Maybe she was finally in recovery and could forgive Darren too.

'Look!' Violet said. 'Isn't that the old lady with the dog we saw last time, Mum?'

Looking along the beach, Lou saw a solitary figure, her long white hair blowing in the breeze, her skirt trailing in the water. A dog was running ahead, then stopping to wait for her. 'It's old Agnes,' she said. 'We don't often see her here. She usually walks on the dog beach.'

The woman drew closer, then stopped. 'So, you're Fleur's daughter,' she said, peering at Iris. 'And you decided to forget the past?' she said to Lou. 'There are good times ahead if you follow your heart, not always an easy thing to do. And be sure to take care.' She glanced up at the sky as she said this.

Lou's eyes followed hers, but all she could see was the changing colours of the setting sun. It was a sight that always delighted Lou and made her glad to be alive.

'Thanks,' Lou said, realising that old Agnes was now walking away. 'You take care too.'

Back in the cottage, Lou looked out some of her old childhood books for Violet, while Iris leafed through the photo albums Lou had retrieved from the attic. When Blair arrived, Lou was sitting with Iris and Violet sharing memories of times when she and Fleur were growing up in Pelican Crossing.

'Hope I'm not interrupting,' he said, clearly seeing the albums strewn across the floor.

'Not at all. We can do this anytime. Mmm, smells good. We should eat while everything's hot.'

Before long, they were seated outside in the courtyard with plates filled with fish and chips, Tilly prowling around their ankles meowing loudly.

'To family,' Lou said, holding up her glass of white wine.

'To family,' the others chorused, Iris and Blair doing the same with their glasses and Violet with her glass of milk.

'And new beginnings,' Lou added, meeting Blair's eyes. How would it be to be able to do this as often as she wanted? She couldn't wait to tell Iris her idea, but something held her back.

'I'd like to catch the news,' Blair said, when they'd finished eating, 'check on the cyclone.'

'You don't really think we're at risk?' Lou asked.

'I spoke with Joe Harris this afternoon – he's the local mayor,' he said to Iris.

'And a neighbour of mine,' Lou added.

'Anyway, he said we should be prepared. He's putting together guidelines for the community. They'll be in tomorrow's edition of *The Echo*.'

'Oh!' Lou felt her first flicker of fear. This couldn't be happening. The cyclone couldn't reach here, could it?

They went inside, and Lou turned on the television. Violet was the only one who wasn't concerned, having found a ball of wool to tease Tilly with. She and the cat were loving the game.

The three grownups chatted, only falling silent to listen intently when the weather man appeared, standing in front of the map of Australia.

'The cyclone has drifted farther south than was originally predicted. It's now gathering strength and turning the screws on the Queensland coast. Tropical Cyclone Zara is now predicted to make landfall anywhere between Bundaberg and northern NSW later this week. The Australian Bureau of Meteorology has warned it may bring severe hazards and dangerous and life-threatening flash flooding. Make sure you're prepared and have a grab-and-go kit that you can carry by yourself if authorities suddenly tell you to evacuate immediately.'

'What's a grab-and-go kit? And will we have to evacuate? Where will we go?' Iris's eyes widened.

'Joe told me it's all in hand,' Blair said. 'Tomorrow's *Echo* will have all the information we need to prepare for the worst, and where the evacuation centres will be. And the council is planning to set up a disaster dashboard on their website. We just need to keep checking.'

'Surely it won't come to that?' Lou said, conscious she had the bookshop and café to take care of, as well as the cottage.

'Hopefully not, but better to be safe than sorry.'

They were feeling very sombre when Blair turned off the television. 'Would anyone like tea or coffee… or something stronger?' Lou asked.

'Not for me. Violet and I have had a busy day. It's her bedtime and I think I'll turn in too,' Iris said.

'I hope you sleep well,' Lou said, giving her and Violet a hug.

When they'd left, Blair said, 'I wouldn't say no to a small whisky.'

'Sounds good to me.' It might calm her and help stem the panic she'd felt at the realisation that the cyclone might really cross the coast at Pelican Crossing.

'I'll get it. Just tell me where.'

'Thanks. The cupboard next to the sink.'

Blair disappeared to reappear a few minutes later carrying two not-so-small measures of whisky. 'This should do it.' he said, sitting down beside Lou on the sofa and putting an arm around her shoulders. 'Remember this is all a precaution. From what I can gather, cyclones are difficult to predict, and while we may get hit, we may just as easily escape the worst of it.'

With Blair's arm around her shoulders, his warm body close to hers, all thought of the approaching cyclone disappeared. Lou felt safe, safe in the knowledge he cared for her, that her niece and grandniece were asleep in her spare room and Christmas was just around the corner, the sort of Christmas she could only have dreamt about. She took a sip of her whisky, relaxing as the warmth spread through her chest.

'Thanks, Blair,' she said, snuggling into him.

'For what?' he asked.

'Oh, just for being you.'

Forty-four

Next morning, Blair rose early as usual, ready for his morning swim. The sky was clear, the sun bright, a slightly stronger breeze than usual the only indication there might be a change in the weather.

He picked up a copy of *The Echo* on the way home, eager to see what it had to say, and there it was on the front page, a headline which read, *Tropical cyclone Zara intensifies on path to Qld coast.*

Trust the newspaper to use scare tactics, he thought, before reading on to discover that the headline was an accurate summary of reports from the Bureau of Meteorology. Inside the paper was a call for volunteers to assist the SES (State Emergency Service) with filling and distributing sandbags to those most at risk, with a list of low-lying properties. There was also a list of steps to take to prepare for the cyclone crossing the coast.

Worried, he hurried home for breakfast but found it difficult to concentrate. If the cyclone really *was* heading this way, he wanted to do something. Maybe he could volunteer to help with the sandbags. Undecided, he stepped outside to see Stan leaving the next-door villa.

'Stan!' he called.

'Morning, Blair. I was just checking in with Joan, to make sure she'd heard the news. You see the paper?'

'Just did. I thought I might volunteer my services.'

'With sandbags? It's a young man's game, mate. Better to check all the residents in *The Haven* are prepared. Not everyone is as fit as we are. You can help by going around the doors. Ewan and Fred are on it too. Shouldn't take us long. We can help bring in outdoor furniture and make sure they keep watching the news and listening to the radio to check the cyclone's progress and if there's a need to evacuate.'

'Righto!' Blair locked up and started knocking on his neighbours' doors. At first, if felt a little odd to be warning people of a cyclone, when it was a lovely summer day, and some residents resented his interference. But most were grateful, and he was able to assist a few of the more infirm to move their outdoor settings either closer to the villa or into the garage. By the time he met up with the others, he'd introduced himself to many of the residents he hadn't met before, and decided that if nothing came of the cyclone, at least the exercise had been worthwhile in that regard.

'We're heading into town for a beer at *The Grand*. Join us?' Stan asked.

Blair was tempted, but he had something more important to do. 'Not this time,' he said.

Back at his villa, he picked up the paper. First, he'd make sure he was prepared, then he'd check in with Lou to see how she was feeling this morning.

*

Iris was sitting in the kitchen staring at the headline in the paper when Lou walked in. 'It's really happening,' she said, a tremor in her voice. 'What are we going to do?'

'Oh, Iris, I'm sorry. If I hadn't invited you to stay, you'd have been safely back in Melbourne by now. It may not be too late for you to leave.' She'd be devastated to lose her and Violet, just as they were getting to know each other, but this wasn't about her. Lou would never forgive herself if anything happened to them, because she'd asked them to stay.

'Don't be silly. Of course we're going to stay.' Iris's voice strengthened, making her sound exactly like Fleur. 'I'm not going to let you face this on your own. Vi and I can help get prepared while you're at work. There's a list here of what to do.' She opened the paper and read, '*Be sure to have enough non-perishable food for five to seven days, water for drinking and cleaning, any medications, toiletries and first-aid kit, pet food, torches, batteries, protective clothing and closed-in shoes, cash in small denominations, valuable documents such as passports, title deeds, ID, insurance details, photos.* It suggests filling the bath for water to flush the toilet and clean, and to move outdoor furniture and plants. Also to have a battery-operated radio in case the power goes off.'

'I can't let you…'

'Of course you can. We're family… remember?'

Despite the unfolding disaster, Lou felt a sense of contentment she hadn't experienced for years, decades even. She'd accept Iris's help. It was what families did. Lou had been on her own for so long, she'd forgotten what it was like to have someone other than herself to depend on. 'If you're sure,' she said.

'I'm sure. Now, I made French toast for Vi and me, and there's plenty, so help yourself.'

'Thanks.' Lou made herself a cup of lemon and ginger tea and joined Iris at the table, reaching for the paper which Iris had set down. 'May I?' she asked.

'Of course. I've read it so often, I think I know it off by heart. Vi and I will go shopping this morning and maybe catch up with you in the bookshop around lunchtime. Will that be okay?'

'Of course. Depending on how busy we are, I may not be able to join you.'

'No problem. I want to check in on Uncle Stan too, see if he needs any help. He's a lot older and…'

'I understand, though I believe he has a lady friend at *The Haven*. She lives next door to Blair.' Even as she spoke, Lou silently berated herself for being a gossipmonger, knowing how much she hated being the butt of gossip herself.

'Really?' Iris grinned, the cyclone seemingly forgotten for a moment.

*

The bookshop was surprisingly busy. Lou had thought people would be preparing for the cyclone, but it seemed they were more interested in talking about it than in making preparations – or in buying books.

When Blair appeared, a little later than usual, it was easy to slip away to the café, which, like the bookshop, seemed to have attracted locals and tourists eager to discuss the news.

'Did you see the paper?' Blair asked as soon as they were seated and had ordered coffee – no brownies today; neither of them was hungry.

Lou nodded. 'Iris had it at breakfast. She's offered to help me prepare, probably shopping right now.' She glanced around. 'I'm not sure about the shop…'

'I can help you there, and I'm sure Ron and Denny will muck in.'

'Great. How could she have forgotten the two young men who were always eager to help out in any way they could. '*The Haven?*'

'All good there. A few of us went around this morning to ensure everyone was aware and offer assistance to those who needed it. We're on higher ground than you are.'

'Surely…' Lou wasn't sure what she was going to say. She had a sudden image of high waves sweeping across the road and water pouring into her little cottage. Lou had always loved the fact she was so close to the ocean, but now it might not be such a safe location. She didn't want to think about it.

'If there's anything I can do to help…'

'Thanks. You're a good friend, Blair, but… Oh, there is something. The table and chairs in the courtyard. They might be too heavy for Iris to handle. If you could…'

'Consider it done. Will she be home this afternoon?'

'I expect so. She said she'd come in here for lunch, so I can let her know then.'

Suddenly, it seemed, the café emptied, and an air of expectancy hung over them, broken by Denny saying, 'I'm heading out. Ron can manage on his own here now. They've been calling for volunteers to help the SES. I want to do my bit.'

As the door swung shut behind him, Blair gave a sigh. 'I'd be joining them if I was younger, but…'

'You're doing what you can.' Greatly daring, Lou put her hand on his. 'Don't put yourself down. What about Katrina? How is she coping? It's school holidays, isn't it?'

'You're right. I can help out there too. I promised to take the kids to see the pelican feeding. That should still be on. Maybe Violet would like to join us. She and Harper are the same age.'

'What a good idea. It will free up Iris too. I seem to have a lot to thank you for.'

'As always, it's not a problem. I'm happy to be of help.'

*

The cottage seemed full of people when Lou arrived home. Not only were Iris and Violet there, the latter excited at having made a new friend in Blair's granddaughter, Harper. Blair was there too, and Joe.

'What's up? What are you doing here, Joe?' she asked.

'We need to cancel the neighbourhood get-together on Saturday. It's too risky with the reports we're getting of the cyclone, and I decided to drop in on everyone in the row to make sure you know the drill. Seems like you guys are all set, he said, nodding towards Blair and Iris.

'Thanks, Joe. I think we are. I've been helping Iris with all the heavy stuff,' Blair said.

'And I've filled the bath with water and been to the shops for supplies. It's amazing how quickly the shelves have become empty, the bread was almost all gone, and I managed to get the last pack of toilet paper,' Iris said. 'People are going crazy.'

'The government has promised to arrange for distribution centres to work overtime to restock,' Joe said, 'but it's good to know. Gill and I have been working all day, though she did plan to make a quick trip to the shops in her lunch hour. You will keep an eye on the council website?'

'Sure thing,' Blair answered for all of them. 'And I'll be dividing my time between here and my daughter's, though she has her husband to help take care of things.'

'Iris and I will be fine. We don't need a man to take care of us,' Lou said, adding, 'Though it's good of you to help,' when she saw Blair's crestfallen expression. While she appreciated his help, she'd managed on her own for years – she'd had to.

'I'm sorry about Saturday, Joe,' she said. She'd been looking forward to it. It had been her friend, Livvy, who had instigated their regular get-togethers on the beach, and they were always a good opportunity to let off steam with a group of friends. Even with all the flurry and news about the cyclone, it hadn't occurred to her that their neighbourhood gathering would be affected. 'Maybe we can do something after it's all over?'

'I hope so. If the cyclone does cross the coast here at high tide, you need to be ready to evacuate, and there may be no beach left afterwards.'

It was a sobering thought. Lou scanned the large open area of her cottage. What would happen to it if all the predictions were correct? It didn't bear thinking about. 'Thanks for coming round, Joe,' she said. 'Can I offer you a drink?'

'Thanks, but no. I still have a few more people to see, then I need to make sure Gill and I are prepared too – as prepared as we can be.'

They were all silent for a few moments when Joe had left. Iris was first to speak. 'I've filled the pantry with tinned foods in case of a power cut and cooked a pork leg roast for tonight. There should be enough left for sandwiches in case…'

'You'll stay for dinner, Blair?' Lou asked.

'Thanks. We should watch the news first to check…'

While Lou showered and changed, and Iris set the table, Blair had turned on the television. They were all huddled around it when the weather report began.

'Cyclone Zara has slowed down while tracking towards land and is predicted to cross later than expected, bringing fresh dangers. Millions across Queensland are bracing for the impact and sheltering in their homes as the cyclone edges towards the coast. The cyclone's slowdown may prolong the nervous waiting game for millions of residents in two states, as the first effects are starting to be felt. Early on Thursday, heavy spurts of rain and sudden gusts are expected to hit the small coastal towns of Pelican Crossing and Bellbird Bay where some predictions have Zara making landfall. The slow-moving category three system is right now 325 kilometres north of Brisbane and is currently moving at just ten kilometers an hour.'

When the screen changed to show the sports reporter, Blair turned off the television, and they all stared at each other. Lou's stomach churned. What had seemed an impossibility had suddenly become very real.

'Are you okay?' Blair asked.

'I think so. I guess we should get some of those sandbags they're filling and… what about the shop?'

'Maybe there too, and you can have Ron and Denny tape the windows.'

'I can do the ones here,' Iris offered.

'Mmm.' Lou couldn't think straight.

They sat down to eat but, despite the delicious aroma of the roast pork, no one was hungry. Even Violet seemed to have been affected by the tension in the room. Afterwards, Iris put Violet to bed, and Lou and Blair sat together on the sofa.

'Are you sure you want to stay here?' Blair asked, his arm around Lou's shoulders. 'You heard the news, what Joe said. It would be safer for you at *The Haven*. There's room for Iris and Violet too.'

'No, I want to stay here, but maybe Iris and Violet…' Regardless of the potential danger, Lou knew she couldn't leave, not unless she was forced to by an evacuation order.

'Okay,' Blair said, but Lou could see he wasn't pleased. It was good of him to be concerned, but this was her home, and she'd worked hard to establish herself here.

'Will you close the shop?'

'Maybe.' Lou was struggling with what she should do, but concern for her employees might be the deciding factor. They had homes to take care of too… and families. 'I'll give it a couple of days.'

When Blair left that night, his hug seemed tighter than usual, and his kiss more tender than before. After he'd gone, Lou stood, her arms wrapped around herself and stared up at the clear sky. The moon and stars twinkled just like they always did. It was difficult to believe the warnings, difficult to imagine all this changing.

Forty-five

The next few days passed uneventfully. Apart from the news on television, there were no signs of the cyclone's approach, but everyone was on edge, waiting for it to happen.

The bookshop had become busy again, this time with people stocking up on books to read in the event of a power cut. Jigsaws were also popular, with many looking for ways to occupy themselves if they were stuck at home with no television.

Ron and Denny had worked hard at making sure the shop and café were as secure as possible for the dangerous weather which was expected to intensify as Zara approached the coast, but so far there was no sign of it. The waiting was making everyone tense, and tempers were frayed. It was difficult to look forward to Christmas with the threat of the cyclone hanging over everything. Even the Christmas carols which still played in the bookshop failed to raise people's spirits.

When Thursday arrived, Lou was home with Iris and Violet who had refused Blair's offer too. Lou had closed *Books and Coffee* until further notice, telling her staff to stay home and look after themselves. She could only hope it would survive whatever the weather gods sent them. All they could do now was wait.

Lou and Iris spent the day keeping Violet occupied with jigsaws and games of Scrabble, snap and checkers. Blair texted several times. He had given in to Katrina's urgings and left his villa to join them. They were all waiting too and with two children to keep busy, they must be more anxious than Lou and Iris.

Finally, the day was over, and still no sign of the cyclone – apart from a few gusts of wind. Violet had gone to bed, but neither Lou nor Iris felt they could settle. They'd been on tenterhooks all day, too worried to speak about what was in the forefront of both of their minds – *what would they do when the cyclone hit?* The local sports hall had been designated as the main evacuation centre for the town and, as instructed, they had prepared bags of essential items – the grab-and-go kits Iris had wondered about. They were sitting by the door, ready to be picked up if necessary.

'I think we need a drink,' Lou said, going to the kitchen and pouring two measures of whisky. 'It may be a bit strong,' she said to Iris as she handed her a glass, 'but it's what we need to get us through this. I doubt we'll sleep tonight and… if it does hit, goodness knows when we'll get a decent sleep again.'

'I'm glad I'm here… with you,' Iris said, as she curled her feet under her in one of Lou's armchairs. Lou was seated more sedately in the other one, clasping her glass in both hands. She was remembering another time she'd sat like this. She had been with Blair in his villa, and she'd just heard that her sister was dead. It was the night he'd first kissed her. It had only been just over a week ago, but so much had happened since then. She was lost in thought, when Iris spoke.

'There's something you never told me, Aunt Lou.'

'What's that?'

'What did Mum want to apologise for? It must have been something dreadful for you to have returned all her letters.'

Lou flinched. She'd hoped Iris would never ask her this, would have been satisfied to know Fleur had her forgiveness. She stared across the room, lit only by the Christmas tree in the corner, bought at Violet's urging and providing Tilly with endless pleasure, and took a deep breath. 'It was all so long ago. Darren and I were in the same year at school. Fleur was younger, my little sister. We – Darren and I – were dating, had been for some time. It had started when he invited me to the Year Twelve formal and by the time we were in our twenties everyone expected us to get married. I did too.' She stared into space, the memory of those days she'd tried so hard to forget suddenly seeming very close. For a moment, the familiar room disappeared, and she was back in the past, seeing the triumph in Fleur's eyes, the embarrassment in Darren's as he told her he was in love with her sister. She forced herself back to the present.

Iris was watching her, her eyes widening.

Lou continued, 'Fleur always got what she wanted, always had. As the youngest daughter she was spoiled. She'd been a premature baby. My parents didn't know if she'd survive. They were grateful, I guess. I'd always given in, let her have my toys, my books. But this time it was Darren she wanted… and there was nothing I could do about it. So that's why I returned her letters, didn't want to read about their new life together. It was only as I grew older that I realised I didn't feel bitter any longer, that I wanted to see her again. I never stopped loving her, she was always my little sister, but it took me a long time to forgive her.'

'Wow, Aunt Lou. And Dad? Did you forgive him?'

'That was harder. I thought he loved me… I guess he did, in his way, but once Fleur…' She shook her head. 'It's all water under the bridge. You didn't need to know.'

'But now I do. I can't believe Dad did that to you… What Scott did to me, though it wasn't with my sister. It was my best friend. As soon as he learnt I was pregnant, he said he didn't bargain on a kid. He left soon after. He's never seen Vi, never will, as far as I'm concerned. He gave up any rights to her when he left. No wonder you cut off all contact with Mum… and Dad. She never changed, you know. She always knew how to get what she wanted… from Dad, from me, from anyone. It's why I came here to meet you. Yes, I was curious about the aunt I'd never known existed, but it was Mum, exerting her will, even from the grave. She didn't forget you. I told you I found newspaper articles about Pelican Crossing, about *Books and Coffee*. I think she regretted being estranged from you, her only sister.'

'So much wasted time,' Lou said. 'I wish now that I'd read her letters, hadn't been so bitter, but I was hurting, and it was easier to return them, to try to forget. I could have been part of your life…'

'I'd have liked that. I was happy, growing up, but other kids had grandparents, aunts, uncles. I sometimes wondered why I didn't, but when I asked Mum or Dad, they always said we were enough for each other and didn't need anyone else.' She sighed.

'I'm sorry, Iris.'

'It's not your fault. I'd have done the same. To think Mum…' She shook her head. 'Dad always gave in to her. He was weak like that. I always thought it was because he loved her so much.'

'I'm glad they were happy together. I don't think I could have borne it if…'

'They were… as far as I could tell. You never really know about your parents, do you? I didn't think Mum could keep a secret, yet she kept you a secret for all that time.'

'You're here now, that's all that matters.' *Was this the time to tell Iris her idea?*

'I wish we didn't live so far away,' Iris said, 'but we can visit again, and maybe you could come to see us in Melbourne.'

Lou took another deep breath. 'About that, I've been thinking. I'll be sixty-five soon and I don't know how much longer I'm going to be able to stand on my feet all day, every day. I've been worried about what will happen to *Books and Coffee* when I have to give it up.'

'But surely… You're not…'

'Not yet, but the day will come. So, I wondered… how would you feel about moving here… to Pelican Crossing… to be here to take over the bookshop when I'm no longer able, maybe help out in the meantime, learn the ropes… or I'm sure you could get a position in our local library.'

Iris didn't reply, and Lou thought she'd made a mistake. *Of course, Iris didn't want to leave her life in Melbourne to move to this small town. She was trying to figure out a polite way to decline.*

When she did speak, Lou got a surprise.

'Oh, Aunt Lou. It would be a dream come true. Do you mean it? You'd like me to work in your bookshop, that wonderful bookshop, to take it over when you retire? Though I hope that's not for many years yet.' She jumped up and threw her arms around Lou. 'Oh, thank you, thank you!'

For a moment, Lou was too overcome to speak, then she said, 'I think this deserves another drink.'

Both women were beaming as they toasted their decision with another measure of whisky.

'Vi will be thrilled,' Iris said. 'She loves it here. After meeting Blair's granddaughter today, she was very envious to hear that Harper's school offered surfing lessons, and how Harper was learning to be a surf lifesaver. There's nothing like that in her Melbourne school. She loves the beach too. We'll have to go back to Melbourne to pack up our life there and I'll need to give notice at work, put the house on the market. I'll be sad to see our family home go, but I'd probably have had to sell it anyway. It's old and too big for Vi and me. Oh, Aunt Lou! I still can't believe it.'

'I'm so glad you're onboard. I was worried you might not want to leave Melbourne. I could have understood if…'

'No, now Mum's gone, there's nothing to keep us there. And we have family in Pelican Crossing – you and Uncle Stan.'

Lou smiled. It was all going to work out. 'I guess we should try to get some sleep,' she said, rising and looking out the window. 'It still looks calm out there.' While the threat of the cyclone had retreated during their conversation, it was still there, and there was no telling what tomorrow would bring.

Forty-six

Against his better judgement, Blair had spent the night at Katrina's, and the three adults had sat up late, watching the Bureau of Meteorology website, only going to bed when it looked like nothing had changed, and they knew they had to get some sleep so as to be alert next morning.

After a restless night, he was eager to see what the news was this morning. While Katrina's main concern was that the children's Christmas might be spoiled, Blair was concerned about the fate of the cottages across the road from the ocean and the bookshop in the centre of town. When his phone rang as he was getting dressed, he grabbed it, hoping it was Lou.

'Dad.' Chelsea's voice came as a shock. 'How are you, and Kat and the kids? We've had a dreadful night of wind and rain. I've been thinking of you all up there.'

'It's still calm here,' he said, staring out the window to where a couple of people had been brave enough to take their dogs for a walk. 'Have you checked the news this morning?'

'Not yet. Last I heard they were still predicting landfall today or tomorrow. How's Kat coping?'

'Worried about it ruining Christmas.'

Chelsea laughed. 'That's Kat. But it still could, couldn't it?'

'It's a possibility. You're too young to remember Darwin. A cyclone hit there on Christmas Eve back in 1974. I was in my teens, and I'll never forget it. Everyone said it was the year Christmas didn't come to Darwin. There was even a song about it – *Santa never made it into Darwin*. Let's hope it doesn't happen here. I'm feeling optimistic.'

'Hope you're right. It's raining here but if it's safe to travel, I plan to drive up. I won't wait till Christmas. Stay safe!'

'You too, sweetheart, and drive carefully. Don't take any risks.'

'I won't. You know me. Give Kat my love.'

'You could speak to her yourself.'

'Not now. I'll let her know when I'm on my way.'

'Okay.' Blair could never understand the relationship between the two sisters. They'd feuded as teenagers, which Prue said was only natural, but now they lived reasonably close to each other, they didn't appear to meet very often or even keep in touch regularly. Maybe it was because they had taken different paths, and their lives had gone in very different directions. It would be good to see Chelsea again, to have the family all together at Christmas. Blair couldn't contemplate the possibility of the cyclone putting paid to that.

Thinking of family, sent Blair's thoughts to Lou, and *her* family. He wondered how she and Iris were coping, how they were spending their time. He was aware she'd decided to close *Books and Coffee*, and that Ron and Denny had ensured it was protected as well as possible from the ravages of wind and rain. She must be worried but being Lou, she'd put on a brave face last time they spoke, determined to see it out in her cottage unless forced to evacuate.

Blair could hear the television when he left the bedroom, and when he entered the living room, it was to find Brett and his grandchildren sitting in front of it, eyes glued to the weather map. Even Harper and Noah appeared to have forsaken their iPads to watch the track of the cyclone.

'Anyone want breakfast?' Katrina called, popping her head in. "Oh, good morning, Dad. Sleep well?'

'As well as I could, given the circumstances,' Blair said. 'Breakfast sounds good.'

'I made scrambled eggs and there's plenty of toast and coffee. I hope we don't lose power.' Her forehead creased.

'It may not happen, honey,' Brett said, switching off the television and going over to give her a hug.

'The cyclone or a power cut?'

'Both. Let's just enjoy a few days together.'

'Why can't we go to the beach?' Harper wailed. 'The sun's shining.'

'What do you think, Dad?' Katrina asked. 'They've been cooped up here since yesterday morning.'

'Maybe a short walk. I can take them,' Blair said. He'd be glad to get out of the house himself. He wanted to call Lou but didn't want Katrina to overhear him. He'd dearly like to drop round to see her, but not with his grandchildren in tow.

'Yay!' Harper and Noah said together.

After breakfast, Blair and the children left. At Noah's insistence, they headed for the harbour, their initial high spirits at being outside tempered by the sight of many of the shops closed and reinforced with sandbags. Beside the newly renovated Surf Club, a group of men were busy filling sandbags, and residents were lining up to collect them. Blair recognised the two young men from *Books and Coffee* among those shovelling sand into bags.

Stopping for a moment to gaze out at the ocean, the high waves deterring all but the keenest or most foolish surfers, Blair asked Noah, 'Still interested in a swim?'

'No, Grandad.' The little boy shook his head.

Blair laughed, but it was no laughing matter. Next day, it would be high tide, and if the cyclone crossed the coast then, Lou's cottage, along with lots of others would be in danger of flooding from the resultant surge of water.

'Ready to go back now?' he asked, as a gust of wind threatened to lift them off their feet.

'Look!' Harper said. 'It's Vi. Can I go over to talk to her?'

Blair followed her pointing finger to see Lou with her niece and grandniece, also battling the wind.

*

To her surprise, Lou had slept well. It had been a relief to tell Iris about what Fleur and Darren had done. She'd kept it bottled up for so long, only sharing it with Blair. At first, she'd been hesitant to reveal their betrayal to Iris. She was their daughter, after all, and might have been upset by Lou's bitterness at the time. But her understanding, fuelled by her own experience, had allayed Lou's concern.

Then there was Iris's agreement to move to Pelican Crossing which had thrilled Lou and set her mind at ease. It was something to look forward to and made the idea of retirement seem less threatening.

Despite the wind which seemed to have strengthened overnight, nothing had changed since yesterday, and Lou wondered if she'd been overhasty in closing *Books and Coffee*. But it was probably best to take precautions, and it freed up both Ron and Denny to volunteer with the SES.

After breakfast and watching reports from the Bureau of Meteorology, Iris checked out the Higgins Stormchasing website on Facebook which reported dangerous flooding farther north and warnings to expect more treacherous winds and rain as the cyclone drew nearer to the coast. Lou shivered but realised she'd been right to close up.

'Can we go out?' Violet asked. 'It's not raining here.'

Lou and Iris looked at each other. Lou knew how difficult it must be for Violet to be stuck inside with them for another day of playing board games and doing jigsaws. 'Maybe for a little while. What do you think, Iris?'

'Sounds good to me.'

A few minutes later, they set off, Violet holding tightly to Lou and Iris's hands as they were buffeted by the wind. It was fiercer than Lou had expected. There were a few trees over the road, blown down overnight. They were almost at the harbour where many of the boats were being tossed around, and Lou was about to suggest they ought to turn back when she saw Blair walking towards them, a grandchild in each hand.

'Am I glad to see you,' Blair said, as Violet slipped her hand out of Lou's to join her new friend. 'I was worried about you… and Iris.'

'We're fine, more than fine,' Lou said with a smile. 'But we were about to turn back. It's wilder than I expected.'

'I don't blame you. I was thinking the same. It could storm.' He glanced up at the sky which was clouding over.

'Why don't you come back with us for coffee? I can make smoothies for the kids.'

'Yes, please, Aunt Lou,' Violet said, she and Harper already chatting happily.

'Well…' Blair hesitated, looking up at the sky again, '… maybe for a quick one. We don't want to get caught in a storm, but it would be good to get out of this for a short time.'

'Good.' Lou wasn't sure why Blair's agreement made her feel so good. She could only assume it was because she missed their chats over coffee in the café.

Back at the cottage, Iris fixed smoothies for the three children while Lou made coffee, then Iris took the children through to the living area to play a game of Uno, leaving Lou and Blair alone in the kitchen.

'How's it working out?' he asked, gesturing to where happy sounds were coming from the other room.

'Good, better than good, actually. Iris and I had a long talk last night. She wanted to know what her mother's apology was all about, so I told her.'

'And?' Blair looked concerned.

'It was good. Her ex did the same to her as Darren did to me, only she was pregnant with Vi at the time. And she's agreed to move to Pelican Crossing.'

'Oh, Lou! I'm so pleased for you. You'll have your family around you.'

'After all those years. It takes a bit of getting used to.'

'But you're happy about it?'

'Very happy. It won't happen immediately. They have things to sort out in Melbourne, but it *will* happen. It means that, when I decide to retire, Iris will take over the bookshop. It's a weird thought, but I'm sure I'll get used to it.'

'You will. It takes time, but now I wonder how I ever had time to go to work.' He chuckled. 'The young one will keep you busy, and she and Harper seem to have struck up a friendship.'

'Yes, when we told Vi about the move, all she could talk about was how great it would be to go to Harper's school and learn to surf.'

'You're referring to her as Vi now?'

'Now they've moved in, it's easier, and Violet sounds too formal. I'll just be glad when this blasted cyclone is over,' she said, her mind reverting to the threat hanging over them.

'I think we all will.' Blair sighed. 'The last reports suggested the delay means it may intensify before making landfall.'

Lou felt a cold shiver run down her spine. She loved her cottage and the thought of it being swamped by sea and sand made her blood run cold.

'It may never come to that,' Blair said as if reading her mind.

'I hope you're right. It'll soon be Christmas, but it doesn't feel like it.' She shivered again, despite the warm day.

'Let's believe it'll all be over by then, and we'll be safe. You never did reply about the Christmas carols. You could bring Iris and Violet along too.'

'Oh!' Lou had been surprised when Blair had suggested they go together. Now, looking at his familiar face, at the way his eyes crinkled when he smiled, she knew she was in danger of becoming fond of him, too fond. She didn't have a good history with men… even though there had only been one in her life, it hadn't ended well. But the annual carol singing was something Iris and Violet would enjoy, Violet was already friends with Harper, and Iris would need friends of her own age in Pelican Crossing. 'I guess we could join you,' she said with a smile.

'Good. I'm becoming more and more drawn to you, Lou. If it wasn't for this blasted cyclone… and your family moving in…'

A new and unexpected warmth surged through Lou. She cleared her throat, pretending not to be affected.

Then, right there in her kitchen, in the middle of the morning, with her family and his grandchildren in the next room, Blair drew her into his arms.

Lou's pulse began to quicken, and her heart hammered at the thought of what it might mean if they became more than friends. A kiss was one thing… and she'd enjoyed Blair's kisses… wanted more… but if he wanted to take it further… He'd been married, was experienced in… she swallowed. She was too old to risk her heart again. She pulled away. 'I don't think…' she said, sending a glance towards the doorway into the living room.

'Probably not.' Blair grinned. 'But the time will come.'

Lou tried to smile back, but all she could think of was that she wanted to get away, to be by herself, and to think about this.

Forty-seven

Lou was still thinking about what Blair had said, long after he and his grandchildren left, thinking of how he made her feel and the implications of the more intimate relationship he would obviously expect.

'You should have these.'

Lou saw Iris was holding a bundle of letters. They were the ones Fleur had sent to her, the ones she'd returned.

'They're yours,' Iris said, handing them to Lou.

'I...' Lou choked up. She'd never expected to see them again, imagined Fleur would have destroyed them, but they were what had brought Iris here to Pelican Crossing, these and the newspaper articles Fleur had kept. Her sister had known more about Lou's life than Lou had known about hers. 'Thanks, Iris.'

Dinner was over, Violet was in bed, and Lou and Iris had been watching the news and weather forecast. Nothing had changed. The cyclone was still out at sea with the trajectory to make landfall in one or two days, though it now looked as if it might happen farther south.

'I'm off to bed now, Aunt Lou. Will you read them?'

'I'm not sure.' Lou fingered the bundle which she'd placed on the coffee table. They were her last link with her sister.

She waited till Iris had gone, till she'd heard the bathroom door open and close, the bedroom door close. Then she poured herself a glass of wine, sipping it slowly as she eyed the letters. As if understanding her indecision, Tilly had joined her on the sofa and had stretched out beside her. Finally, Lou could bear it no longer. She had to know what Fleur had written. Picking up the bundle, she noticed they had been packed together in date order, the first one written only a week after Fleur and Darren had left. Gingerly she slit it open.

Two hours later, Lou was in tears, the letters scattered around her where they'd fallen as she read them one after the other. Tilly, having become tired of being ignored, had wandered off. At first, Fleur had written to apologise for falling in love with Darren, saying she knew how much Lou cared for him, but that she couldn't bear to live without him and that he loved her too; they couldn't help themselves, they were soulmates. She was sure Lou would understand and find someone else. Lou snorted and threw the letter down. She almost gave up but after another sip of wine, forced herself to continue reading. Later letters told of their marriage, their life in Melbourne, Fleur's failure to understand why Lou hadn't replied, had returned her letters unopened. The final one was angry, bitter, telling Lou this was the last time she'd reach out to her.

'Oh, Fleur!' she said, tears streaming down her cheeks. 'If only…' If only she'd read the letters? If only she had reached out sooner, had found out where Fleur was living, if only Fleur had lived to know Lou had forgiven her? Lou wasn't sure which of these she meant. But it was too late for any more regrets. She had to live with the consequence of her actions, and to look on the bright side. She had a niece and grandniece who would be spending Christmas with her, and moving to Pelican Crossing, someone to take over the bookshop when she was ready to retire. She needed to count her blessings instead of focussing on the past and her regrets.

Lou gathered up the letters and packaged them into a bundle again, unsure what she wanted to do with them. But for the time being, she'd keep them safe, the last words Fleur had written to her.

This dealt with, Lou's thoughts returned to Blair. What was she going to do about him? But she was too tired to worry about that now. She picked up the bundle of letters and headed to her bedroom.

*

Next morning, Lou was awakened by her phone ringing, and Tilly, who'd made her way into the bedroom overnight, kneading her shoulder. Seeing Blair's number, she pushed herself up against the pillows.

'Blair, is something wrong?'

'Quite the opposite. Have you seen the news this morning?'

'Not yet.' Lou peered at the bedside clock. It was only half past six.

'Sorry, did I waken you? I couldn't sleep and have been following the news for the past couple of hours. The cyclone has changed direction and moved out to sea.'

Lou suddenly felt energised and wide awake. 'It has?' she said, her voice rising with excitement. 'It's over, it's really over?'

'So it seems. We may get rain, but nothing like what we'd have got if it had made landfall here or even farther south.'

'So, I can reopen the bookshop,' Lou said, almost to herself, trying to figure out how she'd manage to get everything back to normal. But she'd have Ron and Denny to help, she reminded herself.

'You certainly can, and the council is reminding everyone that the sand should not be put on the beach and are requesting residents to put it on their gardens or return the sandbags to the council waste site. Joe must have been up half the night updating the council website and the disaster dashboard.'

'Oh, good. I was just wondering about that.'

'If you're reopening, I'll try to pop in sometime this morning, but it may be difficult. Chelsea is on her way, and I'm not sure when she'll arrive.'

'No worries.' Lou wasn't sure if she was ready to see Blair again just yet. She was still processing what had happened last time they'd met.

'Oh, and the carols can go ahead too.'

'Right.' Lou remembered agreeing to attend the event with Blair and his family, but that had been before…

After sending a text to Ron to let him know about re-opening, Lou walked into the kitchen where the radio was blaring and Tilly, having left Lou while she was talking to Blair, was busy eating. Violet was sitting at the table, and Iris was making breakfast.

'The cyclone has gone out to sea, Aunt Lou,' Violet yelled over the noise of the radio, 'but Mum says we still can't go swimming.'

'The sea will still be too rough, Vi, but I'm sure you'll be able to find lots of other things to do.'

'Can we go to see Harper?'

Lou sighed. While she was pleased about Violet's friendship with Blair's granddaughter, it wasn't going to make things any easier for her. 'You'll see her at the Christmas carols the day after tomorrow. Will that do?' she said. 'Her aunt is visiting and probably wants to spend time with her,' she added, remembering what Blair had told her.

'I suppose.' But Violet didn't seem satisfied.

'I'm opening the bookshop again today. I texted Ron, and he and Denny will get the café going and get rid of the sandbags,' Lou said, deciding to let Iris cope with her daughter. 'Why don't you come there for lunch. I should be able to get away. I don't imagine we'll be busy today. Everyone will be getting things back to normal.' As she spoke, Lou realised there were things to be done here too.

'I'm on it,' Iris said. 'I can move the outdoor furniture back, empty the bath and check what else needs to be done.'

'Thanks, Iris. That would be great. I'd be lost without you.' And she would, Lou thought. Having Iris and Violet here had helped her get through the past few days, and Iris was a big help around the house. After so many years of living on her own, with only Tilly for company, she'd never expected to feel so comfortable having other people around.

*

Lou was right. There were only a few customers in both the bookshop and the café, giving Denny time to remove the sandbags and take them to the council waste site.

It felt good to be back in the shop, the lights of the Christmas tree twinkling in the corner and Christmas carols in the background giving it a festive air. It was as if the threat of the cyclone had never happened, difficult to believe that they'd spent the last two days in fear of the entire town being destroyed.

Lou was busying herself with setting up a new display of books when a familiar voice said, 'I'm glad to see you open again. How are you?'

'Rach!' Lou swung around to greet her friend with a hug. She was just the person she wanted to see. Rachel was a good listener, could keep a secret and was known among her friends as a source of good advice. And Lou was in need of advice. 'Am I glad to see you.'

'Well, I must say I didn't expect such an enthusiastic welcome. I was passing, noticed you were open, and came in to say hello. It's good to get out of the house again. Luke's walking the dogs, so I decided to come into town to see what was happening.'

'Do you have time for coffee? I need to talk to you.'

'Always.' Rachel looked puzzled but didn't say more as she followed Lou to the café where only a few tables were occupied.

'Hopefully, things will get back to normal soon,' Lou said, glancing around at the empty tables. 'Thank goodness Zara has gone off to sea and we can enjoy our Christmas in peace,' she added, ordering coffees from Ron.

'Now, what gives, and how's that lovely man of yours?' Rachel asked when they were seated at a table by the window with their coffees and freshly baked strawberry and white chocolate muffins.

Lou winced. 'He's not mine, but he's what I want to talk to you about.'

'I'm all ears, and you know I can keep whatever it is to myself.'

'I do. It's why you get to hear everyone's innermost secrets.'

Rachel laughed.

'Well, Rach, it's like this.' Lou cleared her throat and took a sip of coffee. This was going to be more difficult than she'd anticipated. She wanted to talk to Rachel, get her advice, but finding the right words was proving a challenge. She decided not to think about it, but to say what was in her mind. 'It's Blair. I don't know what to do.'

Rachel took a sip of coffee and cut her muffin into four before speaking. 'How do you feel about him?'

'I like him… a lot. He says he likes me too.'

'So, what's the problem? You're friends… more than friends?'

'We've kissed.' Lou blushed.

'And?'

'That's the problem. It's obvious that Blair wants more, wants to…' She blushed again. 'I may have misunderstood but he implied that… after Christmas… we might… Oh, Rach! What if I can't… if I don't…

if I'm a disappointment to him?' There, she'd said it, revealed the worry which had been uppermost in her mind, the fear which had been there ever since Blair had said, 'The time will come'.

Rachel peered at Lou. 'You have… you and Darren… didn't you?'

'We only… once, Rach. I've always wondered if Fleur and he… if she was a better…'

'Your sister was a scheming bitch. Sorry, but it is what it is… or was. She had quite a reputation back then, and Darren was a sitting duck. But Blair's not Darren. From what I know of him, he's a gentle, intelligent man, and in my experience, love will conquer any lack of experience. A loving man will take account of it and make you feel wonderful, as if you are the only woman in the world.' She gazed into space as if lost in a world of her own.

Love? Lou examined her feelings. *Was that what she felt for Blair? Was that what he meant when he said he was drawn to her?*

Forty-eight

Blair called Lou as soon as he deemed suitable after he'd read the news the cyclone had changed direction and was now headed out to sea. Even so, he'd wakened her and was distracted by imagining her naked body lying in bed, so much so that he'd had trouble making conversation.

He couldn't wait to see her again. Last time they'd spoken, he'd tried to be clearer about his intentions, but she'd pulled away. The timing had been wrong, with Iris, Violet and his grandchildren in the next room, but he was hopeful that next time… He'd been cautious about revealing his feelings up till now, but he wanted Lou to know his intentions. After Prue's death, he'd never expected to feel this way again, but he was falling in love with Lou and wanted her to know it.

Although he was pleased to see Chelsea, it was a pity she had arrived last night, and he'd have to forego his morning coffee with Lou, but he intended to drop into the bookshop as soon as he could get away.

'I suppose you'll be going back to your villa now?' Katrina asked at breakfast, when she could make herself heard over Harper and Noah's chatter – they were thrilled with the arrival of Chelsea who always spoiled them.

'I think you have enough people here without me,' he said with a grin, 'and I have things I need to get on with.'

'I assume you're talking about that book you say you're writing,' she said rolling her eyes.

'You've started writing it, Dad?' Chelsea asked. 'Oh, I'm glad. I know it's been on your mind for a long time.'

'Thanks, Chels, and yes, I'm beginning to make some progress, though it's going to take some time. I still have a lot of research to do.'

'I don't know why you're bothering,' Katrina said. 'But I know you don't pay any attention to what I think.'

'It's Dad's life, Kat. He's never tried to interfere in our lives, to tell us what to do.'

Katrina scowled and seemed about to reply, but Blair intervened. 'That's enough, you two. I can fight my own battles, Chels, and I do intend to write a fictionalised account of our forebears. The time of the early settlers has always been an interest of mine and what I've discovered so far is fascinating.'

'Well, I need to get on,' Katrina said. 'I plan to go into the clinic today to check on my schedule. Now everything will be opening up again, I'm sure I'll have clients wanting appointments. Can I leave Harper and Noah with you, Chels?'

'Sure. We can go down to look at the ocean and maybe find out what's open in town. What about you Dad? Will you join us?'

'Please, Grandad,' Noah said. 'We can look at the boats in the harbour, and…'

'Okay, okay. I guess I can go home later.' Spending the morning with Chelsea and the grandchildren would put paid to him visiting the bookshop, but perhaps he could make it in the afternoon. Lou would still be there.

Blair enjoyed the morning spent with Chelsea, wandering around the town, his grandchildren hanging on to his and Chelsea's hands. His daughter had brought her camera, and they made frequent stops for her to take shots of the giant waves pounding the beach, the ships in the harbour being tossed by the wind, and a posse of pelicans looking for something to eat.

It was close to lunchtime when they arrived back, and he was able to pack his belongings and head for home.

After restoring everything to normal at his villa and having a bite to eat, Blair drove back into town, this time to see Lou. But when he arrived in the bookshop, it wasn't her but Zoe behind the counter.

'She's having lunch with Iris and Violet,' Zoe said. 'You'll find her in the café.'

Blair blushed. Was it so obvious he'd come to see Lou, and did he care? 'Thanks,' he said, hesitating for a moment before leaving again. He didn't want to disturb their lunch. He'd go to the library and come back later. There was something he needed to check out anyway, before he could continue writing.

*

Although Blair had told her he'd be busy with his daughter, Lou hadn't been able to stop looking out for him, turning towards the door each time it opened, expecting to see Blair walk in and disappointed when he didn't. He still hadn't made an appearance by the time Iris and Violet arrived to have lunch with her.

It was almost closing time, and Lou had given up hoping to see him, when Blair finally walked in. At the sight of him, her heart raced, and she felt a tingling sensation in the pit of her stomach, Rachel's words making her think of what it might be like if they…

'Hi, Blair,' she said, hoping he couldn't read her mind.

'Lou. Sorry I didn't make it this morning. I did come in when you were at lunch but didn't want to disturb you.'

'Oh!' Why hadn't Zoe told her? Then she remembered how busy they'd been when she came back from lunch. Her assistant had probably forgotten, or thought it wasn't important enough to mention. 'But you're here now. It's good to see you.' She tried to stifle the unfamiliar sensations she was experiencing.

'I went to the library and got caught up. Sorry.' He dragged a hand through his hair.

'No need to apologise. We've been busy,' she said, trying to pretend she hadn't been looking out for him all day.

'Well, I'm here now. You'll be closing soon. Have you time for a drink or do you need to go straight home?'

'I…' *Why did her legs suddenly feel weak?* 'I can call Iris to let her know I'll be late.'

'Good.' Blair smiled, sending a shiver down her spine.

What had happened to her? He hadn't had this effect on her before, not until he'd suggested… and since she'd spoken to Rachel. But what if she was wrong and he hadn't meant anything?

As soon as she'd put the closed sign on the door and checked the day's sales, Lou left the bookshop with Blair, trembling as he took her hand. 'A busy day?' he asked.

'Not at first, but after lunchtime it changed. It seemed everyone remembered it would be Christmas in a couple of days, and they still had shopping to do.'

'It'll take a while to get back to normal. We went to the beach and the harbour this morning, and the sea's still fierce. Let's hope it stays fine for the carols tomorrow.'

'Yes.' Lou was puzzled. She didn't know what she'd expected, but not this small talk. Maybe she'd misunderstood him after all and she'd humiliated herself with Rachel for nothing.

By the time Lou was seated in a booth in *The Grand*, while Blair fetched their drinks, she'd decided she'd definitely been wrong about what Blair had meant. Pushing down a keen sense of disappointment, she tried to tell herself it was all for the best. She was almost sixty-five, too old to imagine a man like Blair wanted anything more than friendship from her. It had been a pipedream, a fantasy, lovely while it lasted, but now she'd come down to earth. She would just be glad she'd found a friend and a delightful companion.

'Cheers.' Blair lifted his glass to meet Lou's. 'I'm so glad to see you again. I've missed our morning chats over coffee and… at your cottage, I'm afraid I may have overstepped the mark. I didn't mean to frighten you. I hope I didn't scare you off. I realise my timing was out. It was neither the time nor place to…' He cleared his throat. 'I'm afraid I'm out of practice. I'm glad to have this opportunity to clear things up with you.'

Lou picked up her glass and took a sip. She felt herself turn hot, then cold, as a now familiar shiver ran down her spine. *What was Blair trying to say?*

'You didn't… scare me off,' she risked saying. 'But you're right about time and place.' She swallowed, wondering what he would say next.

'As I think I said then, I'm finding myself increasingly drawn to you. I'd never expected to feel this way again, thought I was over all this sort of thing, but meeting you… I don't expect you to tell me how you feel right now. I know that, like me, you have your family, and Christmas, but… when it's over, can we meet properly, see if this spark

I feel is real, if you possibly feel it too? How about we make a date to have dinner together on Boxing Day?'

Lou thought her heart was going to burst. She ached to tell him that she felt a spark too, but something stopped her. There would be time enough. As he said, they both had their families… and it would be Christmas in two days' time. 'That sounds perfect,' she said. 'Let's drink to that.' She raised her glass to meet his again.

Forty-nine

Christmas Eve in the bookshop was hectic. It seemed as if all of Pelican Crossing had decided to buy books as last-minute gifts, and Lou, Zoe, Georgia and a friend of Georgia's who Lou had called upon at the last minute, didn't stop all day. They were all exhausted when the shop finally closed, glad they had a few days break before it all started again.

Lou was almost too tired to go to the carols event, but she'd promised Blair she'd see him there, and both Iris and Violet were keen to attend.

She felt better after showering and changing before sitting down to eat the salad nicoise Iris had prepared to use up two of the tins of tuna she'd bought when they were preparing for the cyclone.

'Can we go now?' Violet asked, as soon as she'd finished eating.

'In a little while,' Iris said. 'Let Aunt Lou take a few minutes to relax. She's had a busy day.'

'Thanks, Iris, but I'm fine now. That was a lovely dinner. You're spoiling me.'

'Nonsense. It's the least I can do.'

But Lou knew it wasn't nonsense. Iris was continuing to be a big help around the house, and she'd miss her and Violet when they left. But they'd be back, though they'd no doubt want a place of their own. Well, she'd face that when it happened. Once again she felt buoyed, barely able to believe she was enjoying sharing her home

Finally, they were ready to go and leaving a disgruntled Tilly, they set off to walk to Pelican Plaza where the carol service was to be held. There was already a crowd of people there when they arrived, and Lou wondered if they'd be able to find Blair and his family, but Violet called out, 'There's Harper!' and started weaving her way through the crowd. Lou and Iris followed until they reached the spot where Blair, Katrina, Brett and a stranger Lou knew must be Chelsea, were standing, along with Harper and Noah.

After introducing Iris to Katrina and Brett, and both Lou and Iris to Chelsea, Blair gave Lou a hug, much to her embarrassment. 'It's good to see you,' he whispered.

'Good to see you too,' she murmured, just as Joe took the microphone to welcome everyone to Pelican Crossing's annual Christmas carols. Everyone cheered, then his place was taken by the musical group and choir from the local high school.

As Lou joined with others in the singing of new and traditional carols, she felt Blair's hand take hers, a warm glow suffusing her as their fingers entwined, promising more intimate contact when the festivities were over. She was glad it was too dark for anyone to see her blush.

Lou felt a sense of loss when the event finally came to an end with a traditional rendition of *We wish you a Merry Christmas*, and Blair dropped her hand as the crowd began to disperse.

'It's too early to go home,' Harper said, still energised from singing carols. 'Can we see all the Christmas lights?'

'Oh, I don't know.' Katrina looked at Brett for support, but before he could speak, Chelsea said, 'What a good idea, Harper. Do you know where we should go?'

'*I* do,' Noah yelled, grabbing his aunt's hand.

'You'll join us?' Blair asked Lou who, seeing Violet was already haring off with Harper, nodded.

For the next hour, the group wandered around the streets behind the harbour, the children racing ahead and oohing and aahing at the displays of Christmas lights while the adults followed more slowly, chatting among themselves. To Lou's disappointment, there was no opportunity for her and Blair to have any private conversation, but she hugged herself with the knowledge of their date on Boxing Day.

As both Noah and Violet began to flag, Katrina suggested it was time to go home, but first, they stopped at a cart selling hot chocolate which they all enjoyed.

Back at the now deserted Pelican Plaza, Lou, Iris and Violet farewelled the others wishing them a Happy Christmas for the next day, before heading off in different directions, but not before Blair gave Lou another hug and whispered, 'I'm looking forward to our dinner on Boxing Day,' his warm breath on her cheek making her tingle all over.

*

When Lou awoke on Christmas morning, it was to the sound of Christmas carols and shouts of joy from Violet. She couldn't help thinking how different this was from the Christmas she'd anticipated before Iris and Violet's arrival, and from all the previous Christmases she'd spent alone with Tilly.

Pulling on a robe, she followed the sounds through to the kitchen to where Iris and Violet were eating breakfast. Her eyes widened at the sight of chocolate croissants.

'I thought we should have something special for Christmas breakfast,' Iris said. 'Mum and I always…' her words trailed off.

'It's okay to speak about your mum,' Lou said. 'I have happy memories of her too, of our Christmases growing up together.'

'Now Aunt Lou's up, can I open my presents?' Violet asked.

'Let her have breakfast first, Vi.'

'Why don't I bring my breakfast through and have it while you open them?' Lou suggested, making her ginger and lemon tea and putting a croissant onto a plate.

'Thanks,' Iris said. 'Vi's been up since the crack of dawn, but I said she had to wait for you before she opened any.'

'Well, let's not wait any longer, Vi.'

Lou and Iris followed an excited Violet through to where a pile of gaily wrapped parcels sat beneath the Christmas tree along with Tilly who had chosen this as her favourite spot this morning and was curled up among them. Violet immediately rushed forward, sending Tilly scurrying away and making Lou laugh. Poor Tilly was still getting used to Violet's unpredictable movements, so different from Lou's more familiar slower ones.

As the presents were opened, wrapping papers scattered everywhere, the room began to resemble a rubbish tip, and Tilly reappeared to join in the fun. Violet was delighted with her iPad, bundle of books and new outfits, while Lou was thrilled with the unexpected gift of a brightly coloured shawl in soft cashmere.

'Thanks so much, Iris,' she said, a tear in her eye. She couldn't remember when she'd last received a gift at Christmas, apart from the wine and chocolates the staff at *Books and Coffee* always presented to her.

'This is lovely,' she said, holding the scarf to her cheek. 'But I'm so sorry. I didn't… I didn't think to get you a gift. I promise to rectify that.' While she'd bought books and a tee shirt with the Pelican Crossing logo for Violet, it hadn't occurred to her that she and Iris would be exchanging gifts.

Iris chuckled. 'Don't worry about it, Aunt Lou. You've already given me the greatest gift I could have hoped for.'

The two women hugged, then Violet joined in. They stood like that for several moments, Lou making no attempt to hide her emotion. It was such a special day for her, one she'd never imagined. If only Fleur could have been there too… As they parted, Lou wiped away a tear. 'Now, look what you've made me do,' she said, but she was beaming with delight.

'Look!' Violet said, 'Tilly's looking for her present.'

Lou and Iris turned to see where the cat was fossicking among the discarded Christmas paper. They both laughed.

'She already has hers,' Lou said.

'Where is it?' Violet asked.

Lou pointed to the kitchen, and Violet ran off, to return carrying the Fluffy Fox Tail Cat Teaser Wand Lou had presented to Tilly before going to bed the night before.

'Look, Tilly,' Violet said, waving it at the cat who leapt up to grab it, making her laugh with joy.

When all the presents had been opened and the paper tidied away, Lou showered and dressed. Then she put the chicken she'd bought for lunch into the oven, surrounded by vegetables, and they all went across the road to the beach. As Lou and Iris walked along the edge of the ocean, and Violet paddled in the shallow water, Lou silently gave thanks that they'd been spared from the disaster of Cyclone Zara.

They weren't the only ones on the beach. Joe and Gill were out walking with Coco, Livvy and Dan with Dan's old labrador, Cooper, and Erica and Jamie with Erica's spaniel, Bandit. They all stopped to wish each other Merry Christmas, before continuing on their way.

'Can I get a dog when we move here?' Violet asked.

'We'll see,' Iris replied. 'I thought you preferred cats?'

'I love Tilly, but she belongs to Aunt Lou, and I can't take her for walks.'

Lou laughed, but it confirmed her guess that Iris and Violet would find their own place when they moved here.

Back at the cottage, Lou enjoyed the sort of Christmas lunch she hadn't experienced since she was a child, with Christmas crackers, complete with silly mottos and jokes, which had Vi giggling every time, and paper hats which Violet insisted they all wear, making Tilly wary of the crowned humans until Vi gave the cat her own hat which saw her rolling around the floor, batting at it and causing more laughter as it was ripped to shreds. The chicken with all the trimmings went down a treat and the meal was completed with a dessert of trifle, just like Lou's mother used to make, both Iris and Vi commenting on how delicious it was and asking for a second helping despite their groaning tummies. This Christmas was turning out to be a truly joyous occasion.

Afterwards, while Violet played with her new iPad, Lou and Iris took a much-needed rest, enjoying a coffee in the courtyard, grateful that the wind had died to a gentle breeze, cooling the warm day.

'It really is so lovely here,' Iris said.

Lou was taken by surprise when Iris reached out and took hold of her hand.

'Thanks, Aunt Lou,' she said. 'Honestly, to be here in this beautiful place, with you, well, this is the best Christmas we've ever had. And I hope there's a lot more to come.'

The tears in her niece's eyes were enough to make Lou's eyes water. 'You're going to make me cry again.' She squeezed Iris's hand, swallowing the lump in her throat. 'But you're right. Last time I enjoyed Christmas so much I must have been Vi's age. It really is so good to have you both here.'

As the day progressed, Lou became flustered at the prospect of her dinner with Blair next day. While she was looking forward to it with anticipation, she was also beginning to panic at the thought of what might happen afterwards. What if he wanted to… and what if Rachel was wrong? She got butterflies in her stomach every time she thought about it.

'Is everything all right, Aunt Lou?' Iris asked, when Violet had gone to bed and the two of them were sitting in the living room enjoying a slice of Christmas cake and a glass of port while watching Iris's favourite Christmas movie, *Love Actually*.

'Yes, of course. I was just thinking how glad I am to have you and Violet here. I've had some very lonely Christmases with only Tilly and me.'

'No one invited you to join them? None of your friends?'

'They did, but I always pretended it was what I wanted. I guess I was too proud to accept.' Lou thought of how Rachel had invited her every year and how every year she'd declined. Only now she realised how foolish she'd been, staying home alone when she could have been part of a warm family group.

'You didn't want to see your friend, Blair, today?'

'We're having dinner tomorrow.' Lou blushed. Blair had called her when Iris was busy helping Violet pack away the wrapping paper. It had been a lovely call when he wished her Merry Christmas, asked her how she was spending the day, regretted that they were both tied up with their respective families and told her how much he was looking forward to having dinner with her. He'd booked a table at *Crossings* and said he couldn't wait to see her.

'That'll be nice,' Iris said, not taking her eyes off the TV screen. 'I love this movie. The way all the characters come together at the end like one big happy family at Christmastime. Just like us,' she added smiling at Lou.

Lou couldn't help smiling back at this lovely young woman, her niece no less.

'And look,' she said, glancing back at the TV. 'Natalie is there to meet David at the airport, showing her love for him in public. That's such a perfect ending.'

Lou found herself blushing more than ever. Imagine that, showing her… *love* for a man – for Blair – in public.

'I think it's time we had a whisky,' she said, getting up and soon returning with two tumblers of amber liquid.

'To family,' Iris said, lifting her glass.
Lou smiled. 'To family.'

Fifty

To Lou's surprise, she slept soundly on Christmas night, probably helped by the glass of port she and Iris had consumed with a slice of Christmas cake while watching the movie – topped off with a good measure of whisky to settle her nerves. She was awakened by the sound of rain on the window and grimaced. It was the aftermath of Cyclone Zara they'd been warned about. At least it had remained fine for Christmas.

When she wandered into the kitchen after a quick shower and dressed in a pair of jeans and linen shirt, she was surprised it was empty apart from Tilly who leapt up at the sight of Lou and began to meow.

'Okay, Tilly. I can feed you. Iris and Violet must be having a sleep in.' She wasn't surprised. She and Iris had sat up late, and Violet had had an exciting day.

She was making herself a cup of lemon and ginger tea and wondering if it would be too decadent to have a slice of Christmas cake with it for breakfast, when her phone rang. Her heart started pounding when she saw Blair's number. *What if he'd had second thoughts and was calling to cancel their date?*

'Good morning, Lou. Did you have a good Christmas Day?'

Lou relaxed at the sound of his voice. 'We did, thanks. It was very different from those I've had in past years. Violet was so excited. It was delightful to see.'

'Christmas is all about family and children. It's over all too soon. You must be wondering why I'm calling since we're meeting this evening.'

Lou waited.

'It seems that on Christmas Eve, my granddaughter and your grandniece concocted a plan to meet on the beach today, but the weather…'

Lou gazed at the rain which was streaming down the window. Certainly not a day for the beach. She was sorry. Violet would be disappointed. Blair was still speaking.

'So, Chelsea had an idea. She's suggested that Violet and her mother spend the day here. The girls can do their own thing, and Iris can get to know Kat and Chels. What do you think?'

Lou's first thought was that she'd be on her own, with nothing to distract her from the evening ahead but Iris and Violet would enjoy it. 'It's a good idea,' she said.

'Which leaves us,' Blair said. 'I've been meaning to visit the local brewery, and I've checked that it's open today. How about I pick you up after lunch and we visit it before we go to *Crossings* for dinner? Are you able to drive Iris and Violet over to Kat's?'

'Yes… I can do that. And what a lovely idea. I haven't been there. I'm always in the bookshop.' The thought of spending not only the evening with Blair, but the afternoon too sent Lou's mind into a whirl. 'Thanks, Blair.'

'No worries. I'll see you soon.'

'It's raining!' Violet wandered into the kitchen, her eyes still bleary from sleep. 'I was going to meet Harper on the beach. Do you think it'll stop soon, Aunt Lou?'

'It's unlikely, sweetheart, but guess what? Harper's grandad just called to invite you and your mum to her house instead.'

'And you?' Iris asked following her daughter.

'No.' Lou blushed. 'I'm going to visit the local brewery with Blair.'

'Nice.' Iris raised one eyebrow. 'Sorry we slept so late.'

'It's not late, and it's a holiday. Breakfast?' Lou asked.

'I think coffee will do me,' Iris said, just as Violet asked, 'Can we have pancakes?'

'Of course you can.' It was a long time since Lou had made pancakes – not since she'd been a teenager and she and Fleur had made them together – but she hadn't forgotten how.

'Grandma used to make them for me,' Violet said, as she watched Lou prepare the batter.

'She and I used to make them together, when we were not much older than you are now.' Lou wondered if Fleur had thought of her while she made them. She liked to think she had.

After a leisurely breakfast, they all piled into the car for Lou to drive them to Katrina's.

After dropping them off, Lou didn't feel like going back to the cottage, empty apart from Tilly. But she wasn't seeing Blair till the afternoon. Driving through town, deserted due to the holiday and the rain, she found herself at *Books and Coffee*. The Christmas tree was still there, its lights twinkling, but today the shop had a forlorn appearance, as if it knew Christmas was over.

After parking, Lou walked across the footpath, took out her key and opened the door. Once inside, she breathed a sigh of relief. This was where she belonged. She could use the time to take down some of the Christmas decorations, get the shop ready for the sale which would begin when they re-opened in the new year. She'd leave the tree decorations for Zoe and Georgia to dismantle, ready for the tree to be picked up, but she could make a start on the rest. It would take her mind off the afternoon and evening ahead.

It worked for a time, but then all of her reservations came to the fore again. Rachel might have said everything would be all right, but she'd been talking about Lou's experience or lack of it. What about…? She glanced down at her middle-aged body, seeing the evidence of her over-indulgence in Ron's sweet treats over the years. How could she ever have thought she could let Blair see her naked?

She couldn't go through with it. Maybe she could call Blair, say she was sick. She certainly felt sick, imagining what he'd think when he saw her flabby body. She was still trying to figure out what to do, how to tell him, when there was a tap on the shop window. Looking out, she saw Rachel, rain dripping from a large umbrella.

'Come in,' she said, opening the door. 'What are you doing out in this weather today?'

'I could ask you the same. Luke was called to an emergency vet thing, and I'm on my way to Jess's for lunch. I came through town to see if there was anywhere open where I could get milk. Jess has run out. Then I saw you. What are you doing here all alone?'

'Iris and Vi are at Katrina's. Blair's daughter. Vi and his granddaughter have become friends.'

'And Blair?'

'I'm supposed to be seeing him this afternoon to visit the craft brewery, then have dinner at *Crossings*. But I'm thinking of calling off.'

'Why on earth would you do that?'

'Oh, Rach, I know what you said, but… Look at me.'

'I'm looking, and I see an elegant woman.'

'You're too kind. You have to admit that I'm no spring chicken. I've indulged in too many of Ron's brownies and other concoctions and now… I can't…'

Rachel chuckled. 'This sounds very like a conversation I had with Poppy before Luke and I… I was worried about what he'd think when he saw me minus my clothes.'

'What did Poppy say?' Lou was curious.

'She reminded me that all of our bodies change as we get older, that Luke's would have too. She also made a comment to the effect that we'd have more to think about than what we looked like. She was right.' Rachel sighed as if remembering. 'Blair won't expect you to have the body of a twenty-year-old. He's been married. He knows what an older body looks like. I expect he likes you just the way you are. Trust me.'

Lou stared at her friend. Could she… trust her? But Rachel had no reason to lie, and *her* body wasn't that of a twenty-year-old either. 'Thanks, Rach,' she said.

After Rachel left, Lou felt a little better. She even turned on the carols again and began to sing along. By the time she was to meet Blair, she still had butterflies in her stomach but was looking forward to the afternoon and evening ahead and to what it might bring.

*

When Blair arrived to pick her up, Lou felt the now familiar flutter in her stomach, but this time it was accompanied by a sense of anticipation. When Blair greeted her with a hug, she leant into him, and he hugged her even tighter. Tilly, who'd followed Lou to the door, stood for a moment before slipping past them to disappear into the bushes.

'Ready?' Blair asked with a smile.

'Ready,' Lou confirmed, glad to see the rain had eased somewhat.

On the way to the brewery, Blair entertained Lou with stories of his Christmas Day and the various antics of his grandchildren. It sounded as if he loved the chaos they'd created and was delighted to have had all his family around him. He was a lucky man. But she was lucky too, she realised, lucky Fleur had told Iris about her before she died, lucky Iris and Violet had spent Christmas with her, lucky Iris had agreed to move to Pelican Crossing, and lucky to have met Blair. She glanced at the man sitting next to her and blessed the quirk of fate that had brought him into her life.

The visit to the brewery was fun. After a tour of the brewing process, they took part in a tasting of the various craft beers, then enjoyed a glass of one of them in the bar. A young man dressed in shorts and a bright flowered shirt was sitting on a raised section, strumming a guitar and singing Christmas carols with many of the customers joining in. It was a festive atmosphere and one which only heightened Lou's pleasure in the day, her doubts and fears forgotten.

Lou felt she could have stayed there for the rest of the day, joining in the singing with Blair's shoulder next to hers, their knees touching under the table and a sense of all being right in her world. All too soon, it was time to leave and make their way back to her cottage so she could feed Tilly and change for dinner.

Lou was glad there was no sign of Iris and Violet when she pushed open the door to be greeted by an irate Tilly. 'Did you miss me?' she asked the cat, picking her up and hugging her. Tilly only endured the cuddle briefly, before sliding out of her arms and heading for the kitchen to stand over her food bowl.

'How about I make us coffee and feed Tilly while you do what you have to do?' Blair asked with a grin.

'Thanks.' Lou smiled, but the butterflies in her stomach were creating havoc again. Hopefully a cup of coffee might help… and a shower.

The aroma of coffee greeted Lou when she re-entered the kitchen, this time dressed in a pair of black pants and a bright red tunic patterned with white flowers. Tilly, presumably having eaten, was nowhere to be seen.

'You look lovely,' Blair said, coming over to hug her, his lips meeting hers in a gentle kiss. It was as if he recognised her nervousness and wanted to reassure her, but it only increased the flutter of butterflies in her stomach.

The coffee helped a little, then they were in Blair's car again on their way to *Crossings*.

The restaurant was busy with many locals and tourists still in festive mode, as was the restaurant, a large Christmas tree in one corner and the sound of Christmas carols drowning out the noise of chatter. Lou and Blair were shown to a table in a corner and handed menus.

'Champagne?' Blair asked.

Lou nodded. It was still Christmas, after all, and she had a lot to celebrate, not least the man sitting opposite her.

They ordered the seafood platter for two, toasted each other with the champagne, and Lou tried to stifle the worry that still refused to leave her... despite Rachel's assurances.

But, as the meal progressed, her fears began to subside as Blair recounted some of what he'd discovered from his research, and Lou shared her memories of growing up in Pelican Crossing. By the time they were eating dessert – a delicious concoction of fruit, meringue and cream – Lou was feeling relaxed and ready for whatever the evening had in store.

When they left the restaurant, Lou was surprised to see the rain had stopped, leaving a clear sky with the moon and stars shining brightly.

'Fancy a walk along the beach?' Blair asked.

'I'd love it,' Lou said, realising it would be a perfect ending to the day.

They walked along the beach in the moonlight, Blair's arm around Lou's shoulders. Then he turned to her. 'I'm so glad I met you, Lou. I had so many reservations about moving here. I really only did it to please Katrina. But now, I thank my lucky stars that I did. After Prue died, I never expected to fall in love again... then I met you and was blown away. I've fallen in love with you, Lou, and I hope you feel the same way.' He pulled Lou into his embrace, and she could feel his heart thudding close to hers, the strength and warmth of his body making her long for more. Her own heart pounded erratically as their lips met, and it was as if time stood still.

When they pulled apart, Lou was breathless, her lips still throbbing from his kiss, her body aching with a desire she'd never imagined possible. 'I love you too, Blair,' she said, as she heard the sound of carols drifting over from *Crossings*.

This hadn't just been another Christmas, it had been a very special Christmas.

And, later that night, lying in Blair's arms in his villa in *The Haven*, suffused with a sense of wellbeing, Lou discovered that Rachel had been right.

The End

If you've enjoyed Lou and Blair's story, I'd love if you could leave a review on Amazon and/or Goodreads. A few words will suffice, no need for a lengthy review. It will mean a lot to me and help other readers find my books.

I'm thrilled so many of my readers are enjoying this series set in Pelican Crossing and are making friends with my characters.

What's next?

Those of you who have read the earlier books in the series, will remember Rhana, who lives alone and breeds spaniels in her home in the Pelican Crossing hinterland, the next book in the series is her story.

Rhana Black has always been content with her quiet life in the Pelican Crossing hinterland, where she spends her days breeding spaniels. Following a traumatic incident at her school formal and weighed down by her own insecurities about her appearance, Rhana has shied away from any romantic relationships. That is, until a chance encounter with a hot air balloonist changes everything.

Steve Morton has been struggling to move on after the tragic death of his pregnant fiancée. In search of solace, he finds himself in Pelican Crossing, where he rediscovers his love for flying and starts offering hot air balloon rides and scenic helicopter flights along the coast. When he meets Rhana, he is taken aback by the intense emotions he feels towards her.

As Rhana and Steve navigate their complicated pasts and undeniable chemistry, they must decide if they are willing to break their self-imposed barriers and take a chance on love. But with their old wounds and deep insecurities threatening to keep them apart, can they be able to overcome their fears and find happiness together?

You can order here https://mybook.to/somethingPC

From the Author

Dear Reader,

First, I'd like to thank you for choosing to read *A Family for Christmas in Pelican Crossing*. I hope you've enjoyed visiting Pelican Crossing as much as I've enjoyed creating it.

Like all my other books, although it is part of a series, it can be read as a standalone.

If you'd like to stay up to date with my new releases and special offers you can sign up to my reader's group.

You can sign up here

https://subscribe.maggiechristensenauthor.com/readersgroup

I'll never share your email address, and you can unsubscribe at any time. You can also contact me via Facebook or by email. I love hearing from my readers and will always reply.

Thanks again.

MaggieC

Acknowledgements

As always, this book could not have been written without the help and advice of a number of people.

Firstly, my husband Jim for listening to my plotlines without complaint, for his patience and insights as I discuss my characters and storyline with him, for his patience and help with difficult passages and advice on my male dialogue, and for being there when I need him.

John Hudspith, editor extraordinaire for his ideas, suggestions, encouragement and attention to detail, and for helping me make this book better.

Jane Dixon-Smith for her patience and for working her magic on my beautiful cover and interior.

My thanks also to early readers of this book –Maggie, Helen, Karen and Anne for their helpful comments and advice.

And to all of my readers, reviewers and bloggers. Your support and comments make it all worthwhile.

About the Author

After a career in education, Maggie Christensen began writing contemporary women's fiction portraying mature women facing life-changing situations, and historical fiction set in her native Scotland. Her travels inspire her writing, be it her trips to visit family in Scotland, in Oregon, USA or her home on Queensland's beautiful Sunshine Coast. Maggie writes of mature heroines coming to terms with changes in their lives and the heroes worthy of them. Maggie has been called *the queen of mature age fiction* and her writing has been described by one reviewer as *like a nice warm cup of tea. It is warm, nourishing, comforting and embracing.*

From the small town in Scotland where she grew up, Maggie was lured to Australia by the call to 'Come and teach in the sun'. Once there, she worked as a primary school teacher, university lecturer and in educational management. Now living with her husband of over thirty years on Queensland's Sunshine Coast, she loves walking on the deserted beach in the early mornings and having coffee by the river on weekends. Her days are spent surrounded by books, either reading or writing them – her idea of heaven!

Maggie can be found on Facebook, Twitter, Bluesky, Goodreads, Instagram, Bookbub or on her website.
    https://www.facebook.com/maggiechristensenauthor
    https://twitter.com/MaggieChriste33
    https://www.goodreads.com/author/show/8120020.Maggie_Christensen
    https://www.instagram.com/maggiechriste33/
    https://www.bookbub.com/profile/maggie-christensen
    https://bsky.app/profile/maggiechriste33.bsky.social
    https://maggiechristensenauthor.com/